Trinity

A Brethren Novel

Deena Remiel

℘

Dear Alison,
Angels really do
exist, and you're
one of them!
♡
Deena

Decadent Publishing
www.decadentpublishing.com

This book is a work of fiction. Names, characters, places, and incidents are the products of the author's imagination or used fictitiously. Any resemblance to actual events, locales or persons, living or dead, is entirely coincidental.

Trinity

Published by Decadent Publishing Company
Look for us online at:
www.decadentpublishing.com

Printed in the United States of America

"What the Critics are Saying..."

"Wow, what can I say but.... I LOVED IT! I was completely hooked right from the beginning... Deena doesn't disappoint, her story takes you on an amazing journey full of good old-fashioned Good vs Evil in such a new and exciting way. Romance, passion, danger, action, and plenty of gorgeous angel Brethren put your imagination into overdrive. What more can a girl ask for?!?! I BELIEVE IN ANGELS!"

~Stacey Clifford, Sassy Book Lovers

"Trinity by Deena Remiel has a fantastic premise. I love the idea of a magical bloodline providing a savior and I love that angels have created a brotherhood to help. I especially loved that a six year old housed the soul of an ancient warrior that gives her the ability to lead an immortal army...All in all, the Brethren series holds promise..."

~Tara, Night Owl Reviews

"...The suspense never falls short and the dialogue is very well-written. Fans of J.R. Ward's Fallen Angels' and Black Dagger Brotherhood series will fall in love with this series as will any lover of paranormal romance! Deena Remiel is definitely an author to watch!!"

~Destiny Philipose, LoveFantasySciFiNovels

"...Michael makes me want to believe in Angels and Hannah is such a delightful child who is believable. Emma is the protective mother who makes the story sweet with her protectiveness and endearing qualities. I would recommend this book to any readers out there. It sucks you in and keeps you reading late into the night like any fantastic book should do! This Book is now in my KEEP pile!"

~Leanne Gagnon, Books Read 'n' Make Up Done

"Deena Remiel paints the picture and you can't help but keep turning the page... At one point in the book my phone rang in an intense scene, and I actually jumped. To me, I had been in that scene and Agremon was my enemy...By the end of this book, you will know...ANGELS DO EXIST...AND EVIL BETTER WATCH OUT.

~Lindsey Hutchison, United By Books

"Debut Author Deena Remiel sets the thrilling mood...Fast paced, a fascinating plot, and characters you won't forget, this novel will leave readers wanting more!"

~Paranormal Romance Author Kari Thomas

"This book will grab you by the heart and never let you go. It's so real and well- crafted that the story will stay with you. You'll want your own angel!"

~Amber Scott, author Fierce Dawn, Play Fling, and Irish Moon

~DEDICATION~

To my husband and children, who are my real-life angels.

Acknowledgements

It takes a village to raise a novel, and my village is a mighty force. From the inception of The Brethren Series, I've had support from family, old friends, and people who became friends along the way. My family was the first to hear about my endeavor to write a novel. They smiled, gave me space and time, and cheered me on each day as I shared my excitement over how much I'd written.

My beta readers, those friends and family who read the rough, rough draft are a source of motivation and determination to write the best damn novels possible. Auntie A, Mary K, and Elizabeth, I thank you for the time you spend reading and rereading chapter upon chapter and their many incarnations.

The Desert Rose Chapter of RWA has brought me out of my cave and into the real world of authoring and publishing. I thank my sisters, Amber Scott and Kris Tualla, for their tireless tutelage, patience and laughter. My critique partners, Kathy and Varina, were instrumental in teaching me the nuances of revision, and I couldn't thank them more. Judy and Ruth, I thank you for being my first fans, as well as colleagues. My facebook friends and Disciples (fans) are another source of support. I have never had a lovelier group of friends than I do now. They stand strong and decimate my self-doubt.

Decadent Publishing editors are phenomenal. Meredith Cole, Barbara Sheridan, thank you for your attention to detail and teaching me well. Nicole Hicks, thank you for caring so for our baby and giving it a nickname. I eagerly await joining forces once again.

I must acknowledge my publishers. Do authors do that in their acknowledgements? Well I do! Heather and Lisa, I must thank you for being phenomenal publishers and friends. You have provided a wonderful, supportive environment for authors, and I am so pleased and proud to have my series be a part of your house.

~*Deena*

Prologue

*E*ver since the dawn of man, a war has waged between Good and Evil. Good has tried to claim supreme eternal victory, but like the ebb and flow of the tides, Evil rises up periodically trying to usurp Good's reign over the mortal world. Evil has its minions, immortal and mortal alike. Good has the Brethren, angels who were hired by an enigmatic leader to manifest on Earth as men, to fight against Evil, and protect and heal the human race. Time and again they have clashed over the centuries, both suffering great losses, yet Good has always come away triumphant and maintained its sovereignty.

It was during a time of economic and political turmoil that Satan had begun quietly amassing his minions once again. Letting the good and the righteous settle into a comfortable existence, unaware of how tenuous their lives really were.

But not everyone was oblivious. Doomsayers flooded the streets in the larger cities; cults arose in smaller towns promising salvation. And in one of those small towns, a child was born to a mother. Not just any child and her mother, but both born to an ancient, powerful lineage. Fated to fulfill prophecy, both were a part of the key to securing a lasting victory against Evil.

And neither of them knew it.

Chapter One

I'm dead. Emma yawned and rubbed at her dry, bloodshot eyes. *I must be dead. Or maybe I've become one of the living dead.* How else could she explain her zombie-like manner as she walked through her house at nine o'clock in the evening, locking windows and doors, shutting off lights, and nearly passing out at the foot of her bed? At the very least, she was one extremely sleep-deprived single mom who hadn't become so due to an overactive sex life, that's for sure. Oh, she had a nightly ritual, all right, one that starved her body of the healing affects a full night's sleep could offer. And she was certain as she plunged into a deep, dreamless sleep that the ritual would likely continue this very evening.

A blood-curdling scream shattered the peaceful silence of the wee hours. She roused, instantly alert. Her soul, rocked by the echoing scream, seized up like a blown car engine.

"Ow! Son of a bitch!" Emma swore under her breath. She kicked aside the inconsiderate Malibu Barbie. "Hannah, I'm coming! Mama's coming!"

Her stomach roiled at the terror and desperation in her daughter's panic-stricken voice echoing through the hallway.

"I won't go! I won't go! No! I'll never let you take me! I won't do it! You can't make me do it! Mama! Help me! Mama!"

Well hell, this is something new. Usually, when Hannah was having one of her nightmares, she shrieked until Emma talked her out of it and put her back to sleep. Now she's talking in her nightmare, too? Completely at a loss, she raked her hands through her hair as she rushed to her daughter, writhing on the bed.

"Hannah, I'm here. You're okay. Mama's here. Wake up, honey. Sweetie? Mama's here." She repeated these phrases like a mantra, trying to keep her voice as calm and soothing as possible. But who was she kidding? This newly added dimension of these nightmares was sending her over the deep end herself. She hoped her little one couldn't sense it.

"Mama! He's got me! Save me, Mama!" Hannah pleaded in a frenzy of emotion. It looked as though something was tugging on her arms and she was trying to pull them back. And her eyes were open.

Crap! She's never had her eyes open before, either. What the hell was going on?

She sat next to her jerking body and waved a hand in front of her face. Hannah looked at and then past her, as though there really was someone else in the room—someone seated right next to her. *Crap, crap, crap!* As she turned to look beside her, she saw a hint of a shadow, but then figured it to be her own. *Get a hold of yourself.*

"Honey, wake up. It's only a dream. You're okay. You're safe."

Hannah looked back again at her, and foretold in a chilling tone, "I'll never be safe, Mama. Not anymore." And with that, her little angel flopped back onto her pillow and was instantly asleep. What the hell was going on here? She acted as though possessed. Emma stood at the bedside, paralyzed, and stared at her daughter. Utter helplessness invaded her soul. Completely unnerved and sick to her stomach, she dropped to the floor like a rag doll and sobbed until she was spent.

What had happened to her baby girl? Almost six months ago, she had been a carefree, charismatic girl of five. And, for a little girl whose birthday was a week away, anyone would expect her to be bouncing out of her skin with excitement. Now, to look at her these days, she was anxious, withdrawn, and simply drained. Doctors hadn't been any help so far.

Change her routine. Okay.

Don't let her watch scary shows. Fine.

Let's try medication. Well, all right.

All of their suggestions proved fruitless, and left her completely alone with more questions than answers. What was she going to do now? There was no chance in hell that she would tell the doctors about this latest episode. They'd want to put her baby in a psychiatric facility, and she drew the line at that. There had to be another way to stop this nightly assault. But how?

Emma gathered the energy to drag herself onto Hannah's bed. She snuggled close to her baby girl's fragile body, and sank into the nest of Care Bear blankets. As she dropped off to sleep, she prayed, "Please, for heaven's sake, someone help my baby. End this madness."

Chapter Two

"Well, Agremon? Have you brought me the child?"

"Mr. Namirha, sir, I'd like to say yes, but I can't. You know I've been trying for so long now, My Lord, and tonight I got the closest yet to grabbing her, but...."

Namirha scowled and tossed the newspaper he'd been reading to the floor. "Agremon, remind me. Why do I keep you alive? Why do I keep your worthless ass around here if I never see results from your supposed gift? Hmm?"

"Well, Mr. Namirha, sir, you must know my gift for terror is truly great and none can match it. Why, I've kept your followers in line for years now." Agremon puffed out his chest like a preening gorilla. "But I think it's the girl's mother that's causing the problem here. My Lord, there is something about her that's shielding her daughter from me."

"Is that so?"

"I can't put my finger on it, but every time I get to the point where I'm about to take her, the mother comes in and is able to push me away. I don't know how or why. But I'll get to the bottom of it and make sure it doesn't happen again!"

Agremon stood a good distance away from Namirha, not quite trusting the look in the eyes of his Lord and master. He'd worked for him very successfully for centuries, but at the moment, his repeated failures left him open to Namirha's wrath. Knowing what Namirha was capable of was definitely cause for alarm.

"Excuses, excuses! I'm done with excuses, Agremon. Her birthday is a week away for Hell's sake! I need her, and I need her now!" Namirha bellowed. "You get that girl and bring her to me, or I'll have your body roasting on a spit while your head watches from a poleax! Now leave and find a way to get that girl here. Your life depends on it!"

As does yours, Agremon snickered inwardly.

"Yes, my Lord. I'll get her. I promise. Don't worry. All will be as you wish, My Lord, or my name isn't Agremon the Terrible." He bowed and made a quick exit from the throne room.

Agremon knew Namirha's patience was running out. The look of admiration he'd once enjoyed from his Lord had withered to one of downright disappointment. The clock was ticking. If he didn't produce the child soon, he was a total goner. He could kill that mother! If she would have stayed out of the damn room he could have taken the child a while ago. But the damn shrieking always brought her! What could he do?

Maybe if he visited the mother first he could do some damage. And then he could get the girl while the mother is cowering in her own nightmares.

Yes! That's it! It would be a most auspicious evening.

Tomorrow night he'd try again, and this time he'd be damned if he failed.

Chapter Three

"Mama, wake up, we have to get ready for school. Come on, Mama, wake up. Your alarm is going off and I don't know how to stop it."

"Mmmm...okay, honey, okay. I'm up." Bleary-eyed and stiff, Emma slowly moved each limb, testing to see that they were still in working order. "Oh, my word!" she groaned as she tried to sit up, her back screaming with resistance. *Was it seven o'clock already?* She slunk her way back to her own bedroom and turned off the offending alarm that was pounding nails straight through her skull with every beep. Her personal alarm clock followed timidly behind.

"Are you tired, Mama?" Hannah asked. She nodded grimly and patted her back. "I'm sorry I woke you up again."

"Don't be sorry, sugar. I know you can't help these nightmares from coming any more than I can. I just wish we could get a break from them every now and again." She sighed guiltily and caressed Hannah's face.

"But it wasn't a dream this time, Mama! It wasn't! You saved me. You really did. If you hadn't come, that awful, scary man would have taken me to Him forever."

Emma was trying her best to will away any outward signs of frustration and knew it wasn't working. She felt like the absolute

17

worst mother in the world! "Honey, I know it felt real to you, but trust me. It was only a nightmare. Tell me something, though. What did you mean when you said the scary man was going to take you to Him? Who's Him?"

"The scary man who is always in my dream, his name is Agremon. He keeps trying to take me to a man named Mr. Namirha. He wants me to become his daughter. But I'm already yours, Mama. I don't want to be his. That's kidnapping or stealing. Isn't it? And last night, Agremon was really angry with me for fighting him. He grabbed me and was pulling me from my bed, but then you came in and pushed him away. You saved me, Mama!" Hannah cried out and grabbed her so fiercely she thought she'd cracked a couple of ribs.

"Whoa! Anytime, Angel. You know I wouldn't let anyone or anything hurt you or take you away from me." Despite the aching ribs, Emma hugged her tighter, not quite sure at the moment if it was to comfort the grateful child or herself, and then kneeled down to speak to her face to face. "You know, sometimes our dreams can feel so real to us. Sometimes we can convince ourselves that what happened in them really happened. It takes a great mind with a great imagination to think so. You, my dear, have a great imagination. And now that you've shared this dream, you don't have to think about it anymore. You can take a deep breath, knowing it wasn't real, and let it go." She stroked her daughter's long, jet-black hair and kissed her pixie nose. "So, why don't we start getting ready for school now, okay? We'll have a good hearty breakfast, and I'll tell jokes on the way to school. How does that sound?"

"Well, okay, I guess. Do you think I could sleep with you tonight, though?" Hannah asked tentatively. Emma's sleep-deprived brain was no match for the doe eyes peering up at her, nor a trembling mouth.

"Sure, Hannah," she caved. Maybe she would get a better night's sleep if she didn't have to actually get out of bed and run down the hall to deal with the nightmares. And maybe she wouldn't feel like the worst mother in the world for one night.

As Emma drove her ancient pickup truck down the school's dirt road, she paid little attention to the striking, craggy mountains rising up to kiss the sky. She didn't feel the hot breeze wafting through the opened windows, causing sweat to gather around her neck and trickle down between her breasts. No, what she felt was relief washing over her.

She had jokingly called Prophet's Point Elementary School her second home for six years now, but it had only felt like one since Michael D'Angelo, the school's principal, came on board. He was a breath of fresh air for the school, providing a safe, protected place for students and faculty. Quickly, he had become a good friend. Once at school, she thought maybe Hannah would forget about last night and concentrate on her day, her friends, and her schoolwork. The jokes she told on the way to school hadn't gone over so well. Hannah had given her usual polite smile, but that's as far as it went. Was last night's nightmare now going to affect her daughter during school hours, too? How was she to explain it away? *Damn it all if today wasn't going to be a good day for her!*

Living in such a small town made it difficult for anyone to keep secrets. The two of them had kept the nightmare issue a private matter, knowing it would be completely humiliating if any of her friends found out about it. She knew they would be relentless with their questions and their teasing, and she needed an escape. School was that escape.

Emma, on the other hand, was at her wit's end. She needed to confide in someone or she would have a nervous breakdown herself. Only thing was, she didn't know who. Admittedly, she had major trust issues. Once burned, twice shy, as the saying went. But closing herself off to any kind of relationship, be it friend or lover, left her severely lacking in the confidant department. She had vowed never again to desire the pajama party friendships she used to have, or trust her heart to a man, but she reluctantly acknowledged that without opening herself up a little bit right now, she would implode.

The truck now sat under a shade tree, and the two of them held hands while walking into the school building.

"Okay, Angel. I love you. Have a super day learning and playing with your friends. If you need me, you know you can tell Mrs. McNamara, and she'll let you come to my classroom. But, I think you're going to have a really good day. Right?"

"I'll try, Mama. Really, I will. I won't even come to your classroom today," Hannah promised with a smile that didn't quite reach her eyes. She gave her mother a kiss on the cheek, turned around every few steps and waved goodbye. Emma waved back with a smile that she hoped didn't appear as forced as she knew it was. As the classroom door closed, her smile drooped. How could such a tiny girl battle such a big problem...and win?

She walked down the hall a bit further to her own classroom. Leaning against the door, she closed her eyes and took a couple of deep breaths. How was she supposed to focus on today's computer lessons when all she could think about was her little, broken angel?

"Hey, Emma, have you not woken up yet or are you tired from a hot night of steamy sex with a new boyfriend?" joked Maddie as she walked up to her.

"Hey, Ms. Stewart." She waved to her friend and colleague. "Door Number One, please. Late night, couldn't sleep, so I read 'til God knows when." The lie was as good as it was going to get with fatigue keeping her at her breaking point. Since the divorce, lying had become an automatic reflex. She felt a bit guilty but was too exhausted to care.

"So, no real sex for the Mama. Well then, the novel had better have been hot and steamy at the very least," she chided.

"For heaven's sake, girl!" Emma giggled. "Sometimes you can be so brazen!" Whether she knew it or not, Maddie always had a way of putting a smile on her face, and she sent a silent blessing while she turned and opened her classroom door. "See you at lunch, my friend."

"Later, gator! Hey, one more day until summer vacation!

Wahoo!" Maddie shouted as she flitted down the hall to her classroom.

Emma shook her head and sighed. As long as she'd lived here, there had never been the hint of a man around her to stoke the flames of gossip. That's the way she liked it. Everyone knowing your business...she was still getting used to that. Plus, the small town limited one's options where love was concerned. Now Maddie, she hooked a keeper before she moved to Prophet's Point. But Emma had arrived with a baby in her arms and a tan line where a wedding ring used to be. *Don't go there. Not today.*

She unlocked her door and began her daily routine of turning on the Computer Lab's computers and printers, checking the servers, and looking over her lesson plans for the day.

Emma noticed her computer was booting up slower than usual. She looked around the room at the other computers and found they were taking longer as well. Suddenly, a horrifying image of a creature's face appeared on all of the screens; bubbling skin all mottled red and black, eyes that glowed with fire, teeth that looked as though they were made from needle-like shards of glass, and a mouth that was dripping with blood. She jumped back and cracked her elbows against her filing cabinet.

"Ow! Oh my freakin' God!" she cried out. "What the hell is that?"

It was speaking and oddly enough, she could understand it. She inched her way back to the computer, morbid curiosity getting the best of her, to get a better listen.

"Hello, Emma. Why, you get more beautiful the more tired you are. I love the way the dark circles play on your face. I'm coming for you, lovey. I'll see you in your dreams tonight, my precious."

Her eyes widened and she grabbed the back of her chair for purchase.

"You look puzzled, frightened even. Don't you know who I am? Why, I'm Agremon, my precious, Hannah's friend, and now the suitor of your dreams. Until tonight." The computer screens went black, and so did the lights, on Emma.

Chapter Four

Blackness slowly faded into light. Why was she lying down? She blinked her eyes a few times and realized she was on the floor of her classroom. There was someone with her, by her side, urging her to wake up.

"Come on, Emma, wake up. Wake up, please." Michael D'Angelo was gently whisking her waist-length, ebony curtain of hair away from her face when she slowly stirred. "There you go. That's it. Wake up now. Emma, do you know who I am?"

"Yes, I know who you are. You're my principal. Oh God! Did I faint or something?" She struggled to sit up, but he put a firm yet gentle hand on her shoulder that held her in place.

"It seems like it. Now don't get up yet. Just relax while I get you some water." He hopped up, took a bottle of water from her mini-fridge and returned to hand it to her. "Now sit up slowly, that's it. Lean up against your desk here. Take a sip, not too much."

Emma felt embarrassed as all hell, but obliged the man who looked like he'd lost ten years off his life. And then she remembered what led up to her fainting. She trembled as the memories flooded back to her, and she dropped the bottle.

He immediately knelt down next to her and enclosed her hands in his. "Whoa, whoa there, Em. What's got you all in a fright? What the hell happened here?"

"I-I-I think someone's gotten to the computers to play a terrible trick on me, or my imagination's getting the better of me. I'm not sure which. Would-would you please check the computers and tell me what you see, Michael?"

He glanced around. "Well, it looks like the computers are all booted up, ready for your first class. What did you think I'd see?"

"You know what? It was nothing. A silly prank, really, I'm sure of it. Class is going to start soon, and I need to be ready for the kids. So, if you'd help me up, I'll get on with my day, and I'd appreciate it if you wouldn't say anything about this to anyone. It's rather embarrassing, you know? Me fainting, and you, well...you know the rest." Jesus! She was so undone she was rambling on and on, making a bigger ass out of herself than she already felt.

"You know, I don't like this one bit. The school has an alarm system. It never went off between yesterday and today, and you're saying someone tampered with your computers enough to make you faint. I'm going to have someone from the district office come over and check things out. For now, the computers are off limits."

"Now wait a minute. You're overreacting. Let me check things out on my own first before you call in the technology cavalry. Besides, what the heck do you expect me to do if you close this room down? Sit around and twiddle my thumbs all day?" There was no way Emma was going to have her routine changed in any way. She couldn't handle it. This was all she could cling to for sanity's sake.

"Okay. Then at least cancel your first couple of periods today so you can look things over. I don't want any surprises when it comes to the kids' safety." With his hands firmly supporting her elbows, Michael helped her to her feet and watched as she tried to hide the extreme effort it took to make herself appear reasonably stable.

"I agree, and thanks for everything. Hello?" she joked, knocking on his forehead. *Why is he staring at me with that goofy look on his face?* "Are you in there?"

"What? Oh," his voice cracked, "you're welcome. Listen, how about I come by after school and you can give me an update on this computer thing you got going on here? I won't be free until then, what with all the closeout procedures and final meetings I've got scheduled. You can put Hannah in the After School program, no charge."

"Sounds like a plan. See you later, then." And with that, Emma walked her fearless leader to the door. He narrowed his eyes and gave her one lingering glance that she met boldly with a show of confidence she didn't nearly possess, and closed the door. When her heart stopped pounding and her knees stopped feeling like jelly, she planned on finding out exactly what the hell was going on around here.

But first, she gave herself permission to freak out.

Wasn't Agremon the name of the scary man Hannah had spoken about from her nightmares? If it was one and the same, no wonder she had been having such a horrible time of it lately. That man or creature was downright gruesome. And why did he appear on the school's computers? How could something from her imagination show up like this and be so threatening to Emma as well? It didn't seem possible.

A thorough scan of the computers showed nothing irregular at all. No one had tampered or hacked into the system. Maybe it was her imagination working on overdrive, since last night's episode was so different from all the others.

The bell rang, ushering in a swarm of students to the building. Their buzzing voices felt like jackhammers drilling holes in her head. She decided to take her first two periods off, like Michael had wanted her to do in the first place. The kids' homeroom teachers wouldn't mind keeping them. They could use the extra help preparing the classrooms for the summer. She took a couple of aspirin and tried to calm herself down. She looked out the window. The sun was shining and it was a beautiful day. Why let a little techno-horror get in the way, right?

No further incidents occurred except, of course, for the inevitable visit she got from Hannah an hour before the ending bell was to ring. And what was more, she had come bearing pictures she'd drawn today during her art rotation; disturbing pictures of demons and devils crudely drawn, but clearly identifiable. Emma knew it was time to share this whole ordeal with someone, and that someone, she felt was definitely Michael D'Angelo. She couldn't put her finger on the why of it, but after this morning, she felt a curious and unexpected magnetic pull towards him. *Imagine, opening up to a man again. After all these years.* She shook her head, nonplussed. Could she truly trust him enough to share such a private and painful piece of herself? And would he be able to do anything to help?

Prayers did get answered, didn't they?

Chapter Five

*I*t wasn't until an hour after school let out that her principal showed up at Emma's door. But that was okay with her. She'd needed that time to build up her courage. Luckily, Hannah went without a fuss over to the Aftercare Program. With that concern out of the way, she now prayed Michael wouldn't think she was nuts and reconsider continuing her contract for next year. He wouldn't let this interfere, would he? She'd known him for six years now. They had a great professional relationship. He'd always been kind to anyone having a problem and was always willing to help in any way he could. But this, this wasn't your average "run of the mill, hey, can-you-help-change-a-flat-tire problem."

She was taking a huge risk now. This was definitely an issue that crossed over the line from professional to personal. Emma shook her head and rested her forehead on her desk, confidence deflated. What exactly did she expect him to do about her beleaguered daughter's nightmares that anyone else hadn't already tried? He could listen, she reminded herself. Just listen. Wasn't that what she needed right now? Someone to listen to her fears and frustrations about her daughter's well-being.

As if on cue, she heard a light rap on her door, and in he walked. Regret and concern furrowed his brow.

"I'm so sorry it's taken me this long to get to you. We had some bus issues that needed immediate attention. So, what'd you find out about your computers?"

He leaned casually against her filing cabinet looking, well, absolutely scrumptious, like a model for Ralph Lauren. He was a giant, she'd always thought, at six-foot-four or five. He dwarfed her five-foot-two petite frame. Broad shoulders and a narrow waist made him appear like a Greek god. With the relaxed, bohemian nature Prophet's Point was known for, he tended to wear jeans that always hugged perfectly in all the right places and polo shirts that accentuated the fact that he must work out on his time off. With a touch of salt sprinkled through his wavy, shoulder-length black hair, it begged to have hands—her hands—run through it. And his face, well, she mused, it could have rivaled Michelangelo's David. She studied his strong jaw line and high cheekbones, his straight nose and perfectly bowed lips. Six years had done very nice things to Mr. D'Angelo. If only she had the courage to show him she was interested. If only she didn't carry this burden right now. Suddenly, she was aware that he had finished speaking and he'd caught her gazing at him. She blushed from head to toe. His drop-dead smile had her reddening even more.

"Oh, um, I haven't found out much, I'm afraid. But that's actually good news. It means that nobody's tampered with anything here. The bad news is I'm going crazy," Emma quipped, knowing how true those words had become. Her nerves were getting the best of her.

"Hey, no secret there. We've known you were crazy for years." His eyes sparkled as he teased her.

"Ha ha, very funny. Listen, I wanted to thank you for everything you did for me this morning."

Emma hadn't noticed till now how stunning his eyes were. In fact, they were a spectacular blue, azure to be precise, with gold around the rims. How unusual, how distracting.

It was now or never. If she didn't ask him, she'd spend another day with no one to understand what it had been like for her these past six months. "Why don't you come over for some dinner tonight? I make a mean chicken stir-fry. Hannah would be thrilled to see that you exist outside of the school building. You know, even though I teach here, she thinks everyone else evaporates into thin air when school's out for the day. So, what do you say?"

She nibbled nervously at her lower lip. God! What was wrong with her? Why did Michael suddenly have such a strange effect on her? She really didn't need this kind of emotional complication right now. She needed someone to talk to, that's all.

"You know what? I'd like that, actually. Thanks for the invitation."

"Perfect. Well, I'd better shut the computer lab down and head on out ahead of you. You know, to tidy up the place." Emma turned to her desktop computer to initiate the shutdown process. Agremon's face popped into view for the briefest of moments, his arrogant gaze threatening his intent. She nearly jumped into Michael's arms with a shriek.

"Oh, my God! Did you see him? Did you see him?" she cried out, grabbing a fistful of Michael's shirt in the process. He immediately wrapped his powerful arms like a cage around her trembling body and rubbed her back reassuringly.

"Yeah, I did. I did, damn it," he muttered angrily. "We need to talk, Emma. Your invitation to dinner is perfectly timed."

Something had changed about him in those few moments. She couldn't quite put her finger on it, but something had definitely changed. There was a tension she could feel rippling through his arms that concerned her. But they also felt right around her, and were the only things keeping her standing. So for now, she threw concern out the window. *God, but his body feels so good, so solid, so strong!*

"We've got to get your daughter right now and go straight to your house. You're in no condition to drive, so let me, and I can pick you up in the morning for work."

"I'm going to take you up on that offer. Thanks, again." There was awkwardness as he released her from his arms, but they both left it unspoken.

Once she was steady on her feet and the computers were shut down, they picked Hannah up from the After School program. Michael locked his office, and they were ready to go.

"Wow!" Hannah bubbled, bouncing up and down on the back seat. "This is the coolest thing I've ever done, Mama. Why are we riding in Mr. D'Angelo's car?" Emma laughed at how such a little thing, like a car ride from a principal, could make her little girl so excited.

"It's because the truck is having engine trouble, sweetie. Right, Mr. D'Angelo?" She gave him a warning glance. "Now buckle up." *One little white lie won't hurt.* Emma made a concerted effort during the ride home to act normal, and thanked God her principal had followed her lead.

As they pulled up the long driveway to the house, she saw a polite, quiet child transform into a fidgety, argumentative one right before her eyes. Every suggestion she had for her daughter to do or eat for snack was met with whines and complaints, so she gave up. Of course Emma knew why she was being so oppositional, but Michael didn't, and if he was perplexed, he kept quiet about it.

The ranch house, inherited from Emma's parents, was small but sat on six acres of prime real estate with mature palm trees lining the drive and desert landscaping around the perimeter. The rest of the lot was left in nature's hands. The view was spectacular with vistas of the mountains nearly everywhere you turned. She always enjoyed the quiet serenity surrounding her home. As she opened the door and entered the house, though, it was a completely different story. Recently, she had been feeling anything but serene inside. Maybe she was sleep-deprived and imagining things, however, she felt as though all the good vibes that used to be there had been sucked out.

Michael walked in and quickly retreated, bumping into Hannah. "Oof! Oh, I'm so sorry! Are you okay? I must have tripped on the threshold here."

"Oh, I'm okay, Mr. D'Angelo. Don't worry." She ran past him

to the playroom. Emma went directly to the kitchen, washed up, and put on an apron. She returned to the foyer a moment later with a glass in her hand and stared. There Michael stood, like a statue in the doorway.

Geez, what's up with him? Has he changed his mind about dinner? Or is he feeling the same shroud of negative energy in here as I have for months?

"It'll be easier to have dinner with us if you come on in, Michael," Emma joked. "Why don't you take a load off and have something cool to drink while I get it started?"

"Right, yes, that sounds good, thanks," he stammered, and took the glass of iced tea she offered. Their fingertips touched, sending an unexpected bolt of energy between them. Their eyes immediately connected in surprise and puzzlement.

"Wow! The air must be very dry in here."

"Of course," Michael agreed a little too quickly. "Happens all the time at my house. It's the carpeting." He sat down at the kitchen table and silently watched while she cooked dinner. And as they sat for their meal, they stared at Hannah as she pushed the various morsels of food around her plate, with little actually making it to her mouth.

Emma tried small talk, but Michael appeared preoccupied. He did however offer his compliments to the chef. So she gave up on prying any more conversation out of him and turned to Hannah instead to ask what she'd done in school that day. The perennial, "Nothing," was her reply, and she asked to be excused from the table. There was an hour left before her bedtime, so Emma let her go play in the playroom. She wouldn't dare go into her bedroom until she absolutely had to.

Emma was a little concerned. She knew what she wanted to talk about, but what on earth did Michael have to say? He'd been so different since he'd seen Agremon on the computer screen. His mood had darkened. There was a quiet ferocity brewing that cast a vibrating aura over him. It unsettled her. This was definitely a side of him she'd never seen before. But then again, nothing these days was as it had been before.

Rather than barreling into their discussion, they settled into a silent rhythm of washing and drying the dishes. With the last dish washed and the last drop of moisture dried, there was no more they could do to stall the inevitable. They had to talk and they had to talk now. Michael followed her to the room next to the kitchen that she used as a study. He sat on the loveseat that faced a stone fireplace. She closed the French doors so they could be seen from across the hall, but not heard.

Emma crossed over to the fireplace and studied the photographs resting on the mantle. She lightly touched the picture frame containing a photograph of her and Hannah covered in finger-paint and she smiled, then flitted her hand onto another one of them sharing a swing and jumping off together. She rested her hand on the largest in the bunch: a black and white image in a thick, black frame. They were facing each other, forehead to forehead and nose to nose, with beautiful expressions of love on both of their faces. She lost herself for a moment in the fond memory the picture elicited before she turned and joined Michael on the loveseat.

His deep voice dissolved any comfort the pictures had provided. "That face we saw on the screen this afternoon, did you see that this morning as well, when you fainted?" His grave tone sent waves of shivers up her spine.

"Yes, actually. But it wasn't just the horrible face. I know it's going to sound crazy, but he spoke to me. He told me his name was Agremon, Hannah's friend. He isn't a friend, because she told me he's been terrorizing her in her nightmares for months now." She took a deep breath and closed her eyes for a moment. "He said he would visit me in my dreams tonight. And this afternoon, he flat out taunted me."

Michael put a welcomed hand on hers. What she heard herself saying out loud sounded absolutely absurd. But he had seen it, too. And he didn't seem to think she was nuts, so far.

Interesting. Thank goodness he doesn't seem to think I need to be committed.

"Hannah's been having nightmares for months?"

She nodded silently.

"No wonder she seems so withdrawn and anxious all the time. And now the object of her nightmares is after you." He paused. "Listen to me. I need to ask you some questions and I need you to answer them honestly."

"Okay, but really, let's get one thing straight here. If you're going to ask if I've been doing drugs or drinking too heavily, let me stop you right there. I don't do either, ever. And there's no history of psychosis in the family. My imagination is probably on overdrive after all these months of getting little sleep. I'm sure that after hearing about my daughter's nightmares for so long now, maybe they've become mine as well. But I'm an adult and I can handle it. I just need to get some solid sleep." She hesitated. "But, then again, it doesn't explain why you saw this Agremon creature as well, and seem to know something about him." As she began to think on this very troubling idea, she pulled her hand away from his and grabbed hold of the loveseat's armrest instead, as though she were clinging to the edge of a cliff.

"I'll explain everything as soon as I get some answers to some very important questions. First of all, I need to know when you and Hannah were born."

"When we were born? Well, we actually share the same birth date, June sixth." They both loved the coincidence and since it was just the two of them, it made it extra special. "Come to think of it, my mother's birthday is June sixth as well."

"And what time were you both born?" he urged on.

"Well, let me think about that one a minute. Hmm. I think I remember my mother saying when I was a little girl that I was born at 6:06 a.m. and Hannah was born at...you're never going to believe this, but she was born at 6:06 p.m. Isn't that interesting?" She paused, suddenly uncomfortable about the peculiarity and where this conversation was headed. "I never really noticed the coincidence before. Why do you need to know this?" She shifted uneasily.

"Where's your mother now? She should be here, too."

"I wish she could be, God knows, but she's passed on. My

father, as well. So that's going to be a little difficult," she replied quietly.

"God, I'm so sorry. I-I didn't know. Forgive my abrasiveness. How long has it been?"

"They both died before my sixth birthday, actually. There was a terrible skiing accident. An avalanche wiped out an entire group of skiers in Colorado." She shook her head, still amazed after all these years. "My parents were among them. My grandmother took care of me until she passed away unexpectedly a few months after my parents' deaths. I was placed in foster care until I was eighteen." She stood abruptly, smoothed down her shorts, and walked to the fireplace. "And that's where this story is ending. Let's just say they're not memories I'd wish on my worst enemy. So now you know my tragic past. It's time for some answers from you, Michael. You know, ever since this afternoon, you've been acting very strangely. You're not yourself. So come clean. What the hell is going on here?"

Chapter Six

*T*here was a silence as thick as molasses. No, Michael wasn't himself. Not at all. Not since he found Emma lying unconscious on her classroom floor earlier this morning. Disquieting thoughts had been swimming through his mind all day unbidden, and served as frequent distractions. Like how God-awful beautiful she was with that long, wavy, dark-as-midnight hair he could easily imagine brushing across his bare skin. And how her almond-shaped eyes were made for seduction. And her lips. Every time she nibbled on the bottom one, he had wanted to help her. How many times had he thought of her like this since the day they'd met six years ago? He figured he had the longest running crush on a woman in history.

He'd never acted on those feelings, though. It was completely unprofessional, and with these latest developments, it was especially awkward. Although he had to admit, for the first time in the six years he'd known her, he felt consumed beyond measure by her raspy voice, her sensuous body, and her strength of character. He found himself totally enthralled and disarmed.

And then, looking at all the pictures on the mantle tonight added to his discomfort. They were pictures of family, of closeness, of an impenetrable bond, and something he knew he would never experience again. A dull ache welling in his heart he quickly suppressed.

How was he supposed to explain who he really was, and where did he begin to explain who he suspected she really was, who her daughter really was? It was obvious that she'd never been told what she needed to know about herself and her family lineage. Her mother would have done that on her sixth birthday. What about her grandmother, though? Why hadn't she told her? She probably never got the chance.

It was vital that she knew now, or else, Hannah's nightmares wouldn't solely be her own; they would be shared by every mortal on this Earth.

"Okay, I need you to sit down and listen to me very carefully. What I have to tell you isn't going to be easy to hear. It isn't easy to say. I want you to promise that you'll give me a chance to explain, that you won't throw me out or call the police."

"Now you're starting to scare me. What, are you some kind of lunatic escaped from a mental hospital, and you've been living a secret life as the favorite principal in a two-bit town?"

"Emma, please, come sit down and I'll try my best to explain. But you have to promise that you'll listen to everything. Please," he pleaded with an outstretched arm.

"All right," she agreed, joining him on the loveseat. "I promise, now tell me."

"My name *is* Michael, and I really am the principal of Prophet's Point Elementary School. But I also have another job. I was sent here six years ago by the company I work for, Brethren Security and Investigations. There was intelligence gathered alluding to some kind of disturbance here, but nothing specific about who it involved. I've been on alert ever since. I am one of the Protectors of the Good. I am an angel, an immortal."

Emma stared at him, eyes wide as saucers. She opened her mouth as if to respond when he quickly continued, "Uh-uh. You promised you'd hear me out, and I have so much more to tell you." She closed her mouth and Michael could see the cynicism washing over her as she folded her arms and crossed her legs. But he forged ahead undaunted. "This Agremon you're referring to is a really bad guy. He used to be part of the Brethren, but he fell from grace and now works for this Namirha. Dollars to doughnuts, Namirha is an alias for Satan. With what you've told me about your birthdays and Hannah's nightmares, it looks as though Namirha wants her and is using Agremon to get her. Agremon's the perfect guy to get her, too. He's able to turn dreams into nightmares, invade people's imaginations, and take souls while they sleep. When you die in one of his concocted dreams, you die for real. Listen closely. We can't let Agremon get near her again."

"On that I agree." She unfolded her arms, uncrossed her legs, and scooted to the edge of her seat. "Leaving everything else you've told me about yourself aside for the moment, because God knows, I need to; you should know that last night, when I heard her screaming, I walked in to find her in a tug of war with some kind of invisible force." She rubbed her hands on her lap. "When I got close to her, she stopped. She said I saved her from being taken by Agremon to a Mr. Namirha so she could be his daughter. Are you telling me that all that's been happening, that Hannah's nightmares are real?"

"Yes, I am. And it looks like you literally are Hannah's savior. Agremon couldn't take her with you there beside her. Now the threat is clear. Namirha wants Hannah, but why as his daughter? That is the question."

Stunned, Emma sat silent.

"What are you thinking?"

"I think you can obviously understand how all this might sound to me. I don't know if I can believe it, believe you." She nervously combed her hands through her hair. "I mean, what am I supposed to do here, Michael? Are you crazy? Am I crazy, too, if I want to believe you? I mean we're talking about my baby here, my Hannah. She's all I've got in this world." She was quickly becoming unglued, so he turned her to face him with strong yet gentle hands. He cupped her face and looked at her with those piercing azure eyes.

"First of all, I'm not crazy and neither are you. Secondly, I am not going to let anything happen to Hannah or you. And finally, there's actually more to tell. About the two of you. When you hear what I have to say, I think you'll be impressed." He released his hold on her, and she felt instantly bereft, like a vital connection had been cut off. How strange was it that she could be feeling this way about a man, and a seemingly crazy man to boot?

"Okay, okay. Tell me the rest of it. I'm as ready as I'll ever be." Emma breathed in deeply trying to get a grip on things, but who was she fooling? There were no handholds to be found.

"If my guess is right, and I'm pretty damn sure it is, you come from a long line of extremely powerful and gifted women."

"Well, I could have told you that," she joked, desperately trying to lighten up a situation that had become disturbingly dark. She was doing her best to get back on solid ground.

He continued, "When you told me your birthdates, I immediately knew who you were."

"You're not making sense. Of course you know who I am. I've been working for you for six years." She shifted uncomfortably in her seat.

"Yes, I know, that's a part of you. But the part that was lost to you when your mother died is what I'm referring to. Your lineage, Emma, is ancient. Every generation in your family lineage, for as long as history has been recorded, has had a mother and daughter born on the same date, June 6, at precisely the same time 6:06, either a.m. or p.m. Every generation. Usually, on the daughter's sixth birthday, all the knowledge and special gifts are revealed, passed on from mother to daughter.

"Each mother and daughter has had to do battle with evil on a variety of levels. But you didn't get that chance to learn this. I suspect Namirha had a hand in that. You and your daughter are connected to a source of great ancient power and a prophecy foretelling the salvation of this generation. I may be a Protector, but Hannah," he explained, pointing in her direction, "I believe, is meant to be the Great Warrior Child, and you, as her mother, are meant to be the Great Savior Mother. With this knowledge comes great strength and gifts that need to be uncovered by each of you and mastered in order to defeat whatever plans Namirha has in mind. I can help you. I must help you. The fate of the mortal world hangs in the balance."

Conflicting thoughts swirled around in Emma's mind. She stood abruptly and began pacing the floor. Her face flushed and her heart raced. "All right, Michael, I've been very patient, considering. I've listened like you asked. You know," she tittered as her eyes snapped to a copy of Alice in Wonderland on the bookshelf. "I had really invited you over here tonight because I had kept Hannah's nightmares a secret, and after last night, well, I couldn't do it anymore.

"I needed to have someone besides me know what was going on around here, so I could look at that person and find the strength to go on. I thought it could be you." A gulp of air, a slow release, and she turned to face him as her body seemed to hum with unrestrained energy. "Now you share with me a story about who you 'really' are, who my daughter 'really' is, and who I 'really' am, and you know what? I'm not buying it. Not at all, buddy. So I'm going to ask you politely to get your 'immortal' ass out of my house before I do call the police. I suggest you forget about your goodbyes to Hannah, and go. Now."

Damn, it was going so well.

She had misjudged him completely. She stalked towards the front door. Michael grabbed her arm. She looked from his hand on her arm to his face. If looks could kill, she was confident hers would kill him good and dead. He let her go.

"I really don't think I should go given the situation with Agremon. I'm a Protector, Emma. I can protect her."

"I'll protect my daughter, thank you very much. I've been doing fine so far. Now get out."

She opened the door and dismissed him like one of her students. He didn't argue any further.

How could he? Emma slammed the door shut behind him.

She slumped to the floor, elbows on her knees, forehead leaning heavily on the palms of her hands. *How could he do this to me when I'm in such a vulnerable state? Burned again, damn it. I should have known better by now. I should have kept my problems to myself and found a way to solve them that didn't involve others. The man is obviously insane! Immortal, my ass! Special gifts, ancient powers. Fantastical stories...all of it! What drugs has he been taking? But he knows Agremon and Namirha. No, I just can't believe his story is real. And if it is real, well then, I'll find a way to handle it on my own, without him.*

It took a few minutes, but Emma gathered herself together, got back up, and went to the kitchen in search of some aspirin. Hell! There were none left. She really was all alone in this. The one person she thought she could trust had gone off the deep end, nearly taking her with him. Thank goodness she had the presence of mind to throw him out.

What she really needed right now was to shake this disaster off. She needed to be with Hannah and do her routine chores. So she went to the playroom to hang out with her best girl, but as she entered, she heard her playing with her Barbie dolls. She stopped at the doorway to watch and listen because it was so cute when she role-played with them. It reminded Emma of when she was young and had played with her own dolls. Hannah had a Barbie doll in one hand and a Ken doll in the other. Barbie was dressed in her wedding gown, and Ken was wearing a red satin jumpsuit. They were attached to each other with a string, and Hannah had the Ken doll yanking on the string and the Barbie doll was being thrashed around. As Emma watched, her rosy nostalgia turned to shock and dismay. And then Hannah spoke for the dolls.

In a deep voice, she boomed, "For the last time you are coming with me or I will kill you!"

Then she changed to a high lilt. "I won't go, you evil, evil man! I'm never going to be his daughter, ever!"

Hannah used her teeth to rip through the string. "Aha! You see! You can't hold me! And soon, my army of immortals will be here fighting by my side, to send you at last to your total destruction!"

With the deep timber, she responded, "You may have won for now, but you'll never be safe again."

She made the Barbie doll's hands grab the Ken doll and fling him across the room.

"Hannah! What are you doing?"

"Oh, Mama! I didn't know you were there." A blush washed over her face. "I was playing with my Barbie dolls."

"I see, well, I think I'm going to have to do a better job of monitoring the TV shows you're watching." And when had she learned the words immortal and destruction? Emma shook off the unsettling feeling creeping over her. "It's time to get ready for bed, so why don't you get in your jammies, brush your teeth and hair, and come to my room? I remember hearing that some really amazing mother gave permission for one amazing kid to sleep in the queen's bed tonight. Since I am the queen of this house, you must be that amazing kid! So, scoot!"

"Thanks, Mama! I'll meet you in your room, okay, really fast!" Hannah leaped into her arms and nearly knocked her over, ending the love fest with a bear hug. She sprinted to her bedroom in a flash and was out just as quickly.

Emma staggered to her bedroom, weariness suddenly overtaking her, and turned down the sheets. Hannah appeared by the door and came tentatively into the room. She slid quietly into the bed.

"Hey, Mama, where's Mr. D'Angelo?"

"Oh, he had to go, sweetie. He said to tell you goodbye and he'd see you in the morning."

"Oh, okay," she yawned.

In the morning! Shit! He had to pick them up for school since she'd left her truck there. *Not in this lifetime!* She would call and cancel with him, and have Maddie come pick them up instead. Problem solved.

Liar. Her problems weren't nearly solved.

Emma ruffled Hannah's hair and kissed her soundly on the forehead. "Good night, my angel. I'll be in after I look through my

41

e-mail and do some chores. I love you," she cooed in her ear.

"I love you more," Hannah whispered back, and wrapped her arms around her mother's neck.

"I love you most," Emma replied, nuzzling her neck.

"You win, Mama."

"We both do, Angel."

The nightly ritual always made Hannah smile while drifting off to sleep. It broke Emma's heart knowing the smile never lasted very long. She made sure to put the bedside table light on before she left and kept the door wide open.

Returning to her study, her favorite place to unwind, she eased into the overstuffed chair by the fireplace and settled her laptop on her knees. She loved this chair. She had a vague memory of sitting in it as a child with her mother. Now, it felt like she received a comforting hug every time she sat down on its downy pillows. Her tensed muscles slowly relaxed. She decided to close her eyes for a couple of minutes while the laptop was booting up.

No harm in doing that.

Chapter Seven

*M*ichael slammed his hands against the steering wheel as he drove back up the driveway to the street. *As if I should have expected Emma to have reacted any differently?*

He understood her anger, her denial. She should have known who she was when she was six years old, not by accident at thirty. Too much time had gone by. Enough time for a child's innocence to have died and an adult's cynicism to set in. But if he looked at this objectively, how could he hold back? Their lives were in danger, as was the fate of the mortal world. There was no time to be gentle and take it slow.

So Satan has re-surfaced, and Agremon is with him. Agremon's presence intrigued Michael more than Satan hanging a shingle. There was a score to be settled with the fallen angel. Brethren weren't usually in the revenge business, but this development called for an exception. It'd been a long time since the forces of Good and Evil collided. It had been a war to rock both mortal and immortal worlds—Michael's specifically. This time, he wagered, wouldn't be any easier. One thing was certain, Agremon would die.

Unwilling to let Emma and her daughter face whatever the demon had in mind for them, he spun the car around, drove back up the driveway, and parked. He would protect them with every ounce of his blessed immortal soul. And this time, he wouldn't fail.

Michael turned on the radio to occupy his time. He didn't know when he would sense Agremon's presence this evening and wished he'd been able to give mother and daughter his Talismans to wear before he'd been thrown out. But he hadn't forgotten the energy flow that occurred between him and Emma. That would help since he could still feel that connection, microscopic as it was, connecting the two of them together. He would have to be extra vigilant tonight at picking up on the particular thread of fear that would be floating through the air like silky energy waves. "Garbage, garbage, ah, the news. That'll work." He eased his seat back, cranked up the volume, and closed his eyes.

"*...the Arson Squad is investigating. In other news, the religious cult, The Source, that's been gaining popularity overseas, has reportedly found a new home base in Arizona. The cult's leader, Ahriman Namirha, has been seen all around the state this month recruiting followers....*"

Michael's eyes sprung open and he bolted upright in his seat. So this was how Satan's doing things this time around. He had taken on human form and used a cult to insinuate evil into the mortals' minds to cultivate his minions. A rather ingenious plan, even if it did lack some inventiveness.

But what did Namirha need from Hannah? He decided to call Gabriel, one of the other Brethren. If he couldn't figure it out, no one could. After giving him all the information he had gathered, he put his phone away and began a sweep of the area surrounding the house. It was a mental sweep to pick up on any trail Agremon might be laying down as he came to mother or daughter in their dreams. He felt nothing yet. While part of his brain was doing the incessant sweep, another part was checking all of his vital powers, making sure he was armed and ready for whatever was required. He had quite the arsenal of protective gifts, which made him the most powerful Protector out of the three that existed, he, Gabriel, and Urie.

He was going to need his team, as well as the other Brethren teams: the Warriors and the Saviors, and their troops, to defeat Evil and keep Emma and Hannah alive.

Agremon sewed his dream-world suggestions in Emma's drowsy mind and watched with wicked pleasure as she succumbed. He sent a warm breeze to caress her face, and implanted sounds of ocean waves lapping upon the shore. Birds sang songs that hypnotized and dolphins played off in the distance. He massaged her simmering discontent with her life and suggested that this little vacation on the beach was exactly what she needed.

That's right, just ease into it Emma. No need to rush it. Enjoy your little respite for a few minutes. You look extremely hot in that wisp of a bathing suit I so generously provided for you. Maybe I should have you take a little walk along the shoreline. Mmm. I like the way your sinewy muscles move as you take each step. Yes...just like that.

Emma's body moved like a tigress from her chaise lounge as he compelled her to do his bidding.

Emma walked along the pristine beach, the warm breeze seducing her with its fingers burrowing into her hair and massaging away the months of built-up tension in her shoulders. She was lost in the sensual experience. For an instant, she pictured Michael giving her the massage, and then scowled.

Agremon appeared before her like a gruesome tower of flesh, wearing of all things—surfer's shorts.

"Hello, my precious. Well, aren't you looking particularly delectable today? I do have great taste in swimwear, wouldn't you agree?"

"Wh-wh-what? Oh, my God!" Her heart skipped a beat as she stood frozen in place, staring at the behemoth in front of her. His entire body was mottled red and black, and bubbly, like his face, with little thorn-like protrusions all over his arms. He was even more grotesque than he had appeared on the computer screen earlier that day, and she forced the bile back down, scorching her throat in the process.

"Thank the devil I'm not your God, but I could definitely let you worship me like I was. You are one hot mama, you know that? Hey, isn't that what Hannah calls you, Mama? I have a great idea! Why don't I go get her and bring her here with us? We could have a family picnic right here on the beach. It would be so cozy, only the three of us. What do you think?" Fire blazed in his eyes as he ran his tongue over his needle sharp teeth. Blood oozed out of his mouth.

"I'm going to wake up; I'm going to wake up right now. I'm having a nightmare and I'm going to stop it right now," Emma muttered over and over, squeezing her eyelids shut as her body dropped to the sand beneath her.

"You're pathetic if you think you can wake from this dream, precious. This isn't just any old dream. You've got the Master's Original made especially for you. Now let's get this party started."

With a mere wave of his hand, Agremon abruptly altered their surroundings to one of a cemetery. A dense fog hung around them like a shroud, and a cold darkness replaced the warmth of the soothing sunshine. Emma shuddered uncontrollably. He compelled her to stand before what appeared to be a centuries old mausoleum. With another wave, he changed their attire. He was decked out in a funereal suit, and she wore a strapless, sheer, black chiffon evening gown. As awareness finally broke through her stupor, she looked around. For a moment, she almost wanted to laugh.

"If you think turning this into one of those old-time vampire movies can scare me, you're way wrong. I grew up watching those silly movies and loved them." A spark of confidence ignited inside her. *I might live through this nightmare yet.*

"Don't you think I knew that little detail about you? I research my subjects very carefully, precious. Oh no, you're not starring in a campy vampire movie. I've something very special planned for you. I'll be on my way now. I've a date with a little girl I know who loves when I come to visit."

"Don't you go near my daughter, you bastard!" Emma shrieked. She lunged towards him with nails ready to rip him to shreds. He simply froze her in place.

"Have fun! Oh, I believe the mausoleum is where your party is." Agremon raised a finger, spun it around, and pointed to the mausoleum. Her body immediately swung around and began moving jerkily towards the small decrepit building.

"Ooh, you're a fighter. I like a challenge."

Michael picked up on something. The microscopic thread that held Emma to him was definitely humming. It seemed too early for her to be asleep. But then again, she hadn't had much sleep for a long time. If he'd known sooner what was happening to Hannah...what was done was done. All he could do was protect them as best he could now. He raised his own shields so he couldn't be detected by Agremon and got out of the car. Keys in his pocket, phone on vibrate, he made his way quickly yet cautiously up the dirt driveway.

As he approached the house, the humming got exponentially stronger. Something was definitely happening, and it wasn't good. He raced up the path to the front door. It was locked. That wouldn't keep him out. He waved his hand over the lock to open it and crossed the threshold. Where was she? His senses drew him to the study. When he entered the room, he stopped short, barely containing his rage. Her body was crouched in a fetal position on the oversized chair, her laptop broken to pieces on the floor in front of her. He hustled over and felt her skin. She was ice cold, and there were beads of sweat on her brow. Her breathing was shallow and her heart raced. *Damned Agremon!* Michael had to get her out of that nightmare, and fast. The quickest way to get her out was for him to go in. But he had to protect Hannah first.

While reaching into his pocket for a Talisman, he raced to find her bedroom. She wasn't in there. He tried Emma's room next and entered silently, relieved to see Hannah unaffected by the demonic Agremon. He wrapped the protective necklace around her neck and sped back to the study.

Swapping places with Emma, he gingerly rested her on his lap. In order to enter her dreams, as much bodily contact as possible was necessary. He placed his right hand on her forehead and slowed his breathing down considerably.

It took a couple of breaths and he was in. He found himself wading through her past dreams and thoughts she kept to herself. After passing through dreams about test anxiety, disastrous dates, a marriage gone wrong, and an overwhelming sense of distrust of people, he finally came to her current nightmare.

"Agremon certainly has a flair for the dramatic," he muttered dryly as he glanced around. A cemetery of all places. He heard faint whimpering coming from the mausoleum to his right. "She must be in there." He approached the door and was immediately thrown back, landing with a harsh thud on a gravestone. Agremon had shielded it, barring anyone from entering. As Michael recovered, he noticed her name, *Emma Livingston*, written on the gravestone. In fact, as he looked around, every gravestone had her name on it, even the mausoleum.

"Nice touch, asshole," he hissed. Calling upon his protective powers, he spoke the sacred word, *Discaoil*, and dissolved the shield like it was tissue paper. Michael trudged toward the small doorway to the crypt. Of course, it was sealed shut. What would a nightmare be without complications and roadblocks?

"Emma! It's me, Michael! I've come to get you out of there! Hold on!" he called out, hoping she heard him. The seal would take a little longer to dismantle. He reached inward to find the right protection key to unlock it. Once found, he spoke those sacred words, and the door crumbled to rubble on the ground.

Emma lapsed in and out of control. As hard as she fought against going into the mausoleum, she couldn't break free from Agremon's tight reign over her. Her limbs trembled in defiance. Anger was good. She could function with anger, but the fear that followed when the door was sealed shut behind her was crippling.

He knew. The bastard knew.

The dark terrified her. When that mausoleum door closed behind her, she was thrust back in time. She turned into the four-year-old girl who'd gotten stuck in a pitch-black, dank basement closet while playing Hide and Seek with friends. It felt like forever until she was found. Everyone had thought no harm done, but for her, that was the day Darkness became her enemy—an enemy she had yet to defeat.

Emma stood unmoving, paralyzed by her infernal fear, while her scream tried to echo, but came up empty. She had to find a wall, a corner, something to shield her. Being exposed this way in the middle of the room wouldn't be safe. Who knew what could come at her? Agremon did. She knew that now.

He was using her own fears to scare her to death, literally.

Chapter Eight

*E*mma willed her legs to move as she felt around for a wall. She hadn't been able to see much of anything when she had first entered the crypt, and now that she was sealed in, she was surrounded by a stygian darkness. She bumped into something solid and stone-like, and immediately crouched down on the floor in a fetal position. Her body shook, her lips trembled and her mind conjured creepy-crawlies, fantastic monsters, and demons of all shapes and sizes to terrorize her. And they came, one and all in full force, to crawl over her skin, to nip and paw at her, and to literally pull her to pieces.

"I'm going to wake up, I'm going to wake up," she simpered over and over like a mantra while she rocked herself.

A loud rumble sent shockwaves through her body. And, as if from another dimension, she heard her name, insistent and urgent. A giant monster emerged from the rubble and stood before her warped mind. She scuttled feverishly even further into the crypt.

"Get away from me, get away!" she cried out madly, deep in the throes of terror.

"Emma, look at me. It's me, Michael. I'm not here to hurt you. I've come to take you out of this nightmare. Can I do that, Emma? Would you let me? Hannah's waiting for you. You have to let me come a little closer to you so I can help get you out of here, all right?"

"No!" She struggled furiously with him when he picked her up. Her arms flailed wildly, but it was no match for his strength. With all of her energy spent, she had no fight left in her and gave up, going limp in his arms.

"Don't hurt me," she whimpered feebly, and swiped at the imaginary spiders crawling up and down her arms.

"I would never hurt you, Emma. Never."

As he carried her out of the mausoleum, she could feel her tattered gown dragging against the craggy ground. She batted at invisible webs that she was convinced had been woven over her face.

"It's gonna take all of my energy to get us out of this nightmare, but I can do it. Then, I'll get help from Raphael, a Savior, to heal your mind and soul. Until then, you're gonna be plagued with bouts of terror. I'm so sorry. The Talisman I'll give you can help ease that a bit, but it won't rid you of the terror completely." He placed his hand on her forehead, gently closed her eyelids, and breathed slowly in and out.

She awakened and immediately began fighting again. "Let me go, you monster! Let me go!" A hoarse whisper was all that she could muster.

"Emma, I've got you. You're safe now. You're safe." Michael gathered her close, his arms encircling her as he'd done that morning, giving her all of his protection. He nuzzled his face in her hair and kissed her forehead, her temples, and her cheeks.

"You're safe," he repeated.

She looked up at him, finally comprehending it was Michael holding her and not some horrifying zombie. They were back in the study and she relaxed. For the first time since her nightmare had begun, she saw with eyes free of terror yet filled with undeniable understanding and defeat. She clung to him with desperation and sobbed. And he held on.

"It's okay, Emma. Everything is going to be okay. You're safe now. I'm here, and I won't let anything harm you or Hannah."

"Hannah! Oh my God, Hannah! He's gone after her! Michael, we have to wake her up! I won't let him take my baby girl!" Frantic to go to her daughter, she tore away from him and immediately fell to the floor. But sheer determination got her to her hands and knees scrambling toward her daughter's bedroom. "Whoa, slow down." He grabbed her by the waist and stalled her advance. "Before coming to get you, I put a Talisman around her, a protective necklace. Agremon can't get her while she's wearing it. I have one for you, too. Here," he offered, while digging in his pants pocket. "Put it on right now and Agremon won't be able to get to you again either." He held it out to her. Her hands shook so much that he had to help put it around her neck.

"Thank you. I-I-I have to go to her. I have to see that she's all right. Lord, but I can't go to her looking like this! You won't believe what Agremon's dressed me in, the freakin' pervert. Wait a minute. You got me out of there, so you already know what I'm wearing." She paused and took a breath. "Good grief!" she muttered and her head dropped in wretched embarrassment. He gently touched her cheek.

"Emma, look at yourself, sweetheart. He only dressed you up that way in your dream. See? You're still in shorts and a top. No worries." She wasn't totally relieved. After all, he had seen her wearing that Frederick's of Hollywood get-up in her dream. She hoped he had a short memory, but something pressing against her thighs told her his memory was in perfect working order. Maybe she shouldn't be so embarrassed.

"Let me help you up. You still seem a bit shaky." As he coaxed her up off the floor, he held her hands, and she felt a curious surge of energy flow continuously between them. She was standing now and filled with wonder.

"It feels good, doesn't it?" he asked.

"Y-yes, it does, actually. I think I felt this earlier at school, when you held me. W-what is it?" she asked tentatively.

"It's my protective energy connecting with your healing energy. Your powers are awakening. Thank goodness tomorrow's the last day of school. We have a lot of work to do. Now, let's go check on Hannah." He gave her a dashing smile and haltingly let her go.

She was sleeping peacefully as Michael had promised. But Emma wouldn't leave the room, nor agree to get some sleep herself. She hunkered down on the loveseat by her bed and watched.

"I guess I'll get going now that I know you two are safe," Michael said as he made his way out of the bedroom.

"Y-you're leaving?" She shifted her gaze to the man who had come back to save her and her daughter. Against her cynical nature, she found herself disappointed. She actually wanted this man—no, needed this man to stay. "Thanks for coming back for me. I'm sorry about earlier. I've got a bit of a trust issue, which I'm sure you've noticed by now. I promise to work on it. But at the moment, I-I'm not even trusting my own mind," she stammered. "C-c-could you stay, please? I'm not ashamed to say I don't want to be alone. Even with my eyes open, I can feel the terror creeping back in. Frightening images keep coming in and out of my brain. They won't stop. I can't stop them. Oh, God," she shuddered while trying in vain to pound the terror out of her head with her fists. "I-I need you, Michael, please?"

"Sure. I can stay as long as you want. Why don't I sit right down next to you, then? It looks nice and cozy, and I could hold you again, if you'd like."

"Yes, I'd like that, thank you." Relief washed over her, and she watched as he lithely walked back to sit beside her. He quickly grabbed her fisted hands and soothed them open. She gazed into the eyes that continually captivated her, while her own were already brimming with unshed tears. As the drops flooded down her face, he tenderly reached out to catch them.

"Make it go away, Michael," she whimpered, and her breath caught. "Can you make the terror go away?"

"With eyes like yours, looking at me that way, I would make the world go away if you asked."

He reached for her, and in one swift motion, cradled her in his arms. She clung to his sheltering body for dear life, and took a slow, shaky breath. He gently rocked her and stroked her hair, and eventually her heart rate slowed down, her breathing steadied, and she relaxed in his arms.

Emma's last thought before fading into sleep was that Hannah was safe, she was safe, and Michael's protection would guard them through the night.

Agremon eased himself into Hannah's mind and immediately got slammed by a shield. White-hot sparks flew around him, and he shook his hands from the pain of it. *How and when had she become shielded against me? Who would dare to do such a bold and dangerous thing? Are they mad? Don't they know who they're dealing with?* He pushed against the shield, and more white-hot sparks shot in every direction, but it still wouldn't budge. As he pulled away, he absorbed the pain with a wicked grin, and this time he felt the source of the energy.

The Protector! So, he's back. Interesting. What is he doing here? Namirha should be notified immediately. But, he could wait. Agremon had planned to feast off the terror of the little girl before giving her over. If he couldn't do that with Hannah tonight, then he'd find another soul, and another, until his anger was assuaged. Nobody kept him from doing his job.

One way or another, terror will reign tonight.

Chapter Nine

"*All we are saying is give peace a chance. All we are saying is give peace a chance....*" Emma's arm sailed through the air and gave her alarm clock a good whack. Not a very peaceful reaction, but she'd work on that another day. At least she had remembered to change it from that infernal beeping to the radio alarm yesterday morning. Morning? Already? But, it was the last day of school, wasn't it? *Yes!*

She stretched lazily like a cat, but felt like she'd overdone a workout. Every muscle in her body ached. A couple of aspirin would relieve that. Oh, right, she ran out of aspirin yesterday. *Yesterday.* Images slowly crept back into her mind. A grotesque face, walking on a balmy beach, a crypt, black chiffon, Hannah sleeping. *Hannah!*

She turned over in her bed to see an angelic face on the pillow next to hers, and let out a sigh of relief. She was already starting to stir. Her eyes fluttered a few times and then opened sparkling upon her mother.

"Good morning, sunshine. Happy last day of school," Emma cheered, albeit groggily.

"Good morning. Happy last day of school to you, too." She yawned. "Mama, I think I slept through the night. I don't remember getting up at all. Did I get up?"

"No, you didn't, honey. Isn't that awesome?"

"Yeah. Hey, what's this?" Hannah was fumbling with what looked like a medallion the size of a half-dollar. "Where'd this come from?" There was an etching of the archangel, Michael, on one side, and when she turned it over, there was an inscription written in what looked like an ancient language. "It's pretty. Did you give this to me? I bet it's my lucky charm. I bet that's why I slept through the night."

She sure was astute for such a little girl. Suddenly, Emma remembered being held protectively in someone's arms, of Michael giving her a talisman, too. She reached her hand to her throat. There it was. Hmmm, the picture looked just like Michael.

Michael. Where did he go?

"Mama, why are you still in your clothes from yesterday? Did you fall asleep with them on?"

"I guess I did."

"You're a silly goose." Hannah reached over and tickled her mother's belly.

"Hey, cut that out." She giggled, tickling her right back. "It's time to get ready for school, so let's hop to it." With that, she gave Hannah's bottom a tap and sent her on her way.

Emma quickly got out of bed, ignoring the pain that fired through every muscle and bone in her body. She had to find Michael. What would Hannah think if she found him in their house? As far as she knew, he had left after dinner last night. Emma raced around the house like a lunatic, but he was nowhere to be found. And then she heard a light knocking on the front door.

She peered through the peephole. There he was, exuding freshness and looking utterly delicious. She, on the other hand, felt like a train wreck. She couldn't let him see her in this condition! He knocked again, a little louder. But in actuality, he had seen her at her worst. And why should she be concerned about her appearance, anyway? It was only Michael, right? Michael who had saved her ass last night and held her in the most caring way no one had ever done before. She fussed with her hair, pinched her cheeks, and mustered her best smile as she opened the door.

"I brought some bagels for breakfast. I hope you're hungry." Michael stood in the doorway, a toss-up between a sheepish boy and a virile man. It made for an oddly appealing combination.

"I'm famished actually. And Hannah loves bagels. Come on in." She stepped aside to let him pass.

There wasn't quite enough room, and as he entered, his arm rubbed against hers. There was an immediate rush of energy that coursed through her like a runaway train, and she simply stood there dumbstruck, bagels forgotten, door ajar. *This energy feels so good, so invigorating, and comforting at the same time.* Michael's brow furrowed, and he seemed suddenly annoyed, unsettled. He quickly stepped away from her. *Just like a man to back off.*

"Hi, Mr. D'Angelo," Hannah mumbled in her quiet way as she walked into the foyer. "It's the last day of school."

"Oh, well, good morning, sunshine." A broad smile appeared on his face. "I know, isn't that great? Sorry about not saying goodbye to you personally last night, but I thought I'd make it up to you with bagels. What do you say? Do you forgive me?"

"Bagels? You are very forgiven." Hannah's demeanor instantly brightened. "I'll take the bag to the kitchen for you. Can I get everything ready for breakfast, Mama? I know how. I can make it look like a tea party for our last day of school breakfast. Please?"

"Sure, sweetie, go ahead. That sounds terrific."

As her daughter scampered off to the kitchen, Emma closed the front door and turned toward Michael. "You weren't there when I woke up this morning. In fact, I woke up in my bed. You left us. Where did you go?"

Did I really just say that out loud? She couldn't even look him in the eyes, knowing she sounded like an immature, insecure girlfriend of all things, but she couldn't help herself. Trusting men was so out of her nature at this point. She felt part jilted lover and part idiot for actually wanting to have awakened in his arms this morning. *Lord, but I am so messed up in the head!*

Emma concealed the hurt and confusion with annoyance as Michael took a long moment to respond. "I didn't think it was wise for Hannah to see us together when she awoke this morning. So, I put you to bed and went home to change clothes."

"Oh, I see." *I see I'm a total idiot.*

"I only left here about an hour ago. You're both wearing the Talismans I gave you. You should have been fine. You were, weren't you? Agremon didn't try anything again, did he?" Michael placed his hands on her shoulders, and she shriveled under his clinical, probing gaze as he looked in her eyes.

"No, no. We were fine. Just as you said we would be." *And now I'm feeling like an even bigger idiot.* "Hannah slept through the night, actually. And you're right. She shouldn't have seen you, with me, like, you know, the way we were last night. We wouldn't want to give her the wrong idea about us. Well, I've got to get ready or we'll wind up late for the last day of school. Make yourself at home. I'll be ready in a jiffy." She broke free from his hold, but he caught her hand in his as she made her way towards her bedroom.

"Emma, after school today, we'll take her to the park. We'll talk. She's got to know everything. She can handle it. Knowledge is power. And the two of you have much to learn and master."

She nodded, gave him a weak smile while removing her hand from his, and left.

"Geez," Michael muttered as he puttered about the study, looking at the picture frames again.

"We wouldn't want to give Hannah the wrong idea? There was nothing wrong about the way you felt in my arms last night, lady. Not one bit. And there was nothing wrong with the ideas that came to mind as a result of it, either." He picked up the picture of Emma and Hannah swinging. "But then again, that disastrous marriage you had going there has left you mighty damaged. You know what, Miss Emma? I think it's my duty to make the repairs. No matter how long it might take."

Chapter Ten

*E*mma peeled off her clothes and tossed them furiously in the hamper, all the while chastising herself for her immature display. Michael must surely think she's the most neurotic, whacked out woman on the planet. "A few hours in a man's arms and you think you're something special to him?" She pointed heatedly at her reflection. "You are so not ready for any kind of relationship with this man or any man for that matter. Stick to your fantasies, girlfriend. That's all you seem good for these days."

Convinced she'd find lingering marks from Agremon's torment, she stepped back and examined her body, naked except for the Talisman. In her nightmare, she remembered wearing a skimpy bathing suit and a barely there chiffon gown. And in her nightmare, creepy crawlies had scampered intrusively all of her body, pinching and scratching as they blazed their wicked trail. But now, there was nothing remarkable to see. It really had been just a dream, and she had come through it without any physical souvenirs.

She put the Talisman carefully on the counter, ran the shower, and stepped under the water's soothing warmth. As she soaped up, she wished it could wash away all the terrifying images that kept entering her mind. An image popped into her head of Michael, of all people, standing behind her, stroking and soothing her body. For the briefest of moments, he turned into Agremon. She shook her head vigorously and opened her eyes. *Damn! These bouts of terror are wreaking havoc with my mind!* She thought it best to cut her shower short. So she quickly dried off, spent a few minutes pondering which pair of shorts to shrug into that went with her gorgeous, new sequined tank top, and proceeded to squeeze the water out of her thick hair. As she began the arduous task of brushing through the tangles, her brush got stuck.

"Why don't you let me help you with that?"

Agremon suddenly appeared right behind her and grabbed the brush, yanking on it with his hand. He pulled so hard, her head snapped back.

Emma yelped.

She was now bent over backwards and looking into his face, albeit upside down, with horror. "Ooh, so sorry. I meant to actually rip a good chunk of hair out of your head. You must have very healthy hair. What? Surprised to see me?" He spun her around, getting the brush even more knotted in her hair, and gave her a wicked sneer. "You're a very bad girl, Emma. You've made friends with an old enemy of mine. You shouldn't have done that. For that, you will have to be punished. But we'll get to that later. Give your Protector a message for me, would you, precious? Tell him his little trinkets are no match for me. Tell him I'll be taking what I came here for and there's nothing he can do about it." His teeth had pierced his lips and blood was oozing down his chin.

"I'll see you rot in hell before you get near Hannah again!" she avowed through gritted teeth.

"How'd you know where I live? Have you been keeping tabs on me like a jealous girlfriend?"

He languidly licked her face from chin to temple, gave her hair a final yank, and threw her carelessly against the shower door. "You're of no consequence to me. I will have your daughter, and there's nothing you can do about it. I'll let that knowledge be your punishment. After all, you do a much better job at punishing yourself. You make my work so easy."

With an evil wink, he was gone.

Michael knew the instant Agremon had shown up, and quickly put a Level Two protection shield around Hannah, giving her the illusion that everything was fine, and nobody could touch her. Then he raced to the bathroom door and found it sealed like the mausoleum door had been. He heard something crash against the shower door and could only hope Emma was okay. He spoke the sacred words, *An aimsir láithreac*, to release the seal and rushed inside to find her crumpled on the floor in a heap, her hair nested in a frenzy of tangles. A lingering thread of Agremon's presence remained.

How the hell had he gotten to her again?

Emma was shaking uncontrollably, rubbing her cheek raw with her hand. Michael reached her in a flash and tried to loosen the hold terror had on her. He knelt beside her and gently eased her into a sitting position.

"What happened? I know Agremon was here. I can feel it." He noticed the brush stuck in her hair, and she wouldn't stop scraping her cheek with her hand until he grabbed it. She was mumbling something unintelligible. He noticed the Talisman was missing from around her neck. His voice thundered in the cavernous room. "Emma, where's the Talisman I gave you?"

"I didn't th-think I should wear it in the sh-shower, so I took it off and p-put it on the counter by the sink."

Michael looked over at the counter to find the Talisman lying exactly where she said it would be.

"Damn it! You weren't supposed to take it off, Emma, ever!"

"D-don't yell at me. I didn't know."

"I'm sorry. I didn't mean to." Michael's shoulders rose and fell as he took a breath and a moment to compose himself. He continued in a calmer voice. "I guess my directions weren't clear. It's just that, knowing Agremon's gotten to you again, well, it's completely unacceptable and driving me crazy. What happened? What did he do? What did he say? Are you hurt anywhere?"

"No, surprisingly I don't think I'm hurt, just a little banged up, I guess. But my brush, as you can see, is now hopelessly tangled in my hair since he tried to scalp me. But that's the least of it." She grabbed his hands and looked earnestly in his eyes. "He knows you're here, Michael. He's angry with me for involving you in this. He told me to give you a message, that your trinkets are no match for him, and he's taking Hannah. And then, and then, he licked my face!"

She pointed shakily to her cheek. "Don't you see his blood all over my face? I gotta get it off me, right now! I gotta get it off!" Terror had clearly taken hold again as she pawed at her cheek, nearly drawing blood.

"Hey, hey, Emma, honey, I'll help you. Stop rubbing your face, baby. You're gonna make it bleed. Here, let me take this damp towel and I'll show you." Michael gently swiped at her sun-kissed cheeks, and then dabbed at her pixy nose. "There's no blood on you, look. It was just an illusion Agremon created. Your face is as beautiful as ever. You see?" As he showed her the towel, she nodded and settled down a bit.

"Can you get this damn brush out of my hair?" She snuffled, frustrated and disappointed that the man who had promised protection had failed to deliver.

"Sure, hold still so I don't hurt you." She felt his fingers gingerly remove her hair strand by strand from the brush. As he freed the last bit of it, he pointed to the Talisman and looked her straight in the eyes. "Now put that necklace on, and never, ever take it off for any reason. Understood?"

"Understood," she acquiesced, understanding begrudgingly the power of Agremon and the talisman that would keep him at bay. Michael's touch had been so delicate, so caring, that her strong defenses couldn't hold. And with every tress that was let loose, her distrust and disappointment had shaken free as well. Concerns over her crazy attraction to him slowly dissolved into thin air. She gradually rose to her feet, walked to the counter, and put the Talisman back around her neck. She looked at him through the mirror.

"Was he lying, then, about the Talisman being no match for him? He can't get to Hannah anymore, can he?" She was leaning against the counter now. Her legs were doing their best to hold her up under the strain, but they were not completely successful. Neither was the rest of her demeanor. Michael stepped up behind her and wrapped his arms around her waist. She turned within his embrace and held him right back. She heard his heart beating strong and sure, and not nearly as fast as a human's heart would be beating, reminding her she was in the arms of an angel. A true, blue angel. She closed her eyes as waves of comfort and protection surrounded her.

"He won't get to Hannah. And he won't get to you either, ever again. The Talisman has strong ancient power. I've called one of the Brethren, another Protector, who's a genius with intelligence. He'll find out everything we need to know about Namirha's plans. He's also contacting the rest of the Brethren to come and help me out. I don't mess around, Emma. Too many lives are at stake. And there are two lives in particular I've become very attached to." He drew her head back ever so gently with one hand and stroked her lips with the other. His eyes consumed her, and the mutual longing could no longer be denied.

Slowly he bent his head down and his lips grazed hers, soft and gentle as a whisper. As they came together, tiny sparks shot off in all directions, and an aura of rainbow colors formed a protective barrier around them. Unaware of anything but how wonderful Michael's lips felt against hers, Emma leaned aggressively into the kiss. He retaliated by teasing hers open with his tongue. She let out a hungry groan. The urgency of their unexpected desire deepened and they blended into one united entity. Their hearts beat as one, and they breathed for each other as though they did not exist, one without the other. The kiss seemed to last for an eternity, yet in truth it was mere moments.

Gradually, they came apart, lips bruised and swollen from their powerful assault. Energy drained back to its source. Michael's control had come undone. Emma had no idea what she and her growing powers had done to him. He hadn't realized until now that helping was a two-way street. Yes, he was protecting her and Hannah, but whether she instinctively knew he needed it or not, she was saving him, and it hurt like hell. The Savior had been awakened inside her and knew that Michael needed healing as much as she. But from what, he couldn't let on yet.

"Well, uh, I'd better see to breakfast. Hannah's been waiting for a while now. I'll just go to the kitchen and get things rolling again while you finish up in here." Michael gave her a quick smile and withdrew from the bathroom before Emma could respond.

Chapter Eleven

"So I asked Mama if once school is out we could get a pool and put it in the backyard. She said maybe. That's better than no, right, Mr. D'Angelo?"

"I think it's definitely better than no, Hannah. Hey, that's a mighty cool looking necklace you got there. Can I have a look?" Michael asked. She agreed enthusiastically, and leaned over the kitchen table for him to get a better look. He inconspicuously checked it out for any breaches in its shielding. The shields were still holding strong, as they should. "Where'd you get this?" He wondered if Emma had mentioned anything at all about it.

"I don't know, really. You see, I woke up, and it was on me already. Isn't that funny? And I'm never taking it off, either. Know why? Because I slept through the night last night! No bad dreams!" She immediately put her hand to her mouth. Her eyes flew wide open. "Oops! I wasn't supposed to say anything. No one's supposed to know about my bad dreams, Mr. D'Angelo. Please don't say anything. I don't want the kids to make fun of me." She looked so pitiful; he did his best to ease her mind.

"No worries there, little one. On my honor I will never speak of this to another soul in our school. Your secret is safe with me."

"What secret?" Emma came into the kitchen and sat down beside her daughter at the old pine trestle table and planted a huge kiss on her cheek.

"Mama, I kind of told Mr. D'Angelo that I can't sleep and that I have bad dreams. Is that okay?" Hannah tapped her fingers together.

"Yes, honey, that's fine. In fact, after school, we're going to talk more about it together, at the park, all three of us. I think Mr. D'Angelo can help. Now, I see lots of yummy things on this table and I'm starving. Sweetie, the table looks lovely. I'm so proud of you!"

Hannah ate the remainder of her bagel in blushed silence. After the scorching kiss he'd shared with Emma in the bathroom moments ago, Michael found himself preoccupied by troubling thoughts from his tragic past, and chose to avoid her eyes at all cost. And although it felt like he'd already lived through an entire day, it had only been thirty minutes since Agremon had made his appearance. A telling sign that for some reason, as of yet unknown, Michael was off his game. He wasn't a happy camper.

Emma knew that for her daughter, the last day of school meant the end to her daily escape from her nightmares. She'd made sure to tuck her very special necklace under her shirt so no one could see it. As they walked to Michael's car earlier that morning, however, Hannah had told her that she felt she could slay dragons or demons with it on. So maybe being home all the time this summer wouldn't be so terrible after all.

For Emma, her final duties were filling out closeout forms that seemed a mile long and locking computers away in closets. The day went along without too many interruptions, and before she knew it, she was standing outside of the school with Maddie and the other teachers waving goodbye to all the children going home on the buses.

She hadn't noticed Michael come stand beside her. He whispered subtly in her ear, "You all right, there? I thought I sensed a thread of Agremon nearby and then it faded."

"Yeah, I'm okay. He popped up in a few kids' faces as I waved goodbye earlier, but I've decided, no matter what he tries, I'm not going to let him disrupt my life anymore. I let myself become a victim again, and I refuse to stay that way."

Michael raised an eyebrow.

Damn it! She didn't mean to share that much, but she couldn't seem to help herself where he was concerned.

"I'm glad to see you feeling stronger, more self-assured. Why don't the two of you go ahead to the park, and I'll meet you there in half an hour? I actually have a few more teachers' forms to sign-off on, and then, I'm all yours."

His gaze lingered. God, but she was dying for him to grab her and kiss the living daylights out of her again.

"Sounds like a plan, and I am feeling better thanks to you. A half hour, then. We'll be waiting and enjoying the beautiful weather. Don't be late."

"My word is my oath," he replied with a quiet intensity that shook Emma to her very soul. With nothing more to be discussed, they walked back into the school building, he to finish closeouts, she to gather up Hannah.

Emma took the half hour they were waiting for him to catch up on the day with her daughter and doing what Hannah loved: pushing her on the swings. She hoped what Michael had said about her family's history was indeed true. Then, maybe there could be an end to this incessant madness that had become her life. They could be a happy family again, with Good outshining Evil.

Looking at her daughter, she thought she was ready to take on whatever responsibilities she was about to inherit. If it meant lasting security and happiness for Hannah, she'd be willing to do just about anything. The two had returned to their blanketed spot, and she checked her watch, frowning. It was approaching the half hour mark when Michael was due to show.

"Don't start worrying, I'm already here," he teased, walking up to the blanket. He cast a cooling shadow over Emma's face.

"Thank you for sparing my nerves and being punctual. It's

such a rare quality in a man these days. But I guess you're about as rare as they come, now aren't you?" she ribbed.

"So they say," he boasted with a twinkle in his eyes. He hunkered down on the blanket next to Emma. "Shall we get started, then? No time like the present, I always say, and the sooner we discuss everything, with Hannah, the better prepared we'll be for whatever Namirha has in store."

"Sure, and by the way, I told Hannah that Ted's Garage came by the school, picked up the truck and had it fixed by the end of the day. Just so we have our stories straight, okay?"

"All right. Well, I'm gonna have to give Ted's Garage a try then the next time my car is having engine problems. How convenient," he said with a wink.

The afternoon waxed on with the only unpleasant task being the probing of Hannah for details about her dreams, Namirha, and Agremon. She was reticent at first to share anything but came around when a carousel ride was offered as a prize. Then, Michael explained their special gifts and taught them how to recognize exactly how those powers felt when being used. He worked with Emma first.

"Trust that this power is constantly growing inside you. It needs to be harnessed and molded to suit your innate abilities. Close your eyes, hold my hands, and connect with the energy humming through your system. Do you feel it?"

"Yes," Emma whispered.

"Now, imagine there's a little box inside you waiting to be filled. It harnesses the different abilities you possess. I want you to pour a little bit of your power into this box, like you were pouring from a pitcher."

"Okay, I'm imagining, I'm pouring, but I don't know if it's working."

"That's all right. It's working. I can see your aura shifting. Good job. Now, to teach Hannah."

"We're magical, Mama! We're magical!" Hannah squealed with delight. Emma had healed a cut on her knee, and she could tell what was in the trunk of Michael's car. For the first time in months, Emma saw the exuberant, carefree child burst through the carefully constructed wall Hannah had built around her heart.

"I'm magic, I'm magic!" she sang as she grabbed Emma's hands, pulled her to her feet and danced around in circles. They laughed and collapsed on the blanket, breathless, while Michael watched them, a tender smile creeping across his face.

Emma caught a brief moment of melancholia pass beneath that smile and then watched it disappear as quickly as it had come. She wondered if her playfulness with Hannah and obvious love for each other had brought back shades of memories from a past he hadn't shared yet.

The ring of a cell phone pulled Emma out of her reverie.

"Go ahead. Answer it. I'll take Hannah over to the carousel."

"Thanks." He opened his phone. "Michael here."

"Yeah, it's Gabriel. I've got some Intel for you. I think you'll find it very interesting."

"Go ahead. I've been finding a lot of things interesting over the past couple of days."

"I bet. Check this out. Namirha definitely has designs on getting his hands on that girl of yours. I checked with E.L. and it's a sure bet that she and her mother are part of that prophecy we were told about. You know the one about the salvation of this generation. Well, the girl's destined to be a leader, Michael. But not just any leader, our Great Warrior Child. She was born to lead our army of immortals against the uprising of Evil.

"Not only that, we believe Namirha's probably aware of the unusual pattern of numbers in her family's birthdates and times of birth. She is as important to him as she is to us. If he gets a hold of her, on her birthday, which is six days away, he can bind her to

73

him in a blood ritual, at precisely 6:06 p.m. You know what that means?"

"Yeah, Gabriel, I know what that means. All her powers become his and all hell literally breaks loose on Earth." Michael balked with disgust. "I'm not about to let that happen. You can be damned sure about that."

"Don't worry, brother. All teams have been contacted. They're en route as we speak, and are due to arrive within the hour at Hannah's residence."

"Thanks, Gabriel. Now, can you get me some Intel on Namirha's cult? If we can get in there, we can get to him before he gets to us. Man, we could really use Hannah's intuitive powers right now. I'm working on it, but damn, she's so young. She's practically a baby, Gabriel. I'm trying to take things slowly, but when the Warriors come, they're not going to be so patient. And in reality, they shouldn't be. We don't have the luxury of time."

"Listen, Michael, she may look young, but there's the soul of an Ancient warrior inside her. Don't forget that. And by the way, when do we ever get enough time to prepare for war? I'll get back to you on the cult thing."

Emma turned away from watching Hannah on her carousel horse as Michael approached. Wasting no time, she plied him for information. "I'm assuming the phone call had something to do with us."

Chapter Twelve

"Yes, actually, it did. We need to get back to your place, now," he urged. "The rest of the Brethren are coming."

Emma pressed, "Michael, you're making me nervous. Who exactly were you talking to and what did he say?"

"You don't have to fear the Brethren. I was talking to Gabriel, another Protector. He confirmed what I thought about you two. The rest is gonna have to wait till we're back at your house. I don't want the Brethren to arrive before us. Come on, I'll walk you back to your truck."

Summarily dismissed, Emma brooded all the way home. Warning flags were flying around her head as misgivings washed over her. To trust or not to trust; that was the question. This man had completely turned her world upside down.

He was her protection and her heart's enemy all at once.

Moment by moment, she decided, was the only way to stay above water. Plus, she had so many questions, and didn't like being kept in the dark, especially when it involved her daughter. She would definitely be setting him straight about that.

Michael followed closely behind, not looking forward to her

inevitable reaction when he shared the rest of Gabriel's news. Who was he kidding? He could barely get a grip on the idea himself. But Fate didn't care, and certainly never waited for people to get comfortable with their destinies. As he pulled into the driveway, his cell rang. He turned the car off and answered the phone.

"What do you have for me, Gabriel?"

"Namirha's been busy establishing his cult called, The Source. He's got a compound on every continent, if not in every country across the globe. The newest compound, the Global Headquarters, is located right outside Prophet's Point, at the foot of the Superstition Mountains. They broke ground on the main worship center about six months ago, and most followers are living in tents and campers at the moment. No doubt Namirha wants to be as close as possible to the child."

"Yeah, well, that's the closest he's gonna get to her. How do we get in?"

"There's a gathering called the Homecoming at the new compound scheduled for Sunday. No doubt he's trying to increase his minions."

"That doesn't give us nearly enough time to prepare. Damn."

"Hey, brother, we'll be extra careful this time. I remember the last time we tussled with Satan. Nobody wants to see a repeat performance."

"No, we surely don't. See you soon. Oh, and make sure shields are up when coming into the house. It's dripping with dark energy." He closed his phone and wearily rubbed his eyes. The last time. Jesus! The last time the Brethren battled Satan, the Brethren won, but not without a price. Mortal losses were high, even with the Saviors' healing, and he'd paid heavily with the loss of his wife and unborn child.

Michael dared to think upon his wife from centuries ago now, Beth. She'd been mortal, and he'd seen that as perfection. Her life was so...normal, and he craved that after living alone for centuries.

But being mortal turned out to be her fatal flaw. And loving her had turned out to be his.

Agremon got to her head and heart, turning her against her husband as a last ditch effort for Evil to win. One day, she left home with Agremon at her side, Michael's unborn child kicking madly inside her belly. Agremon slaughtered them over the threshold of his house as the Protector innocently walked up the pathway. He thumbed his nose at him and disappeared. He'd never looked at a threshold the same way since.

And now he faced another threshold. Dare he cross it? Emma was extraordinary, gifted. A woman not quite mortal and not quite immortal. With her powers, she was saving him from self-destruction. He'd been alone and in a dark place when it came to any kind of relationship outside the Brethren. And now, here she was, with a daughter he adored—a daughter that would soon be fighting alongside his Warriors for the eternal protection of the mortal world. He was having second thoughts. Could he really afford to let himself feel again? He had already tasted and sampled. Could that be enough? Should that be enough? Or was that immaterial?

Emma had stirred a strong craving within him. The moment he'd first met her, the attraction had gripped him, but he'd learned to ignore it over the years. The taste was now a compulsion not to be denied. Duty came first, though, and his primal needs would have to take a backseat, for now.

Michael walked in as Emma and Hannah were putting their school things away. Emma blocked his path, poking him in the chest determinedly and cautioned, "Don't think you're going to sidestep me again. I've had enough. I told Hannah to go to the playroom. If my daughter's life is in danger, you better damn well tell me everything, and what exactly you and this Brethren group are going to do about it."

A harsh knock preempted his full disclosure. Emma scowled. He shrugged. She walked to the front door and checked through the sidelight. She turned back to him. "The cavalry's arrived, and I'd better get my answers, soon." She swung the door open with authority and greeted her guests.

◌◍

"Hello, gentlemen. Won't you come in? We've been expecting you." Massive walls of hardened flesh stood at attention by her doorway. Emma waved them in and quickly stepped back to allow them entry. One of the Brethren spoke first.

"Thank you. My name is Kemuel." As he walked through the door, he bent his head down so as not to hit the doorframe. "This is Seraphiel, and that's Nathanael. We are the Warrior Generals of the Brethren. We are honored to be here in the presence of such an ancient and powerful family. To train and fight evil beside the Great Warrior Child is humbling."

She escorted them to the family room. "Yeah, right. You must be joking. Did you know my daughter is only about six years old?"

She laughed. He didn't. She stopped.

"You're not serious, are you? He's not serious, Michael?" She turned to him in near hysterics as his words seeped into her brain. But he wasn't looking at her. He was glaring at Kemuel. "Is this what you've been avoiding telling me? Is it?"

She was engulfed by a fiery flush. Her maternal instinct to protect her daughter had kicked into high gear, and the house's energy vibrated in tune with her own surging energy. The men seemed shocked by her outrage. But she only saw frustration on Michael's furrowed brow.

"Not exactly avoiding, Emma. We just keep getting interrupted. Hey, can you give me a few minutes alone with her, please? I didn't get a chance to tell her much yet," he pleaded, rubbing his hands over his face and escorted Emma to the kitchen. "Emma, I'm so sorry. I thought we would have more time before they arrived. I...." He reached for her arms.

She shrugged him off, not wanting to be calmed or comforted at the moment. "Don't you give me that bullshit, Michael! You've had plenty of time to tell me everything. It was one thing when you said we were *from an ancient line of powerful women.*' Even a little cool that we can do some nifty magic. Now you want me to *believe* and *allow* my daughter to be some kind of warrior against evil? It's preposterous, absurd, and absolutely out of the question. She's a child. A baby, *my* baby. I won't have it, I tell you. I won't! There is no way that Hannah is going to get near any more evil than she's already had contact with. You're a Protector, you say. Well, protect her, then, damn it. Don't get her involved in this. For God's sake, Michael! She's all I've got!"

Her eyes welled with tears as she grabbed furiously at his shirt sleeves. He wrapped himself around her and drew her towards him. Emma felt her mind being teased with calmness. She swiped angrily at tears that spilled down her cheeks and ripped away from his hold.

"No! I don't want to be soothed. Not while you're all scheming to send my daughter to a senseless death."

"It's not like that, really. I know you're scared. But that's because you haven't seen what Hannah is capable of. She's your daughter, yes, but she's so much more. Inside her is the soul and power of a great ancient warrior. Your little girl is the only one who can lead us to victory against evil. There is no dou—"
Suddenly they heard metal clashing against metal, and a girl's hearty laughter coming from the living room.

"What the hell? I told her to stay in the playroom." Emma dashed back to the family room where she stopped dead in her tracks. There, in the middle of the family room, was Hannah, wielding a sword against Nathanael.

"Stop it! Stop it this instant! What do you think you're doing?" Hannah spun around, getting in a quick parry.

"Oh, hi, Mama! I was peeking in to see who was here, and all these big guys bowed down like I was a princess or something. They asked if I wanted to play with them. Nathanael is the evil guy, and I'm the Great Warrior Child. Isn't that cool? I'm gonna get him, too, Mama, watch me!"

And with that, she spun back around to face Nathanael, trading swordplay as though she'd been doing it for years. She wasn't playing around with a plastic sword either. She was actually holding one of the Warrior's swords. Without any problem whatsoever. Emma was stunned into silence as she watched Hannah shower blow after blow against him. Nathanael was kneeling on the floor, blocking all of her attacks.

As the swordplay progressed, Emma's stomach clenched into a tight knot while dreadful thoughts of mutilation, severed limbs, and a gruesome early death of her daughter swirled in her mind. It was all too much for her to take in. She charged at her daughter, grabbed the sword from her, and threw it aside. Then she picked Hannah up and whisked her away to her bedroom. Once there, she dropped to the bed and held onto her baby girl with every fiber of her being. She rocked and soothed and petted her precious daughter.

"Mama, what's the matter? Are you okay? 'Cause I'm fine." Hannah pulled back after a moment. "I was having fun. Those guys told me they're my brothers and they're going to help me learn my powers and get Agremon and Mr. Namirha out of here once and for all. They said I am the Great Warrior Child. I feel so much better now that they're here, Mama, don't you?"

"Oh, honey," Emma sighed. "They're not your brothers. They are called the Brethren, and I really don't know how I feel about them being here. I don't like seeing you with a sword in your hand at all, to think of you fighting, putting yourself in such incredible danger. You're my little girl, my angel. I can't imagine anything bad happening to you. I would die first. I want this evil Agremon to go away, but I can't have you fighting. You're just a child. My baby. If anyone is going to fight, it's going to be me."

Hannah took her tiny hands and touched Emma's cheeks while looking intently into her mother's eyes. "It's not only Agremon, Mama. It's Mr. Namirha, too. He's the one who really wants me. But don't be afraid, Mama. I will fight against Agremon and Mr. Namirha and win, because I'll have an army with me. And if I need saving, you can save me, just like you always do." She gave her a big squeeze.

How could a girl who had been so very frightened for the past six months be so very brave now? *She has an ancient, powerful soul inside her. Her powers are awakening.*

Emma reconciled herself to the fact that she had lost all control over their destinies. It did nothing to ease the pain in her heart or loosen the ball of tension in her belly. She prayed that the good guys would win without any casualties. There was a light tap on the door.

"Can I come in?" called a voice softly from outside the bedroom door.

"Yes, Michael," Emma answered, resigned. He'd really screwed up with her, and she could tell by his tentativeness that he knew it, too. Would they be able to get through this and come out the other side intact? She didn't know. What she did know was her heart was in definite turmoil. But this was no time to analyze a budding relationship that was already on the rocks. Her daughter, her baby, had a soul that was actually older than she living inside her, with skills and powers that were sure to amaze her. She had no choice but to see this all the way through at her daughter's side. She stood up and held Hannah's hand.

"Hey. The Warriors are getting restless and would like to get to work with her. There's so much to do and very little time. Will you agree to this, all of this, whatever may come? If you don't, I understand. Hell, if I had my choice, I wouldn't want to see her involved in any of this either. But honestly, we can't do this without her. As crazy as it sounds, I know we can destroy Namirha and Agremon with her leading us."

"Crazy doesn't even begin to describe this whole mess. You know, as a parent I'd always hoped that one day my child would grow up happy, have lots of friends, and be successful. The key phrases here are, grows up and one day. I've just learned that our one day is now. Hannah's sixth birthday is in six days, and instead of celebrating with friends and balloons and laughter, we're looking at going to war against Evil. It's a lot to take in, a lot to commit to. You're asking me to take a huge risk with our lives. If I agree to this, do we get our lives back when it's over? Can we go back to normal?"

"Truthfully, you can never go back to the way things were. Normal will have to look a bit different for you and Hannah. It does for me."

"Of course it does. What am I thinking? You're immortal! What does all of this make us, then? What are we, Michael?"

"That's a good question, and right now, I don't have the answer, except that you and your daughter seem to be the key to Good defeating Evil in this latest battle for world domination. Do you have an answer for me, then? Are you agreeing to move forward with Hannah? With the Brethren?"

"Oh please, Mama! I can do this, I know I can. And I need to. I can feel it deep inside. I've been scared for so long, but ever since I got this necklace, I've been feeling things and thinking things like I was somebody else, somebody more than me. I've been getting stronger inside. I have to do this, Mama. Do this with me."

Such maturity from one so young. But not so young, after all.

It pained her so to say it, but she agreed. "Yes, we'll do this, together. But if anything should happen to this one," she threatened, pointing to Hannah, "Agremon's schemes will seem like child's play when I'm through with all of you."

"Spoken like a Savior, through and through." Michael's voice was filled with respect.

"No, spoken like a mother. I'd bet you my maternal instincts are far more powerful than my ability to heal any day of the week."

"Why don't we get to work on that then? Hannah, you're going to be training with Kemuel, Nathanael, and Seraphiel. They are your generals and will teach you everything you need to know about using your powers." They walked out to the living room. The three men immediately stood, all raising a questioning brow.

"Well, Kemuel, why don't you begin your training?" Michael suggested.

"Excellent. We'll use the backyard. It's the perfect place for this kind of training."

"Can I ask, please," Emma interrupted, "Why swords?"

"These aren't just any swords. On the blades are inscriptions from an ancient incantation book. All warriors have one, as will our Great Warrior Child," Nathanael explained.

"Ah, just make sure there's not a scratch on my child when you're done training today," she demanded.

"These swords will kill only those who have sided with Evil, mortal and immortal alike. As for her training sessions, keeping her scratch-free might be a little hard to do. If she were to get injured from training though, it would be the smallest of nicks or scrapes, and not from any of our swords. They can't harm us. And besides, Savior Mother, you are here to heal her," Kemuel reminded her.

"Well, I'm her mother first, and Mother says train safely, that's all. Oh, and her bedtime is nine now that school's over." She heard a groan come from the group of men. "Don't give me that nonsense. Even warriors need a good night's sleep." Kemuel shot a look at Michael. He returned a placating glance and assured Emma that her daughter would be fine. As the Warriors got down to training, the doorbell rang.

"That must be the rest of our teams."

As Emma answered the door, she was speechless. The men standing before her were as massive as the Warriors, with shoulders so wide they almost had to turn sideways to walk through the doorway. Each had long, beautiful hair of varying shades from blonde to black. And their eyes reminded her of precious jewels.

As they entered the foyer, squeezing into every available space, Emma pondered how they were all going to fit into her tiny ranch home. She had to laugh at that point. Was she really worrying about crowd control? Never mind about the part where a six-year-old would be leading grown men, immortals, into a life and death battle against Evil!

Chapter Thirteen

"Ms. Livingston, we are honored to be in your presence and in the presence of the Great Warrior Child. I am Raphael, Lead Savior, and this is Cassiel and Zadkiel, Saviors as well." They each nodded in turn, and she marveled at how they were so similar in stature and mannerism, yet each had their own individual style. From suit pants to jeans, dress shirts to T-shirts. Combined, they hurt her eyes with their handsomeness.

If these guys don't stop being so formal, I'm going to puke. What's the deal with the royal treatment?

"Well, hello, and please call me Emma," she insisted. "We don't stand on ceremony around here." Raphael grabbed her hand in a firm handshake and immediately gasped, frowned, and let go abruptly. He turned to Michael.

"Listen, Ms. Livingston, Emma, is in seriously bad shape, as is this house. I've gotta take care of these things first before we're able to move forward with our plans. Gabriel has filled us in on everything so we won't be wasting time."

"What do you mean I'm in serious shape? I mean I know I've been getting some terrifying images swimming in my head, but Michael saw to that with this necklace. Right?" She held the talisman in her hands for all to see and stood tall before Raphael.

"The talisman I gave you dampens the effects of the terror

Agremon planted inside you. It doesn't take it away," Michael tried to reassure her. "Raphael will see to that."

"And what's wrong with the house?"

"Well, what we're feeling is a dark energy, very strong. Without our shields to protect us, it would be like wading through a tar pit walking into your home. And like that muck, it is suffocating the life essence, the positive energies that exist in this home from all the people who've lived here before you, as well as you and your daughter. Once your home and you are cleansed, we can continue the training you've begun. I'm going to deal with the house first. That will allow our men to put their shields down. Michael, get everyone out of the house. You too, Emma. I must be alone in the house. And stand as far away as possible."

The two rounded up the men and joined Hannah and her Warriors out back. They all worked their way toward the line where landscaped precision met nature's design. As they watched the house, twilight descended with its exquisite hues of orange, red, purple and gold. Emma glanced at the Brethren who stood in silence and awe of such beauty, then turned back to face her home, wondering what exactly was happening inside. Whatever it was, she hoped it helped.

A flash, like lightning, appeared from inside. And another. Suddenly, the ground under their feet began to vibrate and rumble, and Hannah grabbed onto her mother's leg. The house visibly shook.

"Mama, are we having an earthquake?"

"I don't think so, sweetie." Emma picked up her frightened daughter.

"What's happening, Mama?" she asked in a hushed, high-pitched voice, and flung her arms around her neck like a vice.

"Don't worry, baby," she soothed, and rubbed her back. "Raphael, is taking all the bad feelings out of the house so we can be happy again." She hoped she was speaking the truth.

Michael walked over to her and reached for Emma's hand. She glanced up, surprised to see what she dared not ever hope for from any man—affection, in his eyes. She met it tentatively with a squeeze. Gently, she peeled Hannah away to stand between them.

The rumbling of the Earth had ceased and flashes of light could no longer be seen. The back door opened, and Raphael appeared. He waved them back in, but then dropped his hand on his head and his jaw dropped. Michael and Emma looked at each other with concern, and then scanned the others' faces for anything that would explain Raphael's odd behavior. Their faces held perplexed expressions as well.

"What's going on? Are we being attacked?" she cried out. Michael grabbed her and Hannah and held onto them in a defensive maneuver.

"Brothers! What's going on?" he shouted.

It was Urie who spoke up first.

"Brother, it's okay. We're all a bit taken aback right now, that's all. We didn't know."

"What the hell are you talking about, Urie?" he bristled.

Raphael had finally made his way over to the group of awed immortals. "Michael, we had no idea about this. Why didn't you tell us? This is most interesting. Most interesting indeed."

"All right, enough. What am I supposed to have an idea about that is most interesting?" Michael pressed, his anger simmering. "What gives?"

Gabriel stepped forward and spoke. "Relax. Guys, it's not his fault. He doesn't know. I thought he knew everything since he was dead on with identifying the Warrior Child and Savior Mother." He turned to Michael and continued. "You see, the prophecy we spoke of earlier, well, there is actually a bit more to it. The prophecy reveals that to defeat evil in this generation, it would require the powers of the Great Warrior child to fight against evil, the Great Savior Mother to save the many fallen victims, and the powers of the Great Protector to keep Evil away once defeated. The power of the Trinity—the Great Warrior Child, the Great Savior Mother, and the Great Protector, is what will allow Good to continue to reign over the world."

"Okay," Michael said. "But I still don't see why you're all

looking at the three of us so strangely."

"The prophecy states that the Trinity would be made known when a pure white aura glows around the three chosen ones. Hannah's the Great Warrior Child. Emma here is the Great Savior Mother. And you, my brother, are the Great Protector." Gabriel gave him a shit-eating grin.

"Where the hell did you come up with that load of crap?"

What's the matter with him? Emma wondered. Why was this revelation pissing him off so much?

"You apparently can't see it, but there is an aura surrounding you, Emma, and Hannah that is undeniable. You three are the Trinity, for sure."

"What aura? What are you talking about?" asked Emma.

"Okay, so you're all holding hands. There's a pure white aura surrounding all three of you providing a sphere of protection right now. You can't see it, but we can, and it's nearly blinding. This is mighty incredible. Way to go, brother. Congratulations!"

All the Brethren began stepping forward, offering hearty pats on the back, while Michael and Emma stood dazed and confused. Hannah peered back and forth between the two.

"Why are they congratulating? Are we going to be a family now, Mama? Huh? Are we?" Emma gawked at Michael. She was at a total loss for words. He came to the rescue.

"I consider all of my good friends my family, sweetie."

Snapped back to reality, Emma spoke, with an air of authority that felt unusually comfortable on her. "Well put, Michael. Raphael, I need you to fix me, now. We've got dinner to eat and work to do, and if there aren't any more surprises to be unleashed, I'd like to head on back to the house and get started." Emma softened, "Will you be with me while Raphael does whatever it is Raphael does to me?"

"Of course." He lifted her hand to his mouth to kiss it. "I won't leave your side. But if you'll excuse me, I need a couple minutes here alone with Gabriel." She was wary as he let go of her hand, but walked back to the house with Hannah in tow.

"Gabriel, wait!"

Gabriel turned around and walked back to Michael. "Hey, what's up, brother?"

"Brother, this is totally messed up!" He paced back and forth like a caged tiger. He bent down and picked up a dead branch from a Mesquite tree and started whacking away at some unruly shrubbery. "There's no way I could be the Great Protector, Gabriel. I couldn't even protect my own family, damn it! My own wife, my unborn child, I couldn't protect them. And now I'm supposed to be the Great Protector? It doesn't add up. It's got to be someone else, Gabriel. It's one thing to protect the mother and child right now, and something completely different to protect the world. I need to talk to the boss man immediately. He's got to know this isn't right."

"What good's talking to E.L. going to do, Michael? He's our boss. You know we don't have a say in the tasks that are assigned to us. We can only make good choices along the way. He's got a plan, a reason for doing this to you and not to someone else. Trust E.L. He's never steered you wrong."

"Oh, really? So, disabling my alert system so Agremon could get to Beth wasn't wrong? I disagree."

"You know how I felt about Beth and what happened. But don't you see? If that day never occurred, you wouldn't be here right now, assuming a role that will save this world from Evil. Michael, E.L. knows what he's doing. You're the best man for the job."

"Ha! That's a good one."

"You've already felt what's at stake here. You've had and lost. That's something none of us can say, and in this instance, that's not a plus. Come on, you don't have to think on it right now. Just keep doing what you're doing and I know it will grow on you."

"Yeah, yeah. I wish I had your confidence. Why don't you go on up to the house? I'll be there in a minute. Let me try and clear my head first."

"No problem." Gabriel offered him a hearty thump on the shoulder then started towards the house.

Michael watched as his friend climbed the stairs to the back porch, and then his gaze veered off into the forest.

Prophecy couldn't have dictated the deaths of his wife and child. Could it? For a Protector to be rendered helpless as he watched his family die was cruel and heartless. What must he have done in all his eternal years to have deserved to witness such a tragedy? How was he going to continue in his duty to Emma and Hannah knowing the failure that he truly was? Intentions were only as effective as the actions that backed them up. His actions have not been living up to Brethren standards. And now to be called a Great Protector? Not possible!

He stood by the shrubs, inadequate, troubled, small.

He sensed Emma's presence behind him and he turned. His breath caught as he watched her walk resolutely down the stair, closing the distance between them. Her eyes fixed firmly on his. He could only imagine what she saw in them. Pain maybe, anguish and guilt, for certain.

In hers, he saw redemption.

He couldn't move, stayed by emotions long kept hidden away and suppressed. Emma stood before him, a petite yet strong woman, with a fragile yet fierce heart. He could bear it no longer. He needed to touch her, to absorb the latent power within her. He outstretched his arms in desperation and dropped to his knees, beseeching.

A small cry escaped her lips. She met him on the ground and simply embraced him. He held onto her as he had no other; not even Beth. Like she was his anchor in rough seas. The grief, the helplessness, the fear, and the fury poured out of him and into her. She gasped.

Emma succumbed to the depth and ferocity of emotions assaulting her heart. Michael held onto her as though he were drowning. His horror, his trauma, his eternal anguish seeped into every molecule of her brain. It was then, deep in her soul, that she knew she was the only one who could save him. And it was then that she decided she would.

A single tear managed to escape and trail down her cheek. "I know, Michael. You don't have to say anything. I know, and I'm so sorry. I'm here for you as you've been here for me. And I'm not going anywhere. Never doubt that," Emma professed with an intensity that surprised her.

She framed his face in her hands and gently brushed his lips with hers. It was the kind of kiss that demanded nothing and gave everything. And through this connection, Emma began healing his damaged heart with her powers. She could see tiny tears fighting to escape the corners of Michael's eyes and then dare to cascade down his cheeks. Emma released his lips to sip them away.

He cried out in agony, "Oh God, Emma! No! I can't let you do this for me. Not yet. You're damaged yourself." He pulled away from her and doubled over. She quickly reached out for him and again, he moved away.

"I'm well enough to do this. I must. You can't continue living with your pain and suffering like this. Let me finish what I've started. Come back to me, Michael, please. Come back to me. Let me save you. You've been suffering too long." This time, when she beckoned, he let her hold him. She embraced him and stroked his hair ever so gently. As she sent a warm, soothing sensation through him, he began to heal. She didn't know how she knew what to do, as instinct had taken over. As she worked her healing arts on him, she sensed his pain ease and his grief release layer by layer. She tried to relieve his rage, his need for vengeance, but those threads were far too strong for her to touch with her emergent skills. After a few moments, he stood stronger and more confident.

"Emma," he murmured and found her lips once again. This time, the kiss did demand. He claimed her, body and soul, branding her so that no one could mistake his property. Her arms flew around his neck as she accepted his mark, and she deepened the assault. She never wanted to let go and held on even tighter, amazed at how perfectly they fit together, how spectacular their bodies blended into one. A thought flittered through her mind and stuck. He is the one. All is as it should be. Finally, she reigned in her emotions long enough to release from his searing kiss. He leaned his forehead against hers.

They both clung to each other and breathed heavily as he spoke in a throaty voice, "I-I don't know what to say. You know, you know my suffering. And you're still here. You're incredible." He feathered feverish caresses on her forehead. "But now, we've got to fix you. I won't stand for Agremon's terror being inside you for another minute. I'll be damned if I let anything happen to you li—" He choked on the words. "Okay, if we are to be this Trinity, as Gabriel is saying, we've got to be in top form." He took her hand in his and raised it to his lips. As he pressed them into her palm, his gazed pierced through to her soul.

"I'm ready for our destiny, Emma. Are you?"

"Yes, Michael. I don't know, maybe it's my ancient ancestors speaking to me, but something tells me I should be. So with you, with Hannah, with the Brethren, I believe we can conquer Evil. We can do this."

Her hand remained in his as they walked back to the house with a new resolve. Raphael greeted them at the door. "Are you ready to be healed?"

"Yes, Raphael, I am. Is it going to hurt? What should I expect?" she asked tentatively. Her stomach lurched as she contemplated all sorts of bizarre treatments occurring.

"You'll feel a little lightheaded after I've removed Agremon's threads from your mind, but after that you'll be astounded by your heightened senses. I'd still wear Michael's talisman, though. You still need to be protected. I doubt Agremon will stop trying to get what he needs by any means possible."

"All right, then. Let's get on with it."

The three of them walked into the family room to find it loaded with the rest of the Brethren. The healing took place in her bedroom. As promised, her Protector was by her side for support. It really was as Raphael said it would be. When he placed his hand directly on her forehead, she immediately felt lightheaded and grabbed onto Michael. Then, Raphael waved his palm about an inch over her heart. Healing energy surged through her and eased her spirit.

The whole process only took about five minutes. And the difference in Emma's focus, her attitude, and the way she absorbed the world around her was immediate. Everything was so sharp and crystal clear. Colors were more vibrant, sounds that she hadn't heard before were audible. Smells were more intense. All was as expected, Raphael had assured her. All of her senses had been enhanced as her powers awakened. Agremon's hold on her mind had created a barrier that now no longer existed.

"Dinner's here!" shouted Hannah. As the trio came out of the bedroom, Hannah ran up to them and grabbed Emma's and Michael's hands. There was an immediate surge of energy and the place lit up like the Fourth of July.

"Whoa! Would everybody kindly let go, please. You're blinding us with your aura." Raphael shielded his eyes. They immediately let go of each other. "Now then, Michael, you're going to have to add a little something to those talisman necklaces Emma and the Warrior Child are wearing. Some kind of incantation that will allow you three to use your aura when needed and still shield the rest of us from the blinding light. Until you've got something, I suggest you don't hold hands at the same time, okay?"

"Sorry, brother." He chuckled. "I'll get to work on it right after we eat dinner. Let's go."

Dinner was remarkable in that it was completely unremarkable. Emma sat at the head with Michael to one side and Hannah on the other. The rest of the Brethren behaved like any other hungry bunch of men gathered around a table. They allowed themselves for the briefest of time to converse on all things mundane, like who their picks were for the World Series, and taunted each other over previous escapades gone awry. She could almost forget they were immortal. She scanned the table and thought, this is so...normal. But unfortunately she knew it was a façade, and it would soon fade.

Normal had gone on an extended vacation, and there were no signs of it returning anytime soon.

Chapter Fourteen

*H*e loved the name, Superstition, and the fact that it was assigned to a mountain made it that much more dramatic. Namirha could play off the name and hook followers in a snap at the Homecoming on Sunday. The building of the Global Headquarters was proceeding right on schedule. He could think of no better way to celebrate than with the ritual binding to the child known as Hannah. She was his road to infinite glory and total domination of the world. Namirha looked out the window of his limo towards the mountain, towards the very top. When he ruled over the world, no longer would the mountain tops be reserved for the righteous. Oh no! They would be cast out and he would be exalted! Of course, he could always vacation in the depths of Hell. He did so enjoy it down there.

"Agremon!" Namirha roared. Agremon appeared instantly in the limo, and knelt before Namirha. "Get up and report."

"Well, my Lord, I've hit a bit of a snag. I got the mother out of the way, but I believe the Brethren are now involved. I saw the Protector's talisman around the child's neck. With that shielding her, I couldn't get close. I shall find another way. The Protector, known as Michael, and I have history. I plan on using it to my advantage."

"You know, I'd like to help you, Agremon. You've been so

resourceful with keeping the followers in line. And I recognize how hard you've been working to get the child. Now, with the Brethren involved, things could get very, shall I say, uncomfortable for me and my minions. So, let me do this for you. Let me remind you what is in store for you should you fail me in this monumental task." With a wave of his hand, Namirha delivered a blow that slashed through Agremon's midsection. His organs slowly oozed out onto his lap while he looked on in horror.

"What's the matter, Agremon? Why are you so shocked? You know you won't die. No, I wouldn't do that to you. But can you imagine the rest of your eternity living through this over and over again? How about I add a little bit of this as well?" He waved his hand again and Agremon's skin tore away from his body, leaving muscle and sinew exposed to the air. He shrieked in abject agony. With another wave of his hand, Namirha returned Agremon's body to its original state. "What do you think, Agremon? You bring me the child, or spend the rest of eternity reliving these past few moments over and over again."

Breathless from the pain of torture, Agremon spoke through gritted teeth. "I will get the child, my Lord. And I will see the Protector pays for my pain and labors."

"You are to do no such thing. We are not ready to do battle with the Brethren. After the homecoming we will need to train the new followers. If there is a battle to be fought, it shall happen after the blood ritual with the child. I can't have anything disrupt my plan. You are not to engage the Brethren, yet. Do you understand, Agremon?"

"Yes, my Lord. I understand. But understand this, if I can't touch the Brethren, and they have the child, you may miss your only chance to rule this world."

"Find a way to get the child here, Agremon. Mark my words, I will rule over this world, and no Brethren or sorry excuse for a fallen angel will stop me." Namirha pointed a bony finger at Agremon and zapped him out of the limo. Where he zapped him to, he had no clue, nor did he care.

Agremon spat on the dusty ground, right outside the worship center. Nearly foaming at the mouth from anger, he went on a rampage through the followers' tents. Someone had to be asleep. All he needed was one, just one to terrorize and release his anger upon. He stalked through the rows and rows of tents, ruminating over his plans.

Michael, the Protector, would surely pay for this latest undressing by Namirha. He would see to it. The hell with waiting! Agremon the Terrible was done with all the thwarted attempts to get the child. He'd get her all right, but he was definitely going after Michael, too.

For now, someone was sleeping. Someone who wasn't a true believer yet, who needed to be scared into submission. Frightening a mortal, that would make him feel a whole lot better.

Chapter Fifteen

*D*inner had been finished a long time ago. Michael added a sacred incantation to the talismans Emma and her daughter wore to dampen the brilliant aura the Trinity created, and Hannah was now up to her eyeballs in swordplay with her warriors. They had decided to start with sword fighting since she had shown such a proclivity towards it when they had first met. Her mother could tell she was having the time of her life with these men. She was more animated than she'd been for the past six months. The Brethren didn't treat her like a child, but rather, like one of their own.

It was the strangest thing to see from an outsider's perspective, but to these men, these warriors, it was Hannah's body that was six years old. Her soul on the other hand, held the wisdom and the power of an ancient warrior. As she trained, the little girl that was Hannah seemed to be pushed aside, allowing the Ancient Warrior soul out. Her mother looked on in wonder as she observed the subtle transformation of her baby girl into the ancient warrior. She could scarcely imagine what it must be like to be an ancient warrior's soul trapped in a little girl's body. To even acknowledge that such a thing could occur was simply mind-boggling. Yet here she was, watching her daughter deftly swing a sword as though it was a natural extension of her arm.

But Hannah still was that little girl, and it was time for her to go to bed.

"Gentlemen, it's time for our little warrior to go to bed now. Tomorrow's another day, and she needs her rest." Emma signaled for Hannah to drop the sword and head inside.

"Hannah has shown great talent for the sword," Kemuel reported. "Tomorrow, we will work on her mind. Good night, Great Warrior Child. Sleep well."

"Oh I will, Kemuel. I've got a magic necklace to help me," she boasted with a huge grin.

"Why you've got Michael's special talisman. It is certain you will have a peaceful rest."

"Let Agremon try to get to me tonight. Why, I'll—I'll..." she stammered.

"Okay, kiddo. Let's head on in. No more thinking about the A-man before bed. Thank you for taking good care of her during training. I don't see a scratch on her at all. But I do see a couple of scrapes on you, Kemuel," Emma observed, looking him over and finding herself quite amused.

"As I said, she has shown quite a talent for the sword and fighting," Kemuel replied flatly.

"Yes, well, we'll just go on in then. You should have Raphael take a look at those." She took her daughter by the hand and went into the house.

"I got him real good a couple times, Mama, real good," Hannah gushed.

"I'm so proud of you, honey, I think," she responded awkwardly. Was this really something to be proud of? She hadn't a clue. Emma approached Hannah's bedtime for the first time in months with ease. After all, they both wore Michael's talisman now, and they had a houseful of angels. It couldn't get more secure than that.

Emma walked back into the family room where the Brethren

now congregated. "So what's next?"

"Well, we need to start planning our offense. We're going to infiltrate the Homecoming gathering on Sunday to get close to Agremon and Namirha. Since they're looking to increase their flock, I think we're in a great position to be counted as one of them. Make sure you're all wearing biker clothes. We'll no doubt draw some attention, but if we appear as bikers, our size shouldn't be a problem. There are about five hundred followers already camped out on the site, so we could easily blend in with our own tents."

"That's fine, Kemuel, as long as Hannah isn't counted amongst them. You'll have to go over my dead body to take her anywhere near that encampment."

"Don't worry. You, Michael, and she will be staying right here," Raphael interjected. "The positive energy flowing through this house is enhancing the speed of your success at training. Do you know anything about this house, the land that it's on?"

"Only that it belonged to my mother. I inherited it after she passed away."

"There's something special going on here," Gabriel chimed in. "If I may?"

"Go ahead, Gabriel. You're the master of intelligence," Raphael proclaimed. "Lay it on, brother."

"Well, your house and the land it sits on are part of a large energy vortex. Have you heard of those before? Since you live here in Arizona, I would think you have."

"Yes, I know a little. Great spiritual energy flows down certain magnetic lines. There are many supposedly in Sedona."

"Correct, and one of the strongest lines flows southward, right through your property. It's enhancing both of your powers many times over. So, Raphael will train you tomorrow, Kemuel and the gang will work with Hannah some more, and Michael will work on protecting this place like Fort Knox. As for me, I'll go back to my computers and get the latest information on our resident evil man. I'm actually going to head out now." Gabriel got up then and headed for the door, opened it, and walked right out without so much as a wave or a goodbye.

"Abrupt bugger, isn't he?" she commented.

"Yep, that's Gabriel for you," Michael replied. "Doesn't like goodbyes all that much."

"Well now, that leaves eight of you to battle it out for the couches, chairs, and floor tonight. I'm sorry my place isn't bigger."

"Don't worry about us. We won't be sleeping," Raphael said. "We'll be standing guard around the perimeter of your property through the night."

"You can't possibly think you can stay up all night and then train all day. You're mad!"

"Emma, we never sleep," Raphael answered simply. "We're angels."

"Oh, right, what was I thinking?" she responded, feeling like a total fool. But really, who knew angels didn't sleep? It's not like someone would have an opportunity to question an angel regarding their sleeping habits.

"I'll be staying in the house, if that's okay with you, for extra protection," Michael offered.

"Yes, that would be great, actually. I know we have the talismans to wear, and I haven't had any more trips down terror lane since Raphael cleansed me, but still, I would feel much better."

She looked at him, he looked at her. She knew it was the lamest excuse in history and ventured that he was thinking the same. But she wasn't going to admit it, especially not with the other Brethren in the room. With handshakes and good nights spoken, the Brethren made their way out the door. Emma and Michael watched them through the kitchen window as they faded into the night, and were now alone, left to deal with the impact of the day's events and raw emotions. So much had happened in so little time that it left her dizzy.

"So, can I get you a cup of coffee or something?" Emma finally asked, her voice near breathless from the deafening silence that had grown between them.

"Or something," Michael replied, as he gathered her up in an embrace that took the rest of her breath away. His eyes hypnotized her with their deep oceans of blue and gold. And then, he kissed her. Oh so gently at first, nibbling at her bottom lip, masterfully parting her lips so he could enter and taste her. Then he slowly raised the temperature to blistering.

At first, her arms hung limply at her sides. But as his seduction deepened, she found her footing again, and her hands slid up his arms, caressing and gripping Michael's back and shoulders. She couldn't seem to get enough of him as she fought with his tucked-in shirt. And then, she won the battle. Touching his smooth skin, his taut muscles clenched with every brush of her fingers. He lifted her off the floor, never once breaking their kiss, and she was surprised to find herself planted on the countertop.

"Oh God, Emma, do you know what you've been doing to me?" he growled. "Driving me crazy, woman. That's what." His lips left a feverish trail from her jaw line down her neck. "I need more of you, Emma. So much more."

Emma took his face into her hands and looked at him, his expression blurred by her own desire. She threw all caution to the wind. "My bedroom, Michael, take me there, now." She could barely speak anymore, she could barely think. He swung her up in his arms, never taking his focus off of her, and made his way to her bedroom.

He closed the door with his foot, and proceeded to lay her on the bed. Michael stood motionless.

Unwilling to let his uncertainty ruin the moment, Emma rose to her knees and slowly unbuttoned his shirt. What she revealed was every woman's fantasy, and yet he was here, with eyes and a body only for her. Muscles strained from the sexual tension and showed off their sculpted beauty. Emma couldn't stop herself. She leisurely ran her hands up and down his hard stomach and chest, teasing his taut nipples.

Michael brought her face up to meet his and ravaged her mouth with a kiss so deadly Emma thought she might never recover. As he eased back, he ripped off her shirt.

Emma hadn't worn a bra, and he'd known that all damn day. But finally, he was going to see and touch and taste what he'd been craving so desperately. *I can't believe I'm finally standing here in front of the most beautiful woman I've ever known. Six years! Six years I've dreamed of this moment. And now, she wants me, too.*

"You're so beautiful, Emma, so damn beautiful. And I've wanted you for so very long." He reached out to hold her to him, skin to skin. Flames shot through his body from head to toe.

"Make love to me, Michael," she pleaded and then, merely whispered, "I need you so much it hurts."

No more words were necessary as he took her then and there. This was no unhurried, rainy Sunday morning kind of lovemaking. It was frantic. It was feral. It was his hands and mouth in a frenetic quest to explore every inch of her, and both of them in a heated battle to become one.

Emma's reactive body pushed his to the brink of madness. As he reached the climax of their lovemaking, Michael groaned in ecstasy and wings sprouted from his shoulder blades; large, snowy white, iridescent wings that reached from his shoulders down to his feet.

"Oh God, no!" he moaned. He looked at Emma in utter dread and tore away from her before she could say anything. He jumped off the bed, but didn't know where to go, so he staggered his way to the farthest, darkest corner of the room, turning his back to hide his humiliation. Through the blood shushing through his ears, he heard sheets rustling. He prayed Emma would leave the room and let him collect himself. Instead, the wooden creak of the floorboards told of her approach.

"What's wrong, Michael? Have I done something wrong?"

A gentle stroke of his feathers sent him reeling. His breath hitched. The stroking immediately stopped.

"I'm so sorry! Did I hurt you?"

"No. It—it feels so good, you touching my wings. I'm sorry. It's not you. It's me. I should have controlled myself better back there."

"What on earth do you mean? Michael, explain to me why you've sent yourself to the corner like an errant schoolboy."

"You're probably so sickened by the sight of me right now. I'm an abomination. Give me a little time...to hide my wings. Can you turn away? Don't look at me and don't say anything, please. I'll get myself together and go stand watch with the others. No one has to be the wiser." Damn it all! Why couldn't he keep his wings under wraps this time? He'd been able to so many times before.

"Oh Michael, I'm the farthest thing from sickened a person can be. You're an angel, for heaven's sake! You're supposed to have wings. Where are you getting this crazy notion that you're an abomination and that I'd be sickened by them?"

"I learned early in my immortal life that showing my wings unfortunately never produces the desired effect of awe and peace in you humans. In the past, they've left the women who supposedly loved me shocked and repulsed. I never showed them to Beth. She never knew I was an angel."

Emma stroked his wings again ever so gently. He turned around, in all of his naked glory, and saw fire smoldering from deep behind her eyes. Because of their threaded connection, he could sense that a yearning had taken hold of her like none she'd ever experienced before. Her voice trembled as she spoke. "This human thinks they're beautiful. You're beautiful, and truly the answer to my prayers. And now, I'm yours and you're mine, Michael. Never mind the women in your past. I'm your present. Come back to bed with me. Stay with me, make love to me again, my angel."

Her words soothed him. He delved deeper into her thoughts looking for assurances that what she said was true. Over the thousands of years he'd been manifested, here was the first time he could believe. He could trust. She would accept him for all that he was. Physically perfect, yet emotionally damaged.

Michael drew her to him, held her close, and he floated them across the floor back to the bed. And as he laid them both down, his wings encircled them like a cocoon. He made love to her as though it was the first time, but now, he took his time. He languished in the floral scent that was uniquely hers, and luxuriated in her well-toned body sliding sensuously over his. She watched him and writhed rapturously as he explored every inch of her and tasted every morsel of her. And when they came together as one and she cried out his name, he was convinced he knew her better than she even knew herself.

"I think I love you, Michael," she sighed as she drifted off to sleep.

"God knows, I love you, Emma." He placed a light kiss on her temple and whispered against her ear. "I've never known before the rapture a simple touch could bring or the joy of sharing all that I am with another whose heart is kind and true. You've brought these gifts to me. You've awakened the man inside the angel."

Chapter Sixteen

*B*efore the sun rose, he reluctantly left Emma's bed so he could slip into the guestroom, lest Hannah wake too soon and catch him in her mother's bedroom. He didn't think this was the time to have to explain their relationship.

"Hey there, where're you going?" A drowsy voice murmured from behind him as he reached the door.

Michael walked back to the bed and knelt next to her lying in naked perfection. He couldn't help but weave his fingers delicately through her sleek, black hair and place a whisper of a kiss on her lips. "Emma, honey, the sun will be up soon. I didn't think you'd want your daughter to wake up and possibly find us in bed together. I'll go into the guestroom so she won't have a clue. It's okay."

"I hadn't actually thought about it. I've been a bit distracted, you know." She had a gleam in her eyes. "Michael, we're fine. She loves you. You're one of her favorite people. She wouldn't think unkindly of you just because she may see you walk out of my room this morning. In fact, I'll bet you she'd do her little happy dance if she found us both in here when she wakes up this morning. Put on your boxers, and I'll put on a nightgown. Then we'll be ready for her. And until she comes in, which I'm sure she'll come in, we can—talk."

"We can talk, huh? Okay then." He stepped awkwardly into his boxers while watching Emma float a nightgown over her head. "We can talk about how I love your sexy body and the way it responds to my slightest touch." He pounced on her and she let out a sigh as his hands took a lazy sojourn over her body. His eyes captured hers with a look of possessiveness. "We can talk about how you set my body on fire to the point of madness, and how you soothe my spirit and heal the damaged parts of my soul."

Emma responded with a kiss so sweet and complete he'd forgotten to breathe. "God, Michael! Nobody has ever said anything quite so romantic to me before. And certainly, no one has ever made me feel the way you make me feel." She leaned up on an elbow, bit her bottom lip, and continued. "You know, after Ron, my ex, left us high and dry for my best friend, I didn't think I could trust or feel this way about any man ever again. But you're not just any man, are you?"

"No, I'm certainly not," he agreed with sincerity.

She rested her head back down on his chest and her arm on his stomach. Michael could feel tension working its way through her shoulders, so he began massaging them lightly.

"Truth be told, it scares me to trust again. It scares me a lot. For years now, distrust has been my default. And then there's this whole Trinity business and our lives on the line to save the world. I'm not sure what the hell's going to happen there. And the little matter of you being immortal and I'm—well, I don't know what on earth I am. Honestly, Michael, regardless of how we feel about each other right now, I don't know how this can ultimately work out."

Pausing, she lifted her head and gave him a solemn look. "What I do know, and I'm telling you straight out I'm taking a big risk saying this to you, so you better not screw around with my heart; you're everything I want and need in a partner, a lover, and as a part of my family. As you've seen, I can be pretty protective and possessive about my family."

"My, but you've been busy thinking in the few minutes you've been awake. And I kinda like the cavewoman side of you. A man like me could get used to being your possession."

Emma ensnared his lips with hers for a quick demonstration of the cavewoman she could be. Michael laughed and responded with his best caveman impersonation. He tangled her hair around his hands to pull her nose to nose with him and grunted. Then, he eased his hands out of her hair.

"Listen, in all seriousness, your ex-husband and your ex-best friend are assholes, and they'll get what's coming to them eventually. You shouldn't have let them have this kind of power over you for so long." She nodded in agreement and turned away. "As for us, I know we'll work it out. I'm going to take a big risk here myself. Look at me." He gently caressed her cheek. "I gotta tell you, I can't imagine being without you. There's no way I'll let anything come between me, you, and Hannah. Not my immortality, not Agremon, not a chance in Hell."

"Speaking of Hell and Agremon," she pointed out, sitting up a bit. "Tell me more about him. I'm curious. What made him turn away from the Brethren?"

Michael shifted himself to sit by her side. He gathered her closely to him while he spoke. "Well, Agremon was a Savior, originally, but he was never satisfied with those powers. He saw the warriors as the ultimate immortal and became extremely jealous of their gifts, so much so that he began spending most of his time on a quest to acquire those gifts as well.

"E.L., our boss, wasn't happy at all. Every group has its own gifts and no one is allowed to have more. It's like checks and balances, you know? Well, the boss man had a big sit down with everyone, including Agremon, and laid down the law again for everyone to hear. Agremon protested, got really angry, and stormed out, cursing E.L. and the rest of us as he left. He said he'd find a way to gain all of our powers and damned us all to Hell.

"You can imagine how quickly Satan got wind of that and took him immediately into his service. He's been working for him ever since. His appearance has changed since working with The Brethren. He once looked as we do, tall and formidable, and not too shabby in the looks department," he bragged with a toothy grin. "As you can bear witness to, what he looks like now only mirrors the evil that lives inside him. And as you've seen, he's acquired incredible power, as well. One thing he hasn't got is a Protector's powers. And I know it pisses him off in the biggest way. I don't know the why of it. He can't break through our Protectors' shields. Only if...." He stopped himself.

"Only if someone has deadened your abilities to sense him, right?" Emma offered.

"Yeah, well, Gabriel tried to explain why E.L. did that to me. I'm not ready to accept that explanation yet, but it doesn't matter much now, does it? What's done is done, I am what E.L. needs me to be, and Agremon will pay for what he's done to me and my family, eventually. I imagine Namirha probably is getting good and aggravated with him now, since he hasn't been able to deliver Hannah to him. That could make Agremon so nervous and frustrated that he begins making mistakes. That's all I need is one simple mistake on his part and he's null and void in the history books."

"But how can you do that? He's immortal like you, right? I thought immortal meant living forever."

"Yes, he's immortal, too, and we can live virtually forever; however, there is a way to kill us, for good. Since I am a Protector, I was given the key to that knowledge." He paused. Something occurred to him. He sat up. "You know, I always wondered why E.L. didn't give the key to Gabriel and Urie, too. I'd thought maybe he didn't feel they were ready yet. But now that I'm supposed to be this 'Great Protector', it makes sense somehow that they don't know. I am the ultimate Protector, and I alone hold the key to life or death for the Brethren. Lord Almighty, he really socked it to me, didn't he!" He shook his head in disbelief, and worried the whiskers on his cheeks with his hands.

Emma sat up as well, faced him squarely, and took his hands in hers.

"It is quite an awesome responsibility, Michael, I agree. But I have confidence in your abilities. I've known you for six years, and you've been a phenomenal principal, always making right choices, the hard choices, for the good of the school community. I've no doubt you can handle this, too." She turned toward the window. "Hey, look. The sun is rising."

She rose from the bed and walked to the enormous picture window that looked out onto the mountains. He followed behind her, and surrounded her with his embrace. They stood together in silence for a few prized moments. "It's stunning, isn't it, the way the sunrise makes the mountains appear different minute by minute? I never get tired of watching it change its hue. I hope the guys are able to take it all in, as well. It's a strong reminder that hope, faith, and goodness still prevail in this world."

"I couldn't have said it better myself. I do believe you were meant to be one of us. I think it'll be good to have a mother around all these men, you know."

"Please don't tell me I'm the Brethren's 'Wendy', like in Peter Pan. I don't think I could handle being a mother of nine 'boys' who want bedtime stories!"

"The only one you'll be telling bedtime stories to is me!" Michael asserted and started ravishing her throat with kisses. She squealed, and he found her chin, then her lips. She turned into him, the playfulness forgotten, replaced by his growing need. But that need was going to have to wait. Out of the corner of his eye, he saw the other Brethren beginning to make their way back to the house from all corners of the property.

He reluctantly stepped back from her and simply pointed out the window when she gave him a puzzled look. She pouted when she saw the men coming. She turned back to him and sighed.

"Reality sure has a funny way of interrupting a really good dream," she contemplated.

He wrapped his arms around her again. His lips pressed against her hair. "This isn't a dream, Emma. What we have is real, what's happening to us is real. Prophecy dictates it so. Lucky for you, I like ya a lot."

"Oh, really? Well you're lucky I like you a lot, too," she retorted and nipped his chin with her teeth, then soothed it with her tongue. "I guess we should wake up Hannah. I almost hate to since she hasn't slept this long in months. But I know we have a busy day ahead of us. Duty calls. Let's go wake her up together."

They quickly washed and dressed, then went to her room. Nothing could have prepared them for what greeted them as they entered. Rather than still sleeping as Emma had thought, Hannah was up, dressed, and at her play table, drawing fiercely on a tablet of paper with her crayons. Her face had taken on a much more intense and mature look. She finished the drawing, tore it away from the tablet, and tossed it vigorously to the floor, to join the dozens of other pictures littering her carpet and bed. All the pictures were of monsters and demons. Sometimes they were lined up like army platoons at the base of a mountain range, the Superstition Mountains to be exact. Some of the pictures were of those very platoons setting fire to the towns around the mountains.

Hannah was so absorbed in what she was doing that she didn't stir when the two entered her room. Michael picked up her drawings to get a closer look. Emma peered over his shoulder and grabbed a fistful of his shirt. He touched her hand and sent waves of comfort to ease her mind. The drawings he held were frighteningly explicit and detailed, with people drawn as though they were on fire themselves, running from houses and buildings that were already ablaze. In another set of pictures, she saw the Brethren warriors, dressed in black leather pants and wings unfurled, fighting against creatures that were half human-half demon in appearance. He picked up a final set of pictures where the Brethren were losing the battle against these creatures. Angels were lying on a battlefield of sorts, their bodies sluiced open and their innards oozing out onto the ground.

Emma spotted one last picture peeking out from under Hannah's bed. This picture disturbed her most of all. She had drawn Namirha standing imperiously over an altar, with his arms in the air, holding a bejeweled knife with its blade pointed down over a body. Not just any body, Hannah's body, lying on the altar, like a sacrificial offering. A woman was drawn at the base of the altar reaching up in futility to stop the sacrifice. She had drawn her mouth open as if she were screaming. A man, an angel, had also been drawn lying face down next to the woman, his back bloodied. Beside him was one bloodied wing. The other was being held by none other than Agremon. He had been drawn with the wing in his hands, plucking off the feathers and an evil, triumphant grin on his ghastly face.

Emma was clearly distraught by what she'd seen, but before she could get her daughter's attention, Michael drew her out of the room and into the hallway. He touched her cheek with the back of his hand and sent energy currents down the threaded connection they had forged during the night.

"Listen, Emma, I know this is very disturbing. But, it's also great news. Hannah has tapped into her powers of intuition and is seeing into Namirha's plans."

"Tell me it's not the future we're looking at here."

"I can only say that it is one of many possible outcomes of plans being made by Namirha. Today, we're going to make sure the warriors work on honing her skill. Her pictures are great, but we need specific details on the plans he means to carry out on his ultimate mission. This is very encouraging, however disturbing it may be."

"It's frightening, you know? It's horrifyingly frightening that this could be what's ahead for all of us."

"That's why we're here, honey, to make sure those pictures don't come to fruition. If you're ready, put your best smile on and let's say good morning to your daughter." She secured a wary grin on her face and nodded.

They walked back into the room, and Hannah instantly turned around in her seat with a smile of her own and stood up. Her face had thankfully returned to her normal cherubic glow of a child.

"Good morning, Mama!" She jumped up into Emma's arms to give her mother a hearty hug and kiss. She leaned over toward Michael, so he took her into his arms. She gave him a hearty hug and kiss as well. Then she wriggled out of his hands and started gathering up the pictures. "These pictures are scary, Mama, so if you don't want to look, that's okay. I'll put them away until later." Emma tried her best to stifle her laughter. "That's okay, honey. I think I can handle it. Why don't you tell us about them over breakfast?"

"Okay. But it's a scary story, too. I just wanted you to know." As they made their way to the kitchen, the Brethren were coming in from their overnight watch. They were loud, they were brash, they were hungry, and their very presence filled up every ounce of space available. One might be claustrophobic at such a time, but not Emma. She was safe, secure, and comfortable. As the men washed up and changed clothes, she and Michael got breakfast ready. Hannah was fiddling with her pictures. It looked to Emma as though she was putting them in some kind of sequence. When the men returned, they immediately saw the pictures and abandoned the bountiful breakfast. They swept her off to the family room where they could lay the pictures out on the floor. Michael and Emma quickly followed behind.

Kemuel spoke first. "Hannah, please tell us about these pictures, and how you came to draw them." She walked over to him and sat down on his lap. She had taken him by surprise and he gave an awkward cough. It didn't seem to faze her in the least to think him a good seat to sit on. She started playing with his eyebrows, raising and lowering them, then moved to playing with his cheeks. He frowned at her and she beamed back, molding his frown into a toothy grin and other silly gestures.

"Well, I woke up this morning and felt like I really wanted to draw something. I got washed and dressed, like a big girl, too, and I took out my crayons and paper and started drawing. The funny thing is, when I started drawing, pictures came into my head like a movie. I started drawing like I never did before." She paused and got off of Kemuel's lap.

As she walked away and started pacing, she immediately appeared different from the Hannah of only moments ago. And as she spoke, her voice had become deeper, more mature. The Ancient Warrior's soul had somehow come forth.

"Kemuel, Michael, all of you. These pictures are what Namirha has planned. He has amassed an army of monumental proportions. Demons, monsters, and mortals are assembling to do his bidding. The Homecoming tomorrow is a smoke and mirror ploy to gather his mortal flock. By the sixth of June, all will have arrived at The Source's headquarters waiting to descend upon the surrounding towns, including Prophet's Point. The pictures show his intentions to destroy the towns and their people who have not been turned. He intends to destroy the Brethren, as well, rendering the rest of the mortal world completely vulnerable to his desires and at his mercy."

"You left out the fact that he also plans to gain your powers by killing you on his altar. He had no plans to keep you alive as his surrogate daughter," Michael fumed.

"Then we go ahead with our plan to infiltrate The Source tomorrow."

"No Kemuel," the Ancient Warrior countered. Kemuel raised a quizzical brow. "Your plan will not work as it is, not without Michael, my mother, and me going along with you."

"What are you talking about?"

"I need to be with my warriors, Mother, to fight. The Protectors need to be close, to provide shielding, and you and the rest of the Saviors will be needed for healing. If we're going on the offensive, then we all need to go, together. It's Prophecy, and it's the way we'll win."

"Michael, what do you think?" she asked. "Can you shield her enough so that Agremon and Namirha can't detect her? Because that's the only way I would even contemplate letting her go, Prophecy or not."

"Well, we can shield her, no problem."

"But do we really want to? What I mean is if Namirha wants her, maybe that's how we can draw him to us, by letting him know she's there."

"I hate to say it, Kemuel, but you've got a great point. As much as I don't want Hannah exposed, maybe by doing so will flesh him out." Michael took a moment to contemplate options.

"We can shield her at will, so we'll start out with her shielded and when it suits us, when we're ready, we'll drop them."

"Don't worry, Emma," Gabriel said, reaching out and patting her hand. "She will be well protected. Brethren, tomorrow, when we go, no doubt we're going to find that the followers are under some kind of mind control. Let it be until after we've settled in. Then, Saviors and Protectors, you can go around tent by tent healing and helping the people leave safely. The fewer mortals we have to fight in the end, the better. Mind you, when we're actually there, we'll have a better feel for what needs to be done. Be ready to change plans at a moment's notice. Warriors, you will guard the Ancient Warrior."

"Agreed," the rest of the Brethren concurred. As if in unison, they all made their way to the kitchen to eat a breakfast of eggs, bacon, hash browns, toast, and coffee. Now the only one without an appetite was Emma. She took her coffee mug and went out on the back porch. Hannah followed.

"Mother?" Hannah called. She still had that maturity to her voice, and as she walked towards her mother, her stance was that of a great warrior, not of a little girl. As she got closer, right before Emma's eyes, she changed back into the daughter that jumped into her arms just a short while ago. "Mama?"

Emma grabbed her into a fierce hug, then pulled back to take her all in.

"For a moment I thought you'd outgrown that name for me. I don't think I could have handled that, sweetie. No matter what you evolve into during this time with the Brethren, you need to know that I am always your Mama. No matter if you're an ancient soul or a very young one; I will always answer to 'Mama' and come running."

"Oh, Mama!" Hannah hugged her tightly and for a moment, looked at a loss. Then, she gained her footing again. "I need to try and explain what I'm feeling, because I am changing. It's a little scary. I feel like the little me is sometimes being pushed into a corner or box while the big me takes over for the warrior stuff. I don't really mind, for now, because I'm a lot stronger when the big me is out. I really want Agremon and Namirha to go away forever, and the big me can make that happen. I'm afraid the little me is going to be put in the corner for a long while when we go to the headquarters tomorrow. But Mama, when this is over, I want the little me back all the time. I hope I don't forget who the little me is."

"I won't let you forget, then," Emma pledged with a strained smile, and fought back the tears that threatened to expose her own fears. She put one hand over her heart and one over Hannah's. "I promise I'll make sure you come back to me, the way you want to be."

It was a promise Emma hadn't the slightest idea how to keep, but one she was determined not to break.

Chapter Seventeen

*T*he heat of the Arizona summer came on early and strong. By mid-morning, the warriors were drenched from training with swords and mixed martial arts, and had come inside to tackle Hannah's mind. Raphael and the other Saviors trained Emma at the intermediate level of their healing arts, and now she was practicing the meditation required to help her call upon her powers at will.

Michael, Gabriel, and Urie required a more intense meditation session. They needed to be in perfect condition, and meditation enabled them to check, repair, and enhance their powers. Eventually all the Brethren would need to go through the same process. Manifesting and staying in human form had one drawback, the necessity to monitor and keep their corporeal bodies working in synch with their immortal powers. When facing battle, meditating was crucial to keeping both in harmony. Luckily though, while in human form, their bodies were impervious to injury. That is, any injury that could be inflicted by a human. The Brethren could still be injured by other immortal beings like themselves. So, Michael created more protective talismans for everyone.

The only time anyone stopped during the day was when Emma pushed to eat lunch and dinner. Everyone knew better than to go against the Great Savior Mother, so they dutifully congregated around the kitchen table to feed their bellies while the rest of the day was about training and feeding their souls.

Further on down the road, other plans were being perfected. The Source's Homecoming event was tomorrow, and Namirha knew this would be the last and strongest push to fortify his minions for the ultimate battle that lay ahead. Everything seemed ready. The tents were erected, the brochures printed, and the scripts memorized by his elite group of followers, known as the Inner Sanctum. Nothing more need be done except...securing Hannah Livingston away from her mother!

Namirha ranted in his limousine, terrifying his driver. "Imbecile! Good-for-nothing son-of-bitch! I should have known better than to trust the former Brethren. I bet he's been deceiving me all this time, making me think he's one of mine, but really still working for the Brethren! Agremon!"

Agremon's grotesque body immediately appeared on the seat across from him. "Yes, my lord?" he answered nervously. He knew why Namirha had called him. He had not produced the girl.

"Agremon, I've determined that your usefulness to me has ended. Since you've failed at bringing the girl to me, you will now reside in my home in the mountains, in my dungeon, actually, having your skin torn away from your body and reattached at regular intervals for the rest of eternity. Now, don't get all mushy on me. I know it's not every day I let people stay in my home, but given all you've done for me over the years, I figured you're a special case."

Agremon pleaded for his immortal life. "My lord, you can't do this to me! I am so close to finding a way around the protective shield! I know I can get her to you before Thursday! Trust me!"

"Enough! I can't afford to trust you any further, you sniveling idiot! Be gone!" With a wave of his hand, Agremon disappeared from the limo, and reappeared in a dank, dark cell, within the home Namirha had made out of an abandoned mine deep in the Goldfield Mountains. His wrists were chained to the ceiling, his feet chained to the floor. The air was cool around him, and the walls were dripping with a coppery, noxious liquid that surprisingly made him want to gag. As the flaying began, he screamed, "You will die by my hands alone, Michael! I will find a way out of here, and you will surely die!"

Agremon's roar echoed throughout the chamber each time his skin was torn away, and when it reappeared moments later, giving him a few minutes to recover, his mind conjured up bits and pieces of a plan to escape Namirha's wrath and exact revenge on Michael. After awhile, he began to revel in the pain. Every time a piece of him was torn away, it strengthened his determination to get out and exact his revenge.

After what felt like hours, Agremon had steeled himself against the incessant pain and began to enter particular followers' minds; those whose minds were very open to his suggestion. He called to them. One answered immediately, one in particular who had been doing his bidding for a while now, Jared Sikes.

Jared was a lost soul until he was found near death from shooting up heroin outside one of The Source's mess halls about six months back. When he was brought to Agremon's attention, he could see Jared was one of your basic losers, but Agremon could also discern that with the right guidance and incentive, he could turn Jared into the perfect grunt. So after stroking Jared's self-esteem and feeding his addiction, Agremon began using him.

Agremon called to him now, and with what little energy he had left, flashed Jared away from the headquarters and straight to his cell. Yes, Jared had answered, like a lamb to the slaughter. Little did he know, he was to replace Agremon as Namirha's tortured plaything. That's exactly what grunt work was sometimes, wasn't it?

Jared approached him, pupils dilated.

"What is it you would have me do, Agremon? I shall obey." Jared spoke with reverence.

"Come here, my brother, quickly!" Agremon shouted impatiently. "Come stand before me and rest your hands on my hands. I need comfort. I am wrongly accused of a misdeed, and as you can see, am awaiting judgment locked in this cell."

"Yes, Agremon. Anything you say. Will I be rewarded for this deed I do for you?" Jared asked hungrily and licked his dry lips in anticipation of a quick fix.

"Oh yes, indeed, you shall," Agremon asserted dramatically. "Now come, fast, before I lose all sense of reason and completely break down."

Jared lumbered forward. His stringy blond hair fell like a ripped curtain across his pock-ridden face. He flicked it back and laced his hands with Agremon's. Agremon tightened his grip and immediately spoke, in a hushed tone, "I am you and you are me."

Jared gasped as his soul left his body and floated above the two of them. Standing there, helpless to do anything else, his bag of bones waited for repossession. Agremon's damned soul was released and floated as well, and as the two souls passed in the air, Jared could hear Agremon's triumphant laughter. The transfer complete, Jared found his soul bound not only by the demon he was forced to possess, but by the shackles securing Agremon in the cell.

"What have you done?" Jared cried out, wrenching his arms against their bindings. Agremon, now in possession of Jared's body immediately drew back his hands from Jared.

"What's the problem, Jared? When I called, you came. You told me you'd do anything. Well, I need to get the hell out of here, so you're taking my place, naturally. Now, I gotta run, so sorry buddy. Sometimes you get the shit end of the stick."

"Agremon, you're coming back, right?" Jared shouted crazily. "You're gonna switch me back, right? What about my reward?"

"Don't worry, I'll be back. You've got an expiration date. Don't think I want to get stuck in a rotting vessel. No, I'll let you have all the fun. About that reward...." Agremon snickered. "You die." He laughed heartily as he watched the first flaying occur and then vanished.

Agremon approached the boundaries of Emma's property very carefully. He would stay on the outskirts until opportunity presented itself, then go inside and snatch the girl right from under the bastard angel's nose. Talisman, be damned! He itched to win this battle over Michael, just like he had done so many years ago. Rubbing salt in that wound would give him orgasmic pleasure. Hunkering down in the protection of the trees beyond the property line, he waited. He was a patient demon. He'd been patient for six months. He could be patient for a few hours more.

Emma, determined to keep as much normalcy for her daughter as possible, ushered everyone out back to witness the sun's spectacular descent. Given the monumental task set before them all in the next few days, no one spoke but all looked at the ever-changing colors of the twilight sky.

"Remember, the sun also rises," Hannah whispered vehemently. "And we shall rise to this latest challenge and be victorious. Am I right, my Warriors?"

"Yes, Great Warrior Child!" The Warriors roared in response.

"We have a strong plan," Urie pointed out. "We have trained hard and as well as we could, given the lack of time. I am confident we can succeed."

"Well then, I'm tired. I'm going to bed. Mother, Mama, will you tuck me in?" Hannah asked, and reached her hand out for her to hold. The intermittent switching of souls was unnerving, but Emma smiled lovingly at her daughter nonetheless.

"Of course, sweetheart. Excuse me, gentlemen." She grabbed her daughter's hand and squeezed it as they walked back into the house.

The Brethren fanned out to the positions they had held the night before. Michael stayed out as well, just beyond the back porch. He couldn't help feeling hesitant about what was to come. Images of Beth and their unborn child swam through his head. They were innocents, not involved in the least with his duty, and he couldn't protect them from evil. Now, he had Emma and Hannah. He loved them as much, if not more. And they were headed to the frontline. He couldn't even begin to contemplate what he would do if anything should happen to either of them.

Self-doubt was dangerous. He needed to get over it, and quickly, if he was going to be successful protecting the ones he loved.

"A penny for your thoughts." Emma sidled up next to him and snuggled close.

"Hey! I didn't hear you come back out." He swiftly shielded his thoughts from her, slid his arms around her shoulders, and kissed her lightly on her forehead.

"Well, should I guess what has your mind so completely occupied?"

"Oh, it's nothing really. So, did Hannah settle down quickly to sleep?"

"I think she was asleep before her head hit the pillow. I'm concerned, Michael," she admitted, fatigue evident in her voice. "About the toll this is taking on her physically and emotionally. I can't wait 'til this whole thing is over and done with. I still sometimes think I'm dreaming this elaborate dream, and at any moment I'm going to wake up to find everything back the way it was before—before she started having nightmares."

Michael was concerned, too, and gave her a squeeze of reassurance that he truly didn't feel. Maybe if he faked it, he would come to believe it. He couldn't shake this apprehension he'd had since sunset, but was also confident that if anything were wrong, his Brethren team would have alerted him. He fixed a smile on his face.

"She's going to be fine, honey. Come on, let's head inside and see what we can do about these pre-game jitters. I think I know the perfect solution." He lifted Emma right off her feet so they were eye to eye and kissed her. It started out innocently enough, but quickly escalated to one filled with passion. He put everything into that kiss—his need, his desire for her, his doubt. And he knew the instant his thoughts had traveled down the threaded connection they now shared. His shields had fallen. She tore herself away and shook her head, leaving him aroused and edgy.

"Seems I'm not the only one with concerns," Emma chided. He grabbed her back to him and rested his head on her shoulder, then let her go gently.

"Guilty as charged," Michael declared, kicking his foot at an imaginary pebble. They walked up to the house, hand in hand. "I'm going to have to be more careful around you from now on. Your powers are real good, honey. Healing and reading minds. What a great combination."

"Yeah well, when you got it, you got it," she joked. "Now, about those doubts—" She became serious. "Don't go there, Michael. Don't second guess your powers. You know you can see this through to a successful end. I know you can."

"Yeah, yeah...." He shuffled his feet in the dirt, his hands clasped behind his back.

"Sweetheart, do you know you're brooding?"

"I guess I am. So do you think Mama can make me feel all better?" he asked, stopping before they entered the house.

"Oh, honey, that's what Mama does best. I promise." With a smoldering glance, she reached both hands up, grabbed him by his hair and pulled him down for a kiss so scorching it was a wonder the entire house didn't go up in flames. Without missing a step, he scooped her off her feet and carried her to the bedroom. With the door closed behind them, their passion play continued.

He eased her down to stand before him, and looked deeply into the caverns of her eyes, seeing his reflection and finding her soul reaching out and connecting with his. Lost in the deep pools of chocolate that stared wondrously back at him, he found home. His gaze shifted to her lips, those luscious lips, then to her throat, where he could see her pulse quickening with each moment that passed.

"Emma, I can't stand it any longer," he panted in breathless anticipation and ripped his shirt open. He took her hand and brought it to rest on his chest. "I gotta have you. Touch me. Know me again."

She stepped forward and replaced her hand with her tongue, leaving trail marks of seduction all the way to his navel. Michael nearly came right then. He cradled the nape of her neck, leaned over her, and kissed her with all the ardor of a man who'd lost all control. They released each other long enough to hastily shed their clothes. As if they were magnets, they came together in the center of the room, arms entwined, hands feverishly seeking to reacquaint themselves with each other's bodies, becoming one.

"Oh Michael, I'm gonna touch you, and feel you, and know you like no one's done before."

"And you're gonna make it all better, right?" Michael pleaded through the kisses he traced over her lips and throat and down her body to the very core that made her a woman. "You promised you'd make it all better."

"Oh, God! Yes, I'll make it all better, baby." She moaned and dug her nails into his back. As close to the edge as he was, he was still holding out on her.

"Michael, let them out. Let your wings out, angel. I want all of you. No more hiding."

She rubbed her silken body sensuously over his, igniting little fires along the way, from bottom to top, nearly climbing him like a pole. He groaned and released his wings in all their glory. They were glowing from within, something she hadn't noticed the first time she'd seen them. The feathers quivered gently in a nonexistent breeze, and all she could think of doing at that moment was touch them. She stroked them delicately with her fingers, remembering its effect on him before, and she found herself lifted up off the floor.

In midair, Emma found herself cradled in his wings and watched in hazy delirium as he ravished her. Feathers traced teasing trails along her ankles to her calves, and came to a fluttering halt on her breast. His hand took the same path, but lingered at the juncture of her thighs. She opened for him while her hands sought to discover every hill and valley of his well-hewn body. Her fingers traversed across the wide expanse of his shoulder blades and down to the crook of his lower back, making small circles along the way, until she froze suddenly and caught her breath.

Michael entered her while they spun in a slow, sensual spiral. She had never known ecstasy such as this. Her moans and sobs were smothered by his possessive kisses. As they climaxed together, crying out each other's names, a shroud of light so brilliant and pure emanated from their bodies and lit up the room. Emma looked about them, her eyes filled with wonder and awe, and he kissed her cheek. The light slowly dimmed as they finally came to rest on her bed, drenched in sweat and replete beyond measure. The coolness of the sheets eased the fire still burning inside her, and she nestled against him, not willing to disengage from their entanglement. And then finally, she succumbed to exhaustion.

He had wanted to say so much, but found no voice. What more could he say that hadn't been said already? He could tell her he loved her more than his immortal life. But if, no, when they survived their confrontation with Namirha, what would become of them and their love? Was he to go through their lives watching as she grew older and eventually died, and he didn't? He hadn't thought about that with Beth. He'd been in denial, turning his back on what he truly was, an angel, an immortal. He was destined either to be alone without pain, or with someone he loved, and feel the pain of that ultimate loss forever. The answer was clearly before him as he lay in the strong yet tender arms of the woman he loved. He would stay with her as long as her forever was.

Chapter Eighteen

Resolve clear in Michael's head, he turned his attention to the unsettling feeling that wouldn't go away. Since making love with Emma didn't seem to dampen it, he knew better than to disregard it any longer and figured it had something to do with Agremon. Agremon hadn't shown up for a long while, and that bothered him. What was he up to? There had been no sign of him around the property, no threaded signature to give him away. Michael was confident that the Brethren guarding the property would be able to smoke him out with the smallest of indicators of his existence.

He got up from bed, and she immediately reached out in her sleep. Instantly deprived of what had become so essential, her, he grimaced, tucked his wings away, and got dressed. He had a job to do that he mustn't forget; protect the Great Savior Mother and the Great Warrior Child.

So, he decided to take a walk around the house. Maybe cruising about would help him pinpoint the origin of his concern. He peeked in on Hannah who lay silently sleeping. He passed through the guest room, opening up the closet. Nothing. He skulked down the hall to the family room, kitchen, study and playroom. Again, nothing. Not a thread to indicate anything was wrong. He quietly returned to Emma's bedroom. What time was it anyway? He looked at the clock on the kitchen wall. Three thirty-three in the morning.

And that's precisely when all hell literally broke loose.

Emma roused from her sleep by the lightest touch of a hand to her cheek. She smiled drowsily with her eyes still closed and purred, "Come back to bed. I miss you."

"I miss you, too, pretty Mama," the stranger mocked, while reaching behind her head and pulling her upright. "That's why I came back for you."

"Came back for me? Who the hell are you and how did you get in here?" she asked incredulously as she twisted and squirmed under his strong hold.

"Oh, that's right," he said, tightening his grip. "I forgot. I bet you don't recognize me after my makeover. It's me, Agremon, lovey."

"How? How were you able to get to me?" She was confused and frightened, and pissed.

"Oh, just a little matter of possession makes all bets and shields null and void, my dear. Don't you like the new look? Young and lanky is more your cup of tea than old and gruesome, right? Now, Mr. Lovey-dovey Protector will be back shortly. Just so you know, he's going to have to choose between saving you and your daughter. If he chooses wisely, you'll live to see another day. If he chooses poorly, well, you're more a master of your own terror than I, so you can imagine what's in store. You get the picture, don't you? A slow, painful, horrifying death for our Ms. Livingston."

"Why, you son of a—" Emma spat and thrashed madly about. To her visible consternation, Agremon remained unfazed.

"Regardless of what our mighty Protector does, Hannah will be going on a little vacation, as it were, for a few days. While you're busy vacationing in your hellish dreams, she'll be getting better acquainted with her new father, Mr. Namirha. Oh, don't worry about a thing. She's going to have so much fun, especially on her birthday; she's never going to want to leave!"

"If you so much as breathe in her direction I will fucking kill you, you bastard!" she shrieked and renewed her attack, pummeling him with her fists and kicking wildly with her legs.

"I'd like to see you try, love," Agremon sneered as he tightened his hold on the nape of her neck and secured her legs with his own. "Parting is such sweet sorrow, my dear, but alas, I must go and fulfill my destiny. Have fun in your own little Hell." Agremon placed his free hand over her forehead. She fought to remove it, but was no match for him.

"Oh God, no!" Agremon rested her head back onto her pillow, stared a moment at her seemingly lifeless body, and made his way to Hannah's room. Success was moments away. He reached her bed and proceeded to lift her away from her cozy cocoon. He had to be extra careful. Hannah was a feisty one. She squirmed a bit in his arms and her eyes fluttered open.

"Mmm. What's going on? Hey, you're not one of the Brethren. Who are you and what are you going to do with me?" she asked, wriggling furiously in his arms.

"Relax little one, it is I, your old friend, Agremon, here to take you to your new father. He is anxious to see you and take care of you, and make a happy family together."

"Agremon," she whispered, her eyes widening in astonishment. Without warning, she let out a howl that nearly ruptured his eardrums. "Help!"

Michael heard blood-curdling screams coming first from Emma's and then from Hannah's rooms. He stopped dead in his tracks, hearing a familiar voice surround him. Agremon. How the hell had he gotten to his women again?

"Which way should you go, Michael? Which way should you go? Will it be door number one or door number two? Here's the tricky part. If you pick the wrong door, one will surely die

tonight. *So which will it be, Mr. Protector? Huh? I leave you to your decision. I hope you enjoy the music while you ponder your choices. I always find the musical shrill of people's screams to be most helpful when I'm deliberating.*" And his voice was gone.

Emma whirled around madly, looking for a place that would provide shelter against her fears and the unknown. There wasn't a chance in hell that she would go back to the mausoleum. As she searched the cemetery she shivered, noticing every headstone had her name engraved on it.

Darkness fell upon the cemetery, along with a fog so dense she couldn't see her hand outstretched before her. It made it increasingly impossible for her to find anywhere to hide. Her heart thudded against her chest and tiny beads of sweat condensed on her upper lip. *Damn it! Not again. I can't let this happen to me again. Hannah needs me.*

At that moment, she refused to be paralyzed by her fears any longer nor be a victim ever again. Now was as good a time as any to beat down her fears of the darkness. And she sure as hell wasn't going to let Agremon win. She took a deep breath and willed her heart rate to slow down. What had Agremon said? She was the master of her own terror. Well, she was now the master of her own fate and terror had no place in it!

She felt around some more and found a tall headstone that she decided was good enough to sit by, and then tried to figure out how to get out of the mess Agremon had wrought. How does one escape a nightmare created by a demon? She hadn't a clue. That gave her time to think about other things. Hannah. What was happening to Hannah? Would she be able to hold her own against Agremon? Would Michael make the right choice? Of course he would. She swore on her own life that she would seek revenge should anything happen to her baby girl.

Agremon and Hannah vanished before she could take another breath to scream. They reappeared in Namirha's home.

"Where are we?" Hannah asked, her voice barely audible.

"Mr. Namirha's throne room. It's really just a glorified hole in the wall."

There was a large, empty chair at the back of the alcove and a runner made of goat's hide on the ground. Above the chair was mounted a huge ceremonial knife that had sacred inscriptions written along the blade. All along the walls of the alcove were skulls of various animals, and right in front of the chair, a pentagram adorned the floor.

As Agremon was about to call Namirha, he appeared before them, eyes ablaze with hunger and triumph. "What have we here? I do believe I see before me my wayward apprentice and a gift. Agremon, it is you, is it not? You look a bit different. It doesn't quite suit you. You're too soft-looking. I expect to see the real you by sunrise. Now, is this not the child who is to be my daughter?"

"Yes, my lord. It is she, Hannah Livingston." He held her dangling straight out into the air for Namirha to see. "I have defeated the Brethren and taken her from their evil clutches," Agremon boasted.

"I know better than to believe all that rubbish, my dear Agremon. And I am wondering how it is you escaped my care. But no matter, she is here and I am at peace. Welcome, my child. Agremon, do put her down. I believe there are last minute plans that need attending to for tomorrow's Homecoming. See that all is ready."

"Yes, my lord. Thank you, my lord." Agremon bowed and vanished.

Hannah stood stone still. She was finally face to face with Mr. Namirha.

"Come to me, child. Don't be afraid. I am to be your father come your birthday. Oh, and what a birthday it will be, my dear!

We'll have ourselves such a party to end all parties." He clasped his hands together and smiled. "Would you like that? I'm sure you would. Come, give your father a hug," Namirha entreated with all the adulation and warmth a parent would bestow on his only child. He reached his arms out to her and waited.

The child that was Hannah was frozen, and the soul that was the Ancient Warrior took over, gently pushing the terrified child back into a safe little corner of her mind.

The Ancient Warrior soul knew exactly what to do and began to weave a story to save the little girl's life. She spoke in a thin, wavering voice.

"I've always missed having a father. My mother has kept me away from him against both of our wishes. But now, you are saying you could be my father. I think I would like that. I'm scared a little bit. Agremon scares me. I don't think he likes me very much, and I think he would like to hurt me. If you're going to be my father, will you protect me from that scary man?"

"My dear, I will let nothing scare you or hurt you. You will be my daughter. You will be royalty, and all will kneel at your feet or suffer the consequences." Namirha took a few steps toward Hannah. He reached out a hand to her, beckoning her to approach him. She inched forward one step and then another. And she stopped. She had to appear to be wary yet impressionable.

"Royalty, is that like being a princess? Will I be a princess, Mr. Namirha?" the Ancient Warrior asked, feigning a childlike personality and putting a hand on her hip.

"Yes, my dear," he replied, smiling like a crocodile to a frog. "A princess from now on and please, call me father, would you? It would make my heart sing." He stepped closer to her.

"Wow, a real princess! Will I have a crown? Will I have pretty dresses? Will I have people do things for me?" As Hannah threw these questions out, she jumped up and threw herself upon Namirha. Inwardly she shuddered, but he could never know how she truly felt or it would ruin any chance she had to gain the upper hand. Namirha caught her deftly, not showing the least bit of surprise by her assault.

"Yes, yes, anything for you, my dearest daughter!"

Michael raced to Emma's bedside. He prayed that she had become strong enough to battle whatever Agremon had planned for her. He immediately lay beside her, gathered her up in his arms, and proceeded to enter her dreams as he had done before. "Emma! Emma!" he shouted urgently. "Where are you? It's me, Michael!" He noticed that Agremon had sent her back to the nightmare from before. This time, the dark was darker, the fog was thicker, and he hoped that she hadn't been reduced to terror-induced insanity.

"Michael? Did you get to Hannah in time?" she shouted back. He didn't respond right away, not wanting to face her wrath just yet. He imagined an endless barrage of stones hurled at him before he could reach her. "Michael, is Hannah okay?" Again, he gave no answer. "Damn it! I'm over by a tall headstone. Right next to the mausoleum, if you can see anything!"

"I think I know where you are. Stay put. I'm almost to you." Michael could see better than a mortal, which made his task of finding her easier. "Here you are. Thank God! Are you okay? Are you injured? Did Agremon touch you?" His questions came pouring out faster than a waterfall. He reached out to grab her, to hold her; he had feared so much for her safety. But she violently batted his arms away.

"Did you get to Hannah?" He shook his head. "Then what the hell are you doing here? Go save her!" She shoved him. "How could you pick me?" She screeched and shoved him again. "You've got to get out of here. Agremon's gone after Hannah. How could you come for me first and let him get to her? How?" She started slapping at his chest with her open hands, and he took it. "My baby's gonna die at the hands of Agremon and Namirha, and you came for me." Her open hands curled into fists, and she began pounding him with all of her might. "You know I would die before they got their hands on her. You know that! I was fine here. I was dealing. And now she's gone. She's gone and it's all your fucking fault!" He feared she'd gone over the edge as she threw her whole body into punishing him.

Michael winced at the verbal thrashing and absorbed the physical assault, but there was a limit to his patience. He grabbed her arms to stay them, pulled her to him and growled, "Enough, Emma, enough!"

"Get me out of here, Michael," she hissed. "Someone has to save my baby. Since you can't seem to keep us protected, I'll have to do it myself. Some Great Fucking Protector you are."

She was killing his heart and he believed he deserved it. Again, he was deemed powerless in providing protection to the people he loved most. "I'm so sorry he got to you both again. I'll take you back now. But, listen to me. Coming for you instead of Hannah, as hard as it was for me to do, I believe saved both of your lives. Think about it. If I had gone to her, Agremon would have killed you, no doubt. As much as you would have preferred that over him taking her, he still would have gotten to her regardless. And I'm not prepared to go on living my life without you or her. Since I came for you, yes, Agremon took Hannah, but he can't harm her. Not yet. Namirha can't do a thing before her birthday. And we'll be there, near her, in just a few hours. I'm so sorry my protection failed you. I really am. I think once we're back, and we hash this out with the others we'll find out how this happened." With nothing more to be said, he gently embraced her, placed his right hand on her forehead, and took them on a journey back to real time.

They awoke together. Emma spared no time but jumped off the bed and fled to her daughter's bedroom. The other Brethren stormed through the front and back doors.

"What's happened?" Gabriel asked, breathing hard. "For hours there was nothing, and suddenly, for only a split second, we felt Agremon's thread."

"Agremon's got Hannah," Michael replied, hardly able to get the words out as failure threatened to still his heart.

Emma sifted desperately through the covers on Hannah's bed while Michael looked on, helpless and guilt-ridden. "Hannah! Where are you, baby? Mama's here! Mama's...here." She collapsed onto to the floor. Her cries of fury and rage exploded like a shockwave through the room, knocking him and the rest of the Brethren literally off their feet.

As they recovered from the blast of energy, Gabriel suggested a quick meeting of the minds to find out what had happened. Michael fought with himself to go to her. Raphael must have seen his inner turmoil and took the decision from him.

"I'll go to Emma, you go with the others and figure out what the hell happened and what we do next. Clue me in first so I know what I'm dealing with here." Grateful for the support, Michael told him everything he knew and what he'd done, and then he went to the family room where the others eagerly awaited some kind of explanation.

Chapter Nineteen

*R*aphael put a gentle hand on Emma's back. Her pain was so acute, that even with his mighty strength, he had to fight to keep his hand upon her. "Emma, it's Raphael. Let me help you." He placed his other hand on her head and stroked her hair, all the while releasing his own healing energy. He gave her all he could without jeopardizing his own safety. But she needed more. She had released all of her energies with that blast and was completely tapped out.

"Emma, can you hear me?" Raphael urged.

"Yes," she whispered back weakly.

"You need more than I can give. And your protections are blown to bits. You are vulnerable. Cassiel can complete the healing, but you will need Michael to repair your protection."

She slowly turned her face up, her bloodshot eyes still swimming with tears. Soft as a whisper, yet strong with conviction she ordered, "Get someone else."

"You don't realize what you're saying. Michael is the strongest Protector we've got. You're letting your emotions guide you rather than clear logic and reason. Please, let me get him for you," Raphael implored.

She pushed herself up to a sitting position, ripped Michael's talisman from her neck, and threw it across the room. "I said get me someone else! I can't trust him anymore. If he loved me, he wouldn't have tossed my baby to Hell. She's all I have in this world, and he let Evil have her. No, he's just like Ron, making Hannah last on his list of priorities. Well, she's first on mine and always will be. I'd rather die here and now before accepting any protection from him. I will have someone else or I will have no one!" She crumpled back down to the floor having expended what little energy she had been given. Raphael collected her in his arms, her nightgown a twisted mess around her knees, and sat with her.

"Damn it, Emma! You've got to calm down. You're using up energy quicker than it can be replaced. We will get Hannah back. He's right. She's safe with Namirha. He won't harm her or do anything to jeopardize his chance at total world domination. You know very well she's the key. He did the right thing by rescuing you rather than her. As harsh as it sounds, it's true. The sooner you acknowledge that the sooner we can go on with our plans to infiltrate the Homecoming, which we need to be at in a few hour's time."

Silence. It was better than the wracking sobs from moments ago, Raphael thought optimistically. Ten minutes went by without a word from her. She lay in his arms like a ragdoll. And then she spoke in the softest of whispers, with a voice that tugged at the very foundation of who he was as a healer.

"I'm sorry, Raphael. You're right. I'm sorry, so, so sorry." She looked at him with shame in her eyes. Tears slid like ghosts down her face. He stroked her hair once again, giving more of himself than he knew he should, but he wasn't who mattered now.

"Shh, we all understand what you're going through. She is a part of us, too. You must trust that everything that happens, does so for a reason. We plan and God laughs, right? But if you think about it, our plan hasn't been altered that much. Think positive. We're counting on you, as part of the Trinity."

"Send in Cassiel, please. And have Zadkiel work on you. Don't think I don't know what you've done, my friend. You've compromised yourself for my sake. I won't forget that, ever."

"In the scheme of things, Emma, your safety matters above all. Will you see Michael?"

She sighed deeply. "I guess I must. I behaved abominably towards him, Raphael. How will I ever look at him again without feeling shame inside? He will never forgive me. I've lost him. My blind madness for my daughter made me lose faith. And I've lost him."

"Give it time, Great Savior Mother. Love heals." Raphael released her and walked to the door of Hannah's bedroom. "I'll go get Cassiel for you now."

He closed the door behind him, leaving Emma to gather her wits.

Raphael walked into the family room. "Cassiel, head on in, she's ready for you. Well, any idea how this happened?"

"None whatsoever. There was not one thread of Agremon's existence floating around out there, except for a brief second," Kemuel asserted. "Ask anyone."

"What I know," Michael began, "is that I heard his voice all around me, goading me, and telling me to choose between Emma and Hannah. If I chose wrong, one would die. But I never saw him. Emma, I think, will have the answers we're looking for."

He dragged his hands through his hair for the millionth time. His brows deeply creased, guilt and shame were scrawled over his face like a tattoo. He knew he'd done the right thing, but her reaction was ripping him to shreds. He'd lost her trust. He didn't just feel it. He had heard her yell it from Hannah's room. With Hannah gone, and Emma lost to him, how on earth was the Trinity to survive and help conquer Namirha? Lord only knew. As usual.

Cassiel returned, looking a little worse for wear. "Lord Almighty, she's powerful! I tell you, I'm spent, and still I wasn't able to completely get her back to fully-loaded. No wonder she was able to knock us on our asses before! But I'm estimating that by the time we're ready to get going, she'll be right as rain. She needs to rest for the next couple of hours. Hey, Michael, you're up. All that power needs protecting, brother. You might want to put a little extra zing in it, her being all Great Savior and all." Cassiel threw himself on the couch and closed his eyes. "If you need me, you know where I am, just knock." He immediately fell into his meditative state.

Michael turned to Raphael. "She doesn't want me. She doesn't trust me. Better to send in Urie."

"It's okay. I explained things to her, made her see reason. She agreed to see you so you can give her your protection," he consoled, placing a reassuring arm on his shoulder. "All will be well. In the end, all will be well."

As he walked cautiously towards Hannah's room, Michael raised an eyebrow at Raphael. He gently closed the door behind him. Emma lay on her bed, eyes closed, looking beautiful, stronger, but not the least bit at peace. He took a deep breath as he edged closer to the bed, dying to reach out and hold her and never let her go. He fought his desire with all his might and simply gave a little cough to let her know he was there.

Emma opened her eyes and closed them again. She turned away from him and curled up like a ball. A thousand thoughts raced through her mind. It hurt like hell to look at him. She hated him. She loved him. She gave her trust to him, and he betrayed her. Or did he? Letting Agremon take Hannah probably saved them both. Was she humble enough to admit it if it was so?

Maybe she had gone completely crazy. She couldn't help second-guessing everything or letting the cynicism taint her views. Ron's betrayal and their divorce had ruined her. But then how had she allowed Michael to break down her defenses so easily?

"Emma, I've come to replace what you've lost," Michael told

her simply.

She remained in her protective position. "Can what is lost ever truly be replaced?"

"As far as protection goes, I can replace that."

"I guess that is something, then," she squeaked out.

She heard him walk by Hannah's bureau. Her Talisman lay forgotten on the floor. She peeked out from behind her arm as he bent down to pick it up. He was inspecting the piece. She guessed his protection on it had been pulverized by her blast of grief and fury. Well, she had warned him about her maternal powers being stronger than anything.

She damn well proved it.

"I'll rework the incantations into the charm and it will be as good as new, even better actually."

If he's trying to sound professionally removed, it isn't working, poor thing.

"Okay." She wished there was a do-over button she could push.

He began speaking quietly in words she didn't understand. His voice was so soothing and hypnotic that she dozed off for a while.

"I'll need to hold you now, Emma, so you can absorb my protective aura. Are you okay with that?" he asked.

"Hmmm? What? Oh, I'm sorry, I must have fallen asleep. Are you finished?" She turned to look at him standing over her at her bedside and quickly averted her eyes, her shame not allowing her to face him.

"Not quite. I'll need to hold you so you can absorb my protective aura. Are you okay with that?"

"Me? Am I okay with that?" She paused. "Are you okay with that? Can you stand to hold me? I mean, I don't even know how you can stand to talk to me or even help me for that matter." She hiccupped and shifted to sit up. "I'm so sorry, Michael! Can you ever forgive me? Can you ever forgive me for saying and doing the horrible things I am truly ashamed of, for not being stronger? You probably can't." She strangled the sheets clenched in her hands. "Knowing each other as long as we have, having been through so much and meaning more to each other than we ever expected, how does one forgive a lack of trust? But I do trust you, I do! It's me I've lost faith in." She beat her chest with her fist. "It's me who can't protect my own daughter. It's me who is a downright failure! And I turned it all on you." She choked on her sobs, letting her hand fall back down to her lap. She felt so forlorn, like a child lost to the world.

Michael sat down and gripped her arms harshly. She grimaced and he loosened his hold.

"Emma, there is nothing for me to forgive. You have every right not to trust me. What have I done to gain your trust? Huh? I've told you a crazy story about who you are and brought you into this otherworldly realm of angels and immortals. I've let Agremon get to you not once but three times now. I'm the failure here. E.L. never should have picked me for the Trinity. I'm too ashamed to even ask for your forgiveness." He tore away from her and stood by the small window facing the mountains, pounding a fist against the window frame. She was shocked. He didn't despise her? He feels ashamed? *And he's asked for my forgiveness? This isn't right.* She rose to stand beside him and leaned her head against his shoulder.

"Your guilt complex seems to be as immovable as those damn mountains." She pointed out the window.

"Michael, you did what was right. At first, I was too consumed by grief and fear to see it, as any mother would be having her child stolen from her. But Raphael helped me see what I refused to when you presented the bigger picture, and I've had time to think on it and understand the implications of your choice. By choosing me over Hannah, you saved us both. You saved us both. I was so wrong to have said what I said. And you should know better than me that things happen for a reason. All the choices we make, all the roads we take are meant to lead us to an ultimate end which we may not know 'til we're there. I forgive you for your negatively skewed perception of yourself. Can you forgive me my hasty, judgmental, neurotic tendencies and scathing tongue?"

There was a dreadful silence. She was alarmed. They were finished. The first relationship she'd had since her divorce, and it was over before it really had a chance to begin.

And then he spoke. And his voice was beautiful and kind and light. "I think I can manage that, as long as you let me power up your protections," he bargained with a gleam in his eyes as he caressed her cheeks with the pads of his thumbs.

She laughed. "I think I can live with that, too."

"Let me hold you, Emma, and we'll both get what we want." She couldn't deny the longing in his voice and hope in his eyes.

She wrapped her arms around his waist. She sunk into him as he embraced her with his strong arms, and they both sighed. As he enclosed her in his protective aura she shared some of her healing energy with him. Guilt and shame, grief and fear melted away to be replaced with strength and faith, harmony and love. Time paused as they renewed and strengthened their bond.

"You need to rest now." Michael took his talisman that he had woven extra-strong with his protection and placed it gently around her neck. "It's about five-thirty in the morning. We leave for the Homecoming at nine. The Brethren will do some readjusting to our plans while you sleep. Remember, your strength is needed for all of us to succeed. So sleep." He rested her on her bed, kissing her forehead and eyes, her lips, and whispered, "I love you. I don't deserve you, but I can't help loving you."

Emma awoke with a jolt. She didn't know how long she'd been asleep, but she woke up with a racing heart and an urgent need to share what she knew about Agremon. She hurried out of bed, opened the door, and raced to the family room.

"Agremon's not Agremon!" she sputtered out as she came slamming into a wall, otherwise known as Kemuel. "Oof!" He caught her as she rebounded off of his chest and just before she would have fallen back on her ass. She gave him an embarrassed yet grateful smile as she righted herself and made her way more slowly into the family room.

"Emma?" Raphael bristled. "What are you doing up and running around? You should be sleeping and replenishing your powers."

"Raphael, everyone, you have to listen." As she sat down on the coffee table she noticed Cassiel meditating on the far corner of the couch. "Wake up, Cassiel. Everyone needs to hear this." She waited for someone to nudge Cassiel awake before she said anything further. Zadkiel took the honors and gave him a hard shove.

"Hey, easy does it, brother. I'm awake, I'm awake," Cassiel grunted. "Hey there, Emma. Feeling better?"

"A bit, thanks. Listen, Agremon is not Agremon. What I mean is, he sounds like Agremon and behaves like Agremon, but he doesn't look like Agremon. When he came to me, he looked like a young man, kind of scrawny, stringy blond hair, blue eyes, about six-foot tall with a bad case of acne. I don't know how Agremon did it, but he's possessed a mortal's body. He said that possessing a mortal made Michael's talismans and shields useless. That's how he got to me and stole Hannah away."

The Brethren were silent. She looked to each of them, wondering if this new turn of events had them stymied. She nibbled on her bottom lip, again. Nasty habit, but it was better than smoking. Finally someone spoke up. It was Gabriel.

"He can't stay in that body forever. In fact, if I remember correctly, I don't think he can stay longer than twenty-four hours."

"Where does this guy get all his info?" Cassiel marveled.

"Just call me the information guru," Gabriel threw back at him. "During one of my searches regarding fallen angels and their powers, I remember reading that a fallen angel can possess a mortal, but for a short period of time, and then the host body rejects the possessor. Unfortunately, the host body dies once the possessor leaves it. Agremon's able to get past Michael's shields and walk around undetected right now because his soul is, in essence, disguised. What we've got to figure out is how to protect ourselves against him until he returns to his own body."

"You know what I'm thinking?" Kemuel asked. "We find a way to protect ourselves, call him out in the open, and kill him right then and there."

"As much as I would like to see him dead, my brother, Agremon's death would surely put Namirha on alert. With Hannah at his mercy, I'm not willing to risk that, are you?" Nathanael replied.

"No, no, I'm not, but I'm sick and tired of Agremon's crap! I want the asshole dead and gone already," Kemuel grumbled.

"Whoa! We're going to have to stay cool if we're going to think things through properly. Michael, you got anything we can use to shield us from him in his current state?" Nathanael asked.

"Yeah, I do actually. Everyone, stand up and make a circle. Lock your arms together with the person next to you. I'm going to weave an ancient incantation that has saved priests from possession during an exorcism. If I weave it just right, it will protect all of us from anything Agremon tries to do against us." Everyone did as Michael asked, eager to be as prepared as possible.

Michael began a low, slow chant in an unfamiliar language. Given the quizzical looks passing between the other Protectors, Emma figured this was something way out of their league. As he chanted he walked around the circle. Glowing wisps of threads appeared above the circle, woven into intricate patterns that she thought were breathtakingly beautiful in their delicate artistry. And yet, she could tell there was a strength there that was unshakable.

The woven tapestry enshrouded the Brethren and her alike and gently faded as though melting into the very fibers of their clothing. At the same instant, a surge of energy, warm and strong, penetrated her body. Michael dropped to one knee, but was quick to get up, reassuring all that he was fine.

It was time to prepare for the Homecoming infiltration. Gabriel had called his assistant to purchase and deliver the equipment the Brethren would need. They loaded up their trucks with a few tents, sleeping bags and cots, and food.

This certainly isn't going to be a typical family camping trip, Emma mused darkly as she saw swords and amulets being tossed in the Brethren's duffle bags. And then she saw what she had unwittingly placed in hers—a picture of Hannah.

"I'm coming for you, Hannah," she vowed, touching the picture, before she hugged it to her. "Don't be afraid; let your Ancient Warrior soul fight for you. We're all coming, my sweet angel, and we will all end this together."

Chapter Twenty

Namirha was in his temporary office, a glorified tent at Headquarters, putting the finishing touches on his sermon for this morning's service and could feel the masses lining up at the registration desks in front of the enormous tent-like sanctuary. It could easily seat about a thousand people, and by the looks of it, would wind up being standing room only for this, the first of three separate services: one for morning, one for the afternoon, and one for the evening. By then, Namirha figured he'd have all the followers he needed to press forward with his plans to destroy his enemies and rule the world. Yes, his people were coming. He knew they would. How weak of faith these mortals were to their Gods.

Last night, surprisingly, Agremon had come through and given him Hannah. Just how he had escaped to do Namirha's bidding still gnawed at him. Agremon obviously had powers he'd kept hidden. Namirha would be wise to keep a closer eye on him.

And there Hannah sat, at her own desk, drawing pictures of flowers and bunnies. He watched her for a few minutes, amazed that after all this time of hunting her down, he finally had her in his grasp. And the best part was that she had no clue how important her role would be on her birthday. She looked up to find him staring at her. If she sensed it, she didn't let on.

"What are you doing, Father?"

"I'm writing my sermon for this morning's service. You know, I am a religious leader, the head of The Source, my child. I must write a speech that speaks to what people need to ease their suffering and pain, to make them see that The Source can and will provide for all their desires."

"You can do that for everyone? How?" she asked, head cocking to one side.

"All you need to know is that I have a special gift that I wish to share with the world. Now, how is your drawing going, my dear?"

"Well, I think my flowers are okay, but my bunnies look more like little fuzzy devils. Oh well. So will I go to the services, too, Father?"

"Oh no, my precious. You will stay here. There will be a special service on your birthday, though, that you can definitely attend. In fact, I've bought you the most marvelous dress for it. But you'll have to wait until your birthday to see it and wear it. Although, I do have a little gift for you that you may open now. It's hidden somewhere in this tent. Now, I must get going to the morning service, so you stay put. I believe Helena will see to your needs until I return."

He gently patted her head and rubbed her hair between his fingers before he turned and left the room.

❧

Just that small caress allowed the Ancient Warrior to weave a thread connecting Hannah to Namirha's mind. She needed to know if his plans had changed since her abduction. Somehow, she would need to get that information to the Brethren when they came today. She briefly thought of her mother and what she must be going through since her abduction, but quickly pushed it out of her head. Emotions were the last thing she needed to trip her up right now.

Helena showed no signs of entering the tent so the Ancient

Warrior directed Hannah to lie down as though she was taking a nap. She closed her eyes, breathed in deeply and began her journey along the threaded connection to Namirha. This would be tricky, but she had done very well at masking her presence during practice and was confident that she could do it now. Her breaths were admittedly shaky at first. After all, she was about to enter the mind of the Devil himself. The Ancient Warrior's soul took control at that moment of realization, and made sure that little Hannah was safely tucked away in her little corner of her mind. She knew all too well the horrors yet to come; and one so innocent as she should never witness pure evil unleashed.

The thread she traveled was more like a tunnel, dark and slimy, with unadulterated evil thought and intent dripping down the curved sides to the floor below. The Ancient Warrior was able to stay centered throughout the tunnel, narrowly missing touching the evil ooze at points. As she made her way through, getting closer and closer to her goal, she could feel threads of doubt and fear trying to encircle her.

Had Namirha detected her? Could she defend herself if he had? She strengthened her shields to mask her presence, reached out to grab hold of the doubt and fear to find that it hadn't come from Namirha at all, but rather herself. Fine time to white knuckle, she chided herself.

Finally she reached the thread that held Namirha's plans. Ever so gently she teased the ideas away from the others so she could get a better look. *He plans on using everyone who comes to the Homecoming as his mortal army to keep the Brethren distracted from his goal, to kill me on my birthday with a sacred knife in order to absorb my powers and have supreme domination over the world.* Then Namirha would kill the Brethren, as well, ensuring that he would rule for eternity. He had his immortal army ready to take care of that. Suddenly, she felt something. A little niggle at the back of her mind, like an alarm, and she knew she needed to get out of there and fast. Namirha was at the point of recognizing her invasion. She had the briefest of moments to flee back down the tunnel and get out.

Safely out of Namirha's mind, she bolted upright from her "sleep". A strange woman sat in a chair beside her with a vapid look on her face. She patted Hannah's arm mechanically. "There, there. It's all right. You fell asleep and must have had a bad dream. Come here and I'll hug it away."

"I-I'm okay, really. Thanks, anyway," Hannah replied meekly with a small smile. The last thing she wanted was to be touched by that creepy lady. "My father said he hid a gift for me somewhere in this tent. Would you help me find it? Then, I think I'll go and get some fresh air and maybe some water. Yeah, water would be great, too."

"Sure, I'll help you. Mr. Namirha gave strict orders to watch you and take care of you. I won't let him down."

Great.

After Agremon's triumphant return, he quickly flashed himself to the cell where Jared was being held, having so willingly swapped places with his buddy almost twelve hours ago. Agremon needed to do something and quickly—get his body back before Jared's rejected him and he found himself forever floating around like dust particles.

"Hey, Jared! I'm home!" Agremon was met with silence from his body that hung limp in the shackles. "What, no hello?"

He walked closer and smacked his face. A faint grunt escaped from the barely conscious Jared. "Hey, why the long face? No one said it was easy being me. I guess it's true, our experiences shape who we are, and I'm one helluva creature, ain't I? Well, you're in luck, my friend! You don't need to be me anymore! And, did you notice the flaying stopped?"

Another grunt and a whimper. "Are those tears of joy I see? Aw, you don't have to thank me. Don't say a word. I know how you feel. Unfortunately for you, you're not going to be feeling much of anything anymore." Agremon gave him a hearty slap on the back. "Thanks for being a pal, my man. It was fun while it lasted."

Although Jared was trapped in his immortal's body, Agremon took demonic pleasure in knowing his mortal soul had felt all the torture and he was near death's door. He unchained Jared's arms and legs and watched as his body flopped to the floor. He grabbed both of his hands and chanted an incantation similar to the one he had said earlier. "I was you and you were me, and now I set my damned soul free."

Their two souls departed their host bodies and returned to their rightful places. Agremon immediately got up. Jared did not, nor would he ever again. Agremon didn't give him a second glance and flashed to Headquarters to do his cultish duties for Namirha. Agremon was back on top, and just where he wanted to be.

"Hi, and welcome to The Source. Please sign in. My name's Shandy. If you are interested in a longer stay with us, I can help you with that." The girl taking care of Michael's and Emma's registration looked to be about twenty-years old, with washed-out blonde hair, no makeup, and an overall bland appearance. Although she smiled, Emma saw dilated pupils, and for a bright Arizona morning, they should have been pinholes. She was under some kind of mind control.

As she glanced at the other people helping with registration, she found the same to be true about them. All of their eyes were vacuous and lifeless. She wondered if other people registering had noticed like she did, but apparently, they were too busy filling out forms to waste time with that kind of triviality.

"Yes." Michael hooked his arm around Emma's waist. "We were interested in staying a little longer than the service. In fact, we brought stuff to set up camp. Would you be able to show us where we can do that, Shandy? My wife and I would be really grateful." She looked up at him and gave her sweetest smile.

"Yes, we would be so grateful, Shandy. I know coming here

was the right thing to do," she declared brightly. "I can feel it down to my very soul. It's the only choice we have left. But enough of that. We're here and we'd like to stay."

"Okay then, I'll get Jeff over here to show you to a vacant spot. Jeff! Please show these people where to set up camp. They're here to become one with The Source."

"Sure. Right this way, please." He led them to the campsite where they could set up their tent and park their car.

The other Brethren spaced themselves inconspicuously amongst the other lines that had formed to speed up registration. Slowly but surely they all made their way to the same campsite where Michael and Emma had been brought, and were placed 'coincidentally' near each other. Everyone was busily setting up their tents and stowing their gear when a voice suddenly could be heard emanating from the surrounding trees. It was Agremon!

"Services will begin in ten minutes. All followers are to make their way to the prayer tent. Again, services will be in ten minutes. All followers are to make their way to the prayer tent."

"Okay, that was creepy." Emma involuntarily shivered. Michael walked over to give her a reassuring hug.

"Yeah, hearing Agremon's voice all around us definitely ranks up there with all that is creepy. Looking around, I can tell they've got not only speakers in the trees, but security cameras, too. It's not a problem in terms of us getting identified. We're perfectly shielded. It's getting the others out of here unnoticed where those cameras are going to cause a problem."

"Can you guys do anything about them?" she asked as she dug through her bags to start unpacking.

"I'm going to go and tell the others, if they haven't noticed them already. I'm sure Gabriel can do something nifty like set up a loop when we start herding these people out of here. I'll be right back."

"All right, I'll finish unpacking and setting up the tent."

She felt strange, setting up their temporary home with everything in its place, his and hers. Could she dare allow herself to fall for the illusion of this happily married couple down on their luck and looking to The Source as their last hope? Well, it wasn't that far from the truth. Coming here was their last hope to get Hannah back and to purge Namirha and Agremon from their lives.

As far as the married part, well, she still believed in the idea of marriage when two people fall in love. And she believed she had fallen in love with Michael. But she certainly didn't want to believe in something that would probably fall apart when this whole ordeal was done and over with. *Strong emotional situations lead to quick fiery relationships that soon fizzled out.* Well, that reason wouldn't hold. She'd known Michael for six years. They worked together, side by side, on many projects and were a great team. *Yes,* she countered herself, *but you've only truly known all about him for four days! And the biggest issue of them all is he's immortal! You're certainly not going to live forever. How's that for a kick in the pants?*

As she held this silent battle, she nibbled at her bottom lip again, inadvertently folding and refolding the same shirt. She heard the swoosh of the tent door and looked up. Michael stood in the doorway, holding the flap back.

"I have to admit I've been spying on you."

"You have? How very sneaky of you. And what dark secrets have you uncovered?"

"No secrets, I'm afraid, but I have come to one conclusion." He walked in and sat down on the cot next to her.

"Oh really, what is that?" She shifted a bit to give him more room.

"If there was a contest for best shirt folder, I think you'd win hands down."

"What? Oh, ha, look at that. I, um, well. All right, I've got nothin'." She laughed her worry off and quickly changed the subject. "Did you talk to the others? Is everyone set?"

"Yes, everything is fine and the Saviors and Protectors are readying themselves to get as many newcomers as possible to leave the site. It's going to be tricky making sure others don't notice the departures. But with the service about to begin, I think everyone headed towards the prayer tent should be distraction enough."

Emma put the shirt away and picked up Hannah's picture. "God, Michael! We've got to find her. I can't take being separated from her much longer. I feel like a part of me has been cut away."

"I do, too, honey. I do, too." With conviction clear in his voice, he continued, "We'll find her. I know it." He reached out to hold the picture while he put an arm around Emma. Suddenly, both felt a jolt of energy so strong it should have knocked them to the ground, but instead, it sealed them to the picture and to each other. A bright light surrounded them and they heard Hannah's voice. *Mother! Michael! I'm here and I'm safe. I'm in the dark green tent next to the prayer tent.*And then, just as suddenly, the light faded away, leaving them holding the picture of Hannah in their white-knuckled hands.

"Holy crap!" Emma cried out.

Michael gave her a cautionary look and the quiet signal.

"I'm sorry," she apologized. "This Trinity business is freaking me out. But she's here and she's safe. I almost can't believe it. You did hear her, too, didn't you? It wasn't my imagination. You heard her, too, right?"

"Yes, I did. This is great. We now have a connection to Hannah. Let's go." He took her by the hand and they walked out of their tent as though going to the prayer service. They followed her directions as well as the thread that now connected all three together.

There was a definite buzz in the air as they walked through the camp. As expected, newcomers gave off waves of excitement, trepidation, and desperation. Followers gave off a very different energy; waves of subjugation, faith, and of all things, collective thought. That was deeply disturbing, and something that needed discussion when the Brethren were all together.

Michael noticed the other teams already making a dent in the crowd going to the prayer tent. It was obviously easier to keep newcomers from entering than to get followers out of thrall and to safety. Given how many newcomers there were, just this morning, this would have a huge impact on their success later. But still, there were far too many getting by. Mindful of security cameras, he walked over to Gabriel and Urie.

"Hey, we found Hannah, or rather she found us. Anyway, she's okay. We're going to her now, but as far as all of these hordes of people, do you think we could find a way to mask this place so no more people can get in?"

"That's an awesome idea," Urie considered. "But if we did that, we'd have nothing left of ourselves to give Hannah and our troops when they come. Besides, that would be the biggest red flag ever letting Namirha know we were here."

"Wait a minute," Gabriel interjected. "Maybe we could set something in place that would control the amount of people that came in, you know, like to reduce the flow. If we could let maybe every tenth person enter, we would drastically reduce the amount of people we need to usher back out. It wouldn't take that much energy for that. Urie, come back to the tent with me. I've got an idea where I can locate the proper incantation. Oh, and I'll be able to set up a loop on those security cameras, no problem."

Michael walked back over to Emma who was surveying the area as though her life depended on knowing exactly where everything was located. Well, it did actually, so she definitely got points for recognizing that. "Why are they going back to their tent?" she asked.

"We've got a way to reduce the amount of people coming in today. I don't have to tell you what that means."

"Nope. Better odds for us. I like it. I hope it works." She walked further into the site, her hands banging against her thighs in a steady pattern. "I can't stand it anymore. Let's get her, Michael. I need to hold my daughter, now."

He nodded, and without another word, they walked quickly along pathways that circled the prayer tent. There were many tents and campers of all shapes and sizes set up, all unoccupied at this point given that the prayer service was about to begin. There was one tent, though, that stood out from the rest. It was a deep green color and larger than the rest.

"This is it, Michael! I know it," she whispered excitedly. They were about fifty yards away from it now. She pulled on his arm trying to run towards it.

"We can't just go barreling in there. Stop, Emma! Calm down and think." He tugged back and grasped her securely in his hands.

"Jesus, I'm sorry," she sputtered, shaking her head as if to clear the mess away. "I need to get to her. I'm desperate."

"I know, sweetheart. But we gotta play it cool, now. We're almost there, so look sharp. I'll go first. When I signal you, come quickly."

"I'll do as you say, I promise." She took a couple of deep breaths, shrugged her shoulders and rubbed her hands over her face. And then she signaled to Michael that she was ready.

"Here goes," he muttered, and he was off.

Chapter Twenty-One

*T*he coast was clear. Michael waved Emma to come forward as he watched for any signs of Agremon or other henchmen that Namirha probably had nearby. But the place seemed deserted. He listened by the tent's opening as she scurried next to him. He heard voices. One was definitely Hannah's, the other a woman's.

He put his finger to his lips to make sure she stayed silent and motioned that he was going in, alone. She nodded. His Brethren speed assured a quick and silent entrance. He immediately put the woman to sleep with the touch of his hand to her forehead. Hannah remained quiet while he whispered for Emma to come in.

She rushed inside and scooped Hannah up into her arms before Michael could even blink. Hannah clung to her mother. Her smile reached her contented eyes, and she showered Emma with kisses, receiving just as many back.

"Oh, my dear angel, I'm so glad you're okay. I've been worried sick about you. We had no idea what had become of you. Oh, thank God you're alive. Thank God," she murmured incessantly in Hannah's ear.

"Mother, Michael, we have to talk quickly. I've a lot to tell you." They sat on her cot together and she continued, sharing everything Namirha had planned; everything that she had culled from his evil mind. "One other thing; I have to stay with Namirha."

"Are you out of your mind? We came here to get you out of his reach! Michael, talk some sense into her, please!" she begged, grabbing his arms. He didn't say anything. He stood there with a look that told her she wasn't going to like what he would say at all.

"If we take her now, Namirha will know we were here and took her."

"Why can't it be that she wandered off and ran away? You put her guard to sleep, for heaven's sake. That supplies reason enough for Hannah leaving the tent."

"He would still wind up sending his minions out to locate her, and when they found her, he'd tighten security that much more." Michael rubbed a hand over his face, barely hiding his grimly set lips. "No, Hannah's right, unfortunately. She has to stay." And then, his voice brightened suddenly. "Wait a second. We created a binding thread between the three of us with the picture. I know it flowed one way before, but with us all together now, we can create a stronger thread that goes both ways so that we can basically talk to each other."

"I still don't like her staying here," Emma scoffed gruffly. "But if this is how it's gotta be, then how do we go about creating a threaded link?"

"Well, let's all hold hands and I'll do the rest," Michael suggested. As their hands closed around each other's, the power of the Trinity ignited. A pulsing energy flowed through all three like an electric circuit. As Michael spoke the sacred incantation, his lips moved, but he made no sound. Threads of light wrapped around their hands, binding them together, and slowly faded into their skin.

"I'm feeling a warmth seeping into my hands," Emma noted, "like toasty, warm gloves on a snowy day."

However, it was not a snowy day. It was a toasty one-hundred-two degrees at the moment, which Michael knew was making the creation of the link quite uncomfortable for everyone involved. He saw Hannah wincing ever so slightly, but putting on a brave warrior front, she didn't say a peep. No sooner than it had started, the task was complete. Michael saw the relief wash over mother and daughter.

"Oh, Michael, Namirha gave this to me as a gift. I haven't worn it yet. Can you look at it and tell me if I can wear it and still be safe? It looks like some kind of an amulet to me." Hannah held up a necklace that looked similar to his talisman but with different inscriptions on both sides.

"Let me have it and I'll tell you." He reached for it and closed his eyes as he held it in his hands. Hannah watched as creases formed between his brows. "It's a talisman, made by Namirha." He continued his assessment. "There is one layer of power that is a standard protective shield, then an additional layer of power wrapped around that. A dark power meant to wrap around your heart and mind in order to isolate you from the Brethren and your mother." He opened his eyes and look deeply into Hannah's.

"It is strong, but I'm stronger." He waved his right hand over the amulet and it trembled, then stopped. "I've destroyed the thread. It's safe now. It was meant to control you. You can wear this now without fear, but understand, Namirha expects you to behave as though you were under his control."

"Understood, thanks," Hannah replied.

"Well, now what do we do?" Emma asked, biting her nails. Michael could see she was a bit rattled by the business-like manner in which her daughter spoke and rubbed her arm.

"You two go to the prayer service." Hannah hugged her mother one more time. "Keep an eye on who the key people are working for Namirha. I'll stay here and continue doing whatever a six-year-old would do while keeping an eye on Namirha. When you or I know anything, we'll make contact. Make sure my warriors know where I am and that I'm all right. Have someone come here to create a threaded link with me as well. Don't worry; nothing's going to happen to me until my birthday. We still have four days to carry out our plans."

Emma walked out first, but not before turning one more time to look at her daughter. Hannah smiled back. Michael woke up the woman, making sure she would think she'd dozed off from boredom.

Together, they walked back to the prayer tent, and as they entered the huge circus-like structure, she tensed. "Are you sure we're shielded? We can't be detected?" she whispered.

"Yes Emma, I'm sure. We're protected, I promise. We appear to be like any other person here. Let's grab a seat and watch an immortal madman at work." She felt his reassuring hand in hers as they looked for a good place to sit.

They found two seats near the back mixed in with lots of newcomers, perfect for being inconspicuous, and they watched and listened. Namirha was standing on a stage that was lavishly dressed with richly textured fabrics of red and black. There were candelabras on either side, and behind, hanging from the top of the tent and suspended from invisible wires, was a huge red and gold painted pentagram. A knife that had something carved into its blade hung beneath that. In front of the pentagram were six chairs occupied by three men and three women dressed in red robes. Center stage was Namirha, dressed in a black satin robe with a red collar.

Emma shivered as she looked upon the monster who planned to sacrifice her daughter on their birthday. *Not in this life or ever.* Her nails dug viciously into her clenched fists. There was no podium for him to stand before. He walked back and forth across the stage vigorously, waving his arms in fervent gestures to emphasize some point he was making. She decided to listen to the madness.

"I know how you are feeling. Times are tough, my children, no jobs, no homes, no real God to pray to any longer. Your God has forsaken you because He has fallen from grace himself!" At that moment, Namirha pointed to the sky. "That's right! He has failed you all and disobeyed The Source's commandments. Yes, your God bows down to another! The Source is angry that your

God would allow such strife to befall you." He pointed out to the audience, one person at a time. "How careless and irresponsible of Him to let so many of you lose your jobs and homes that took years to acquire while working your fingers to the bone." He clasped his hands together as if in prayer.

"Don't worry my children, for He will be punished for his sins and The Source shall take care of you now." He jumped down off the stage and started running through the crowd, stopping every now and again to look people directly in their eyes. "Who is The Source, you wonder? Can he really save me, you hope?" He threw his arms up wildly into the air. "I am here, my children, welcoming you home to The Source, because I am The Source! I am the one and only! All others bow down to me, and you, my children, will benefit the most from coming home today. Behold the gifts that await you. And there's more when you pledge your faith and souls to me."

Namirha jumped back up on stage and spoke to the group of people sitting on the stage with him. They all got up at the same time, took bags from under their chairs, and began to circulate around the audience. Emma leaned side to side, standing on her tiptoes, trying to see what they were passing out, but she was too short. She looked over at Michael, who was having no problem looking over the heads of the congregants.

"They're passing out hundred dollar bills, along with medallion necklaces; just like the one he gave to Hannah."

"No wonder these people are going crazy." She shook her head.

"Emma, their minds are being controlled by wearing those amulets of Namirha's making. So he's not as strong as he was the last time we clashed. Very interesting. No wonder he wants Hannah so desperately. He's losing his powers."

"Hmmm. Mr. All Powerful is not so much, eh?" she quipped.

More of Namirha's followers came from behind the stage to help give out the money and the medallions to the frenzied mob. People all around Emma pushed and shoved each other to reach for whatever they could get and put the necklaces on without a thought.

"They're blinded by the almighty dollar," Emma snorted in disgust.

"Yup. Namirha knows what he's doing. He's buying their souls."

Michael and Emma took the money and the medallions so they wouldn't seem out of place. They pretended to put the medallions on, but really dropped them to the floor. Their own talismans would serve as a look-alike. When the money ran out and medallions hung from everyone's necks, Namirha spoke again.

"My children, if you want a better life than what you have now, then you must give yourself to The Source. Have faith that The Source will provide for all of your needs and you will hunger no more." At this point his voice changed from a normal man's voice to something beyond evangelical, something dark and sinister and base. "Give yourself to The Source, to me! Let your souls link with mine and you shall be rewarded!"

Namirha raised his arms and reached out over the crowd as if to touch them. His eyes glowed fiery red, and he babbled in what she could only describe as gibberish. She shuddered and Michael grabbed her hand in comfort. She knew he was having no real affect on the two of them, but what was happening was so unnerving, and they couldn't do anything but play along.

Almost at once, everyone in the audience gasped, so they gasped. Then the rest of the group spoke in unison, "Our souls are yours to command. We live to serve The Source, our one true Master."

"Well, isn't this just great," she whispered. "We're now surrounded by hundreds of people that share a collective mind. And all who are here will serve that lunatic up there. Not very comforting at all."

"Don't worry. The Brethren will take care of it. Trust me."

On stage, Namirha had collapsed and the six people that shared the stage with him collected him and whisked him away.

"Whoa, what's that all about? Curious," she pondered aloud.

"He has weaknesses. Weaknesses can be exploited."

"Mark my words," Michael responded fervently. "They will be."

The service was over and everyone was filing out of the prayer tent. Although they looked the same from a distance, Emma and Michael could tell that there was a distinct difference between the people that walked in an hour ago and the people that left now. Their souls were corrupted, taken, absorbed into a collective that would think what Namirha wanted them to think. Emma and Michael mimicked the people's behavior, and made their way back to their campsite.

Safely in their tent, Michael shared first. "We've got to tell the others about everything we saw and heard. What we've just seen shows me we've got a better shot than originally estimated."

"What does that mean? Are you telling me we didn't have a chance in hell of winning here? Cause if that's so, I'm really going to lose it," she spewed, ready for a fight.

"Whoa, easy there, Mama." Michael raised his hands in defense. "You know there are no guarantees here. It's gonna be a hard fight to be sure. He's no slouch in the war department. But he's shown us a weakness we can use to our advantage. We're still gonna have a hell of a fight on our hands but this is good news."

"Well, that's something then." She was mollified for the moment and feeling a bit embarrassed over her sudden violent outburst. Actually being here at the compound was ripping her emotions to shreds. Emma looked at her watch. It was only eleven in the morning. What the heck were they supposed to do now? Just as she was going to ask, their tent door swung open and in walked Cassiel and Raphael. By the time Zadkiel came in there wasn't enough room to even breathe.

"Hey, let's go to our tent," suggested Zadkiel. "It's bigger."

"Great idea. We'll follow you."

Once inside the Saviors' tent, they all sat down comfortably on the cots. Zadkiel started in right away. "So, are we ready to do some de-programming?"

"I'm up for it." Raphael slapped his hands together and

rubbed them vigorously.

Cassiel unsheathed his sword and swung it high above his head. "Let me at 'em! I'm ready."

Michael stood up to cool some hot heads. "Wait, wait. Easy does it. Before we go, Emma and I have some important information to share."

"Oh really? What do you have for us?" Raphael asked.

"You wouldn't believe what we saw at the prayer service. Namirha needs amulets to keep his people in control. How about that! He never needed that before. He gave them out at the prayer service. The people are now wearing them around their necks. He now commands their souls through them. Take off their amulets and I'll bet anything they are free."

"That means Namirha is weaker than we thought. Excellent. He must be craving Hannah's powers something fierce by now."

"Right Cass, plus after he put the whammy on everyone, he actually collapsed on the stage. His helpers had to carry him off."

"Whoa, he collapsed? That's awesome. We're going to have such an upper hand come showdown. All right, anything else, or can we go set some souls free? I'm dyin' over here!" Cassiel whined like a petulant schoolboy and his knees shook with nervous energy.

"You really are too much." Emma shook her head. "No, that's everything."

"Then let's go!" Cassiel jumped to his feet, nearly sending a small camping table flying across the tent floor. "Time's a wastin' and I want to get as many people out of here as possible before the next group comes in."

"Oh! Wait a second. What are Nathanael and the other Warriors doing since they can't guard Hannah?"

"Oh, they're guarding her, Emma," Raphael assured her. "They're keeping a very low profile, blending in with the scenery, if you will. They'll be keeping tabs on all of her movements."

Cassiel held the tent flap open. "All right then, my brothers. Let's go free some souls."

As Emma and Michael walked, a thought occurred to him that was not sitting well. Namirha was definitely in a weakened state, but they still had Agremon to contend with. And he was in rare form these days.

Just how powerful had Agremon become? Michael hadn't sensed his presence in a long time. What if Agremon was somehow able to completely shield himself from Brethren detection? That required a tremendous amount of power and if true, definitely cause for serious concern. What if he knew the Brethren were already there? Only time would tell. Michael filed his thoughts away for the time being, and focused his attention on the hundreds of people needing to be relieved of their amulets. It was quite satisfying to know how many lives would be saved this time around. Some of the younger Brethren had concluded that this war would not produce the kind of bloodbath the past war had delivered. But this war hadn't even begun, and Michael, with his vast experience, knew conclusions made too early could spell disaster later.

Chapter Twenty-Two

The six members of the Inner Sanctum had taken Namirha to his tent, where they sat him upon his chair.

"Are you okay, my Lord?" asked one of the Inner Sanctum members, still wearing his robe.

"Yes, Robert, I'm fine now. My powers sometimes even overwhelm me. All of you should leave me so I can meditate and prepare for the other services."

"Of course, my Lord. If there is more we can do, we will," he replied. He and the rest of the Inner Sanctum left the tent to tend to their duties around the camp.

"Hannah! Helena! Where are you?" Namirha called out.

"Here, Father, here. We are in the corner."

"Whatever are you doing there? Why are you hiding from me?" he asked, his cheeks puffed out and reddened.

"I couldn't get Hannah out from the corner, my Lord, so I stayed with her, as you commanded," Helena simpered, crawling out of their hiding spot.

"I was scared, Father. So I ran to get out of the way. Please don't be angry, Father, please. Are you all right?"

"Yes, yes, I'm fine. Don't ever run from me, Hannah. You don't need to fear me or for me, my child. Helena, take Hannah to our home. I need to be alone now." His voice lacked the strength of conviction, and his hands were shaking with need for Hannah's powers, so he hid them within the folds of his robe. Now was not the time to take her. He would have to wait. Although each day closer to her birthday strengthened her gifts, it was her birthday when she would come into her full potential. That's what he needed, nothing else would do.

With Hannah gone, he meditated and restored his energy, though it was not as replete as before. If he collapsed again at the other services, he didn't care. It added to the drama. There were over a thousand people this morning. If this kept up, his army of mortals in this region would certainly be a force to be reckoned with. Combine that with the millions around the world ready to defend evil. He was sure to take over the world this time and send the defenders of the Good to Hell. His waning power had given him pause, though. He wasn't sure if the charmed necklaces would be enough to keep the foolish mortals under his control for the amount of time he needed. And it was getting harder and harder to keep from sacrificing Hannah before she came into her full powers. His plan would only work if he waited until the precise moment of her birthday. Nothing short of perfect would do. Nothing.

Agremon had some time on his hands. That never boded well for whoever wound up in his thoughts. Right now, he was thinking about Namirha. Oh, he was happy that he was back in his good graces, but Agremon would never forget the punishment he'd endured yesterday. He had seen Namirha collapse on stage and that gave him pause. Ever-scheming, he devised all sorts of ways to undermine Namirha and reign supreme in the end.

He had a plan coalescing. He was confident he could do it, too. Kill all the Brethren, sacrifice Hannah for her powers and absorb them himself, and take Namirha's place as ruler of all evil. He deserved it after all the time he spent acquiring the girl. Namirha sat on his ass spewing orders all the time. Agremon was fed up and wanted revenge for his fickle Lord and Master.

Pleased with himself, he decided to check on the security cameras. Although Namirha had all the followers in thrall, sometimes a rogue thought flashed through a person that made them take pause and doubt their involvement. It was Agremon's duty to reinforce the idea that they should stay, by any means necessary, lest they create a panic in others and start a domino effect of people leaving the compound. As he walked down the trail that led to the security tent, nobody seemed to be concerned that there was a grotesque monster stalking about. That was part of the thrall in action, and made his job easier. He couldn't very well hide out and do his various tasks effectively, nor did he relish manifesting a disguise that pleased others. He didn't like making people happy or comfortable, and it took valuable energy away.

"Get out of my way, assholes!" he roared as he entered the tent. He immediately shoved the two security officers out of the way, and began looking at the wall of monitors, twelve in all.

"Yes, sir!" they both yelled and scuttled to a corner of the tent farthest away from him.

"Now let me see what's happening. We have lots of newbies here, I see. I wonder how strong that medallion necklace is that Namirha gave 'em. Might be that some folks need a little attitude adjusting. Hmmm, all looks good. Wait a minute, what's this? Son of a bitch! Hey you, Grunt Number One, how long have you and Grunt Number Two been watching these monitors?"

"We got on duty at twelve, sir," Grunt Number One responded.

"And didn't anything look a little strange to you two fuck-ups?" Agremon roared.

Grunt Number One cowered back into a corner. "I—d-don't know what you mean s-s-sir," he stammered.

"Don't you guys know a fucking video loop when you see one? The same people keep passing by every ten or fifteen seconds! Same walk, same motions, same everything! Damn it! You guys are useless. Look, watch the monitor. See anything peculiar?" he asked impatiently.

"Uh, well, no."

"Wait for it," Agremon growled.

"Oh."

"Oh. That's all you can say is, oh. You idiotic shit for brains! Get your genius partner over there and get the fuck out before I rip your throats apart and burn you both from the inside out!"

The two men scrambled and fought with each other to be the first out of the tent. This served to make Agremon even angrier, and he wound up incinerating them both on the spot with a quick and strategically targeted, "Ashes to ashes and dust to dust."

They're here. I bet the Brethren are here. But why the loop? Obviously they're shielding themselves or I would have felt their signatures by now. So what is the loop for? In any case, how fortuitous for me. I can step up my game plan. Why bother waiting for Hannah's birthday?

He was already stronger than anyone realized. He'd been absorbing the energy of others for centuries now. Nobody knew exactly everything he could do, and nobody would. It was best to keep certain things secret. Whether Hannah's powers were at full strength or not, they were still strong enough for him to take over the world. After all, what difference could four days really make in the scheme of things?

Agremon made his way out of the security tent and back on the trails around the campgrounds. He was determined to find out why the Brethren had set up a loop on his security cameras. It didn't take long to find out.

As he walked the trails, he noticed some empty campsites—sites that previously had been filled with campers and tents. He walked on nearing the registration area and noticed hordes of people driving out of the compound.

What the hell is going on? Why is everyone leaving? How could everyone leave if they're wearing the amulets Namirha gave out at the prayer service?

Furious, he walked up to a station wagon that was inching its way down the driveway towards the main road, and planted himself in front of it with his hand out signaling to the driver to stop. The man behind the wheel and all of his friends looked at him in horror and screamed like girls. The driver put his foot on the gas pedal and floored it, heading straight for Agremon.

Damn it! Agremon thought. He'd forgotten to change his appearance in his haste and anger. *Oh well, what's a few more mortal deaths, anyway?* He stood his ground and when the vehicle reached him, he simply put his hand on the front bumper and immediately stopped its advance. Tires spun uselessly. He lifted the raging rust bucket, raised it over his head, and threw it to the side like yesterday's trash.

The other cars quickly sped around the horror and even broke gates to get out, not wanting to be the next to suffer the same fate. He walked over and carelessly grabbed one of the broken bodies. He looked around the neck. No necklace. He carelessly threw the carcass aside. He grabbed another battered soul, and again, found no necklace. Where were the amulets?

The Brethren. They're getting to these people and removing them! Brilliant!

He would have applauded their audacity if he weren't so fucking pissed. He needed those people as a shield, to keep The Brethren at bay until he had accomplished his goal. Well, at least he had the followers who needed no such trickery to do as commanded. But now he knew his timetable had changed absolutely. He would take care of things tonight.

Namirha won't know what hit him! The Brethren will be destroyed and he will rule the world! Not bad for a day's work.

Agremon flashed to his cavernous hideaway not far from Namirha's own lair. He had plans to solidify and immortals to rally to his side. And they would rally. They wouldn't care whose side they were fighting on as long as it was the winning side. He'd promise them world domination and they'd be like moths to a flame. And in the end, they would die the same way, for there was no way he would actually share the glory.

The Brethren were able to free nearly all of the people who showed up for the first prayer service, and they considered it a huge success. Now Gabriel was assessing the population controls they had in place for the next registration and prayer service. While he was out, the rest congregated in the Saviors' tent.

They were going over numbers while Emma linked in to Hannah's thread to check in on her. Hannah relayed that Namirha had seen the necklace around her neck and looked very pleased. Beyond that, he paid little attention to her. He was preparing for the next prayer service. She was to return to his tent.

Gabriel entered with a major scowl on. "Houston, we've got a problem," he disclosed in a hushed tone.

"What's happened, Gabriel?" Michael stood up.

"Well, I checked the population controls. All's in working order and it's doing a great job. But as I walked down the driveway, I noticed some heavy duty ruts, like those you'd find when tires went spinning madly. Directly in front of it were footprints that were not human. I looked around a bit more and found broken windshield glass lying all around on the grass and blood in that same grassy area. No car, no people."

"Agremon must have noticed the loop on the security cameras and gone investigating," Urie spewed. "Gabriel, what's going on here? Why the hell aren't we sensing him?"

"He's gaining strength and power." Gabriel rubbed his stubbled face and pinched the bridge of his nose.

"So, now what do we do?" Emma asked, feeling way out of her league as the Brethren plotted.

"We alert the Warriors," said Urie. "We need their troops at the ready. Have them move closer to Hannah. Agremon could be disguised as anybody or himself. They have to keep a close watch on who's going into that tent. We also need a team in the Prayer Tent with Namirha. We don't know if Agremon's told him yet. Beyond that, I think we should wait and see if either makes a move."

"I agree. We don't know for certain that Agremon's found us

out," Zadkiel concurred. "I mean, we're shielded. He can't trace a thread to any of us. If anything, he's going on suspicion. He's going to have to do some searching, and we all know he won't find us."

"Don't be so quick to dismiss his intellect," Michael warned. "You know Agremon is near genius. I wouldn't put it past him to have put two and two together even without tangible proof of our existence here. We can't afford to be complacent. Might I remind you of our last war waged?" The Brethren all dropped their heads down. "Complacency lost many lives for us, mortal and immortal alike. I say we assume the worst case scenario and plan accordingly."

"I agree," Emma chimed in. "I'll tell Hannah right now. She'll be able to sense a shift in Namirha's plans. And she can tell her warriors."

"All right then. Emma and I have already been to the Prayer Tent, so we'll start working on followers who don't have amulets. Cassiel, you and Zadkiel go to the Prayer Tent. Follow the people out, and then start removing the necklaces," Michael ordered. "Meet back here by four o'clock."

"Roger that." Cassiel left the tent with Zadkiel.

"Gabriel and Urie, you'll be with Emma and me on follower detail. Why don't you start on the west end and we'll start on the east end? Hopefully we'll have enough time and meet in the middle."

"Got it," Gabriel replied.

Emma's head was spinning and her stomach churned as she watched the Brethren move out like a pack of wolves. She had a feeling it wasn't going to be easy. Incantations could unlock the binding chains, but free will was a whole other matter. Having studied social psychology in college, Emma knew that their choice, their free will was keeping them faithful.

And that was more dangerous than anything.

Could the Brethren truly turn the followers away from evil? Would they be able to reach the followers' hearts as well as their minds and truly free them from their dark servitude?

175

Michael reached for Emma's hand as they began their walk to the far eastern end of the encampment. She gladly accepted the peaceful contentment his touch provided. His smile told her that her touch, in turn, had provided him with the reassuring feelings of deep and profound love. If she closed her eyes, Emma could almost pretend they were alone in the desert, wandering through ancient ruins, two people in love, holding hands. But the truth of it was too far from the dream, and she couldn't escape it even for a couple of moments.

Michael remained silent next to her. The tension in his hands increased. His left hand curled into a tight fist and his right was doing its damnedest to do the same.

"Ow! Hey there! I don't have these babies insured yet, so can you lighten up on the grip, big guy?" Emma joked. But then she noticed his shadowed expression.

"Oh, God! I'm so sorry!" Michael massaged her palm and fingers and kissed them all gently.

"Michael, what's the matter?" Emma stopped and turned him to her. "Tell me so I can try to fix it."

"You can't, Emma. This you can't fix."

"How do you know if you don't share with me what's going on inside you?" she countered. "I can tell you've shielded your mind from me, so the only thing I can read is your face and your body language. That tells me whatever you're feeling's got to be really bad." He looked around, brought her over to one of the Palo Verde trees near their path, and spoke in a hushed tone.

"If you must know, I've been doubting my boss's motives in all of this. Ever since Beth and the baby, actually. Oh, I've worked for him and done my job to the letter ever since. I mean a contract is a contract, and I signed on to this task knowing full well it was for eternity. But with you and Hannah, there've been too many hiccups in our plans. We constantly have to readjust them. We've never had to do that before, never.

"So I find myself doubting him more and more, wondering what screwing around with our plans accomplishes in the long run. Is he somehow in league with Namirha after all these millennia of opposing him? If so, to what end? Who is he willing to sacrifice for Good to be victorious in this current generation's war? Will he take you, Hannah, or both of you away from me? Will he take countless, nameless loved ones from their own families, as well?

"I don't want to lose you, either one of you. I couldn't bear it. My wavering faith in my boss is allowing dark thoughts to seep into me, and I know, should anything happen to you, I could easily turn, like Agremon did, and not feel the least bit of remorse."

Emma was silent, shocked by Michael's admission. She chose her words carefully. "I don't think there's anyone who hasn't second-guessed or doubted a decision their boss has made at one point or another. And I know that E.L.'s decision unfortunately changed your life forever. But if the other Brethren remain unwavering in their support of him, I have to think there must be something to it. Open your heart, and release your anger and resentment towards him. I truly believe that only then will this darkness that's threatening to invade you disappear. Let me help you. Don't fight me on this. If you can't let this go, then I think it could actually hinder our job here today."

Michael took her face into his hands and kissed her sweetly. "Okay," he whispered. "You win. But we can't very well do this here, out in the open. We're not far from our tent. Let's go back there, do what you have to do, and then let's free these people."

Back in their tent, he lay on his cot. Emma placed one hand on his heart and another on his head, stroking his hair gently. She closed her eyes and began the delicate process of unknotting the intricate threads of guilt, resentment, and fury. He winced and his body jolted, fighting, she believed, against the release of these emotions that had sustained him for centuries.

She increased the pressure of her hand over his heart, breathed deeply, and absorbed the emotions that were finally loosening from their tethers. She wept bitter tears, her body shook with the intensity of his fury, and three words escaped her lips in an unearthly voice. "You shall pay."

Then all was quiet, body and spirit. Emma took a few cleansing breaths and opened her eyes to find him staring at her. "Are you all right?" she asked tentatively. He said nothing, just kept staring at her. "Michael, are you all right? Say something, anything! Let me know you're okay!"

Chapter Twenty-Three

"Oh God, Michael, please say something!" Emma was frantic. Why wasn't he responding to her? And how could she undo what she'd done? She needed Raphael. He would know what to do. "I'll be right back. I'm going to get Raphael. He'll know how to fix the mess I've made. Stay right there. Don't move," she whispered as calmly as she could, but on the inside she was absolutely torn apart. She had this dreadful feeling she'd done something irreparable.

She turned to go when suddenly, his arm shot out and his hand grabbed at her leg.

"Don't go, please," he begged.

"Michael! Honey, are you all right?" She captured his face in her shaking hands.

He lifted his own to steady hers. "I feel...I feel free," he professed incredulously.

"Lord Almighty!" Emma gushed. "I thought I had...well, you don't want to know what I thought I had done to you!"

He jumped up from the bed and grabbed her for a dizzying, twirling hug. "I'm truly released from pain for the first time since Beth and the baby were taken from me. My mind is free of dark thoughts and filled with forgiveness and understanding. I'm sensing a renewed sharpness to my focus and an intensification of my energy. I'm alive, thanks to you!"

Emma smiled broadly as she looked at him with a sense of joy and accomplishment. He kissed her passionately for a good long while, breaking away only to lavish more over her throat, leaving her breathless and with a racing heartbeat pulsing under his lips.

"I love you, Emma," he professed, sounding intoxicated. "God, I love you so much!"

"I love you, too, Michael, so very, very much," she responded as she drew his face up to meet hers. "We've got a job to do now, if you're up to it. As much as we want each other right now, we've got people out there who don't even know they're counting on us to save them and protect them from Evil."

Emma knew he was sexually frustrated at the moment. The bulge in his pants wasn't a banana and the tiny beads of sweat along his pursed lips told her she better step away. But the better part of valor won out as he nodded and leaned his forehead against hers. "To be continued, then, my love."

"To be continued, my angel," she whispered sweetly and showed him what her promise held. When she released him, he sucked in a deep breath and let it out slowly, and then scrubbed his cheeks with his hands.

"If you would get that raunchy picture of me naked in your bed out of your mind right now, mister, it would make it easier to save these innocent people here. Remember them?" Surprise and guilt washed over his face. "Yeah, I can do other things besides heal people now. I can read your mind, too, remember? So get it out of the gutter and back on the important stuff." She gave him one of her patented death stares only a mother can give and waved him on.

Releasing the followers from Namirha's grasp proved to be more difficult than Emma had anticipated. Those who were single, alone but for the community of other cult members, were irretrievable. Luckily, those who had families were easier to deprogram; perhaps because they possessed the innate need to keep their loved ones away from danger. The Brethren were hoping for complete removal of mortals from the battlefield, planning for their efforts to be ineffective, and were winding up somewhere in the middle.

Namirha was rankled. A hapless lizard, crawling by his foot, received an untimely death with a well-placed zap. His second registration statistics were abysmal. It looked as though the first prayer service might very well be the only one to yield any mortal fodder. And where had his regular followers been? Surely they knew that attendance at all prayer services was mandatory! If the final prayer service turned out to be the same as the last, heads were going to roll. He huffed and puffed, pacing across his tent while his Inner Sanctum gazed on with indifference.

"Agremon!" Agremon did not appear. "Agremon! Where is that damned creature?" he muttered. Namirha was beginning to sense something was awry. He turned to his Inner Sanctum. "Go around the encampment, check on things, and bring me any followers who appear suspicious. I want to know why many of the followers didn't show up for the last prayer service and what's going on with registration. And if any of you see Agremon, tell him to get his ass over here immediately. Report back to me by three-thirty. Go!"

If Agremon had had anything to do with this, his last punishment would seem like a trip to Disneyland.

Hannah reached out to everyone. Although she was back at Namirha's lair deep in the abandoned mine, she could still sense him strongly. And what she sensed was unsettling. She closed her eyes and breathed deeply, catching the threads of her people and spoke to them through her mind.

I have news. It is not good. Namirha is furious over the poor showing at the last prayer service. Agremon can't be found, and Namirha is getting wise to the idea of others thwarting his efforts. Right now, he has a suspicion that it is Agremon. He still does not detect us, but it is only a matter of time before he puts things together. He has his Inner Sanctum scoping out the encampment for resistance and tasked them with bringing any resistant followers to his tent. They are also looking for Agremon. They need to return to Namirha with their findings by three-thirty, just before the last prayer service.

We need to locate Agremon. I'm getting a strong sense that plans are starting to shift. Namirha is weakening with every service and is fighting with himself to keep from sacrificing me sooner than my birthday. He seems to think that to sacrifice me now would do him no good. But I can sense his desperation grow hour by hour. I must go now, Helena returns.

The connection was broken and all were left to ponder what their next move should be. With Nathanael and Seraphiel watching over Hannah's movements, Kemuel decided to head back to the encampment to lend his voice to the ever-changing plans.

"Well, we've done the best we could to rid this place of mortals. I say we wait until Namirha starts his four o'clock prayer service, get Hannah out of his reach, and take him down, right there and then. He'll be so occupied with his ranting that he won't notice us until it's too late."

"Not a bad idea, Cass." Kemuel nodded and considered. "He won't have an opportunity to call his immortal minions, then. The more I think on it, the more I like it."

Emma raised her hand. "I'm for anything that gets Hannah out of his clutches and ends this nightmare once and for all."

"I'll go tell the other warriors of our plans. It's almost time for the service. Better get in position. This is it, folks. No turning back. Good luck, brothers and Mother. We shall remain victorious!" Kemuel left and everyone else mobilized for the assault.

Hannah prepared herself for Helena's return. She was an insufferable woman who smothered and babied, but she was easily pliable, and that worked to the Ancient Warrior's advantage. Her companion came in and took up residence on a chair by the tent's entrance.

"Well, I see you have your coloring book and crayons all set up. How lovely. Now, I'm going to sit here and read my book, so if you need me, I'm right here."

"Thank you, Helena." No sooner had she started drawing yet another bunny, a visitor came. Agremon. As he barged into the room he pushed Helena so hard, she slammed against the wall beside her and slumped to the floor unconscious.

Why didn't I sense his approach at all? He broke through her musings with a booming command, "We're going to a party, Gnat. Come."

"No." If he was going to call her a gnat, she was going to live up to that name and be a pest.

"I'm sorry, I didn't hear you right. Did you say no? His nostrils flared and his hands curled into fists.

"Yes, I said no. I don't wanna go. I'm fine here drawing. Does Father know you're here? He's gonna be angry about what you did to Helena."

Agremon charged forward and picked her and the chair she was sitting on up in the air. "I don't need dear old Pappy's permission to do anything. You listen to me, you little wart on a pig's behind, you're coming with me. And don't even bother screaming or doing anything stupid like that. I've had you shielded since I walked in so no one knows the wiser."

The Ancient Warrior knew when to give in and play along, and this was the moment. Whatever Agremon had in store for her, she'd be taking notes to use to her advantage at another opportune time.

"Okay, Agremon, you win. I'll go. But I'm not gonna like it. And the first chance I get, I'm gonna tell."

"Yeah, all right. You tell. Shout to the world! It won't matter anyway. We're celebrating your birthday a little early and wait till you see your present. Nice knowin' ya kid."

He let the chair loose, held onto Hannah and flashed them away.

Kemuel raced through the rough mountain terrain as quickly as his immortal legs could carry him. Time was of the essence. He was nearly at the opening of the abandoned mine, no more than a few minutes from where the other warriors were hiding out, when suddenly, a dark shadow appeared menacingly in front of him. Before he could even fathom what it could be, it drifted over and around him, but could not get closer than about five feet, thanks to all his protection shields. He reached for his sword and began swiping at the shapeless form surrounding him. But it yielded no positive results. And then he heard a familiar voice emanate from the ever-shifting shadow.

"Well, if it isn't Brother Kemuel. It's been a while. Come for a visit, have you? Well, it seems you've arrived a little too late. I was just on my way out. You see, I'm taking a...friend out for a little celebration in her honor. It should prove to be quite the party of the century. Am I right, Hannah?" Agremon sneered.

"Kemuel!" Hannah screamed. Kemuel thrust his sword in frustration until he sensed that her scream was for show, for Agremon's benefit. She sent Kemuel a quick, clear message that she was very much in control, and plotting what her next move would be. "Well, Agremon. What's the fun of a party if there are no guests?" Kemuel goaded. "I should think you'd want a big crowd. I could arrange that, you know. A reunion of sorts could prove to be quite interesting."

"Sorry, old foe. This party's for two, but when it's over, you can be assured that I will take you up on that reunion. I should love to hear what everyone's been up to since our last meeting, so to speak. For now, though, I wanted to let you know that I have plans, big plans. Very soon, Namirha will be working for me. Later." The shadow disappeared as quickly as it had arrived.

Kemuel immediately ran towards the mine opening. He wondered how no one could sense Agremon taking Hannah. The only plausible but disturbing answer was that he had gained more powers than anyone knew of over the years. He was quickly met by Nathanael and Seraphiel running toward him.

"Hannah's presence is no longer in Namirha's lair," Nathanael said.

"I know. I just had a shadowy visit from Agremon. He has her, damn it. We can trace her thread to where he's taken her. He said something about having a celebration. I know it sounds crazy, but I think he wants to do the sacrifice himself! Tonight! We must call in the troops, now. With the nifty tricks Agremon's got, Namirha is no longer the biggest threat. Agremon is!" With that decided, they ran back to the encampment to alert the others.

Back inside the warrior's tent, all sat around while Gabriel reminded them of how, where and when the blood ritual was supposed to happen.

"Now, we know when it's supposed to take place and that Agremon's blown that scheme out of the water. But what's also important to remember is that it can only be done with a specific ritual knife. The one in the Prayer Tent looks like it could be the one. And the ritual must take place at precisely 6:06 pm on a stone slab that has been ritually prepared for the event. This stone slab, has anyone seen anything resembling such a thing around here? It should be out in the open, preferably a raised area." Everyone shook their heads.

"We've been all throughout the encampment area. No stone slabs to be seen anywhere." Kemuel paced the floor and stopped. "What about the mountain itself? Maybe he's got something going on further up the mountain."

Emma raised her voice, asserting herself for the first time as a member of the team. "Before we go scattering ourselves about this place, remember, we can follow her thread. Hannah will lead us to her and Agremon. We have to have faith."

"Her connections have been inconsistent, but she's right," Michael said. "Let's just take a second here to sit and concentrate on Hannah's signature. If she's been able to send out intermittent messages, we may be able to follow them like cookies crumbs. So where is she? Concentrate, everyone."

It was tough going there for a little while. Agremon was very talented with location spells, shields, and diversions. With Michael's help they all reconnected with her thread. As choppy as it was, they were able to get a pretty good read on where the two of them were and that she was well. Hannah was back in the abandoned mine, but in a much deeper section than before, Agremon's lair perhaps. And even that was tentative. They all knew that Agremon could flash in and out of places now and could very well be gone from the mine and turn up halfway around the world before they even took one step.

Nathanael sat on a cot, polishing his sword. "We have to get that knife before he does. After the prayer service is done, when Namirha leaves the stage and everyone is busy leaving, I'll grab it."

"Perfect, Nathanael. Go now, the service is almost over." Kemuel gave him an extra sheath to carry. "The rest of us will start readying our weapons and making a strong connection to our troops." He turned and addressed Emma. "When the battle begins in earnest we communicate with only our minds. It's most effective that way."

Emma nodded her understanding. She got up and walked to the tent's opening.

"Where are you going?" Michael asked.

"I'm just going back to our tent for a minute. I need to check on a couple of things."

"I'll go with you."

"No, no, it's all right," she answered brightly. "You stay here and do what you Brethren do. I'll be fine, honest." She leaned into Michael and gave him a light kiss before leaving.

"Uh, Michael," Kemuel prodded. "She'll be back when she's back. Staring at the door isn't going to bring her here any sooner. Now come on, link up with us." Michael turned to the business at hand and linked up with the others.

As she stealthily made her way to the Prayer Tent, Emma prayed that she hadn't completely lost her mind. But her decision to go it alone at this point was fueled by her frustration and need to save her daughter by any means necessary. She could not turn away from her mission nor let anyone know or they'd have stopped her for sure, especially Michael. Oh, if she made it through this, he was going to kill her! She'd gladly deal with that later. She was about to turn master and disciple against each other to save her daughter. And may they wipe each other off the face of the earth and leave us alone, she thought.

She snuck in the back of the Prayer Tent, not wanting to be seen by Nathanael. She slunk down in a seat and waited for the service to end, occupying herself with looking around. They had indeed done an excellent job of ridding the place of people. Where the first prayer service had standing room only, this one was a quarter filled at best.

Namirha appeared quite agitated and annoyed on stage. She looked past him, at the pentagram hanging down, and then at the space where the knife should have been. *Damn it all! Agremon got to it before Nathanael!*

As followers left the tent and Namirha made his way out of the side door, she darted out and ran around to the side where she would hopefully run into him heading back to his tent. This had to work. There was one hour left before Agremon would sacrifice Hannah!

Emma saw him. He was a hunched over mass of ashen skin and bones, with a face that reminded her of the frightening wooden African tribal masks she'd seen in a museum. A frail old man, to the untrained eye, maybe. But behind the sunken eyes glimmered pure evil, through and through. He was leaning on a man in a robe as they walked back to his tent. "Mr. Namirha! Mr. Namirha, I must speak with you! It's a matter most urgent! Mr. Namirha!"

At first, he frowned at her. *He's probably shocked at my audacity. Good.* But then his look morphed before her eyes, the frown disappearing in favor of a sickeningly sweet smile.

"An urgent matter, you say, Miss...?"

She paused. Should she divulge who she was right then? Would it jeopardize her plan? She had no choice but to offer her name and replied, "My name is Livingston. And yes, it is a very urgent matter. May I speak with you privately in your tent?" *Breathe, Emma, just breathe.*

"Ms. Livingston? That name is so familiar to me. I meet so many people; I bet I've heard your name at a prayer service somewhere. Please, your urgent matter should be shared sitting down in my tent. Come and we'll talk," Namirha coaxed politely. If he knew who she was, he didn't let on. But Emma wasn't foolish enough not to suspect he'd known exactly who she was.

He offered her a chair and his robed helper eased him into a chair at his desk. He dismissed him and turned his attention to her. "So, let's hear about this urgent matter, Ms. Livingston. I must say you've got me intrigued."

"Well, you see, I've come across information regarding a betrayal by one of your people," she began.

"A betrayal? How fascinating!" Namirha replied with the utmost interest. "Do go on."

"Well, you see, Agremon has taken the girl." Emma paused, looking for any reaction. She saw the slightest twitch of an eyebrow. "And that's not all," she pushed on. "He plans on sacrificing her to get her powers, tonight."

"Why, whatever are you talking about Ms. Livingston? What girl, sacrifice, powers? Surely you can't be serious. I run a very clean religious organization here," Namirha sniffed smugly. "You, however, are sounding quite mad."

"Please, Mr. Namirha, we don't have time to play coy, so give up your charade. You know who I really am, as I know who you really are." Namirha's smile faded to a hard glare. "You took my daughter from me, and now Agremon's taken her from you. If you're smart, you'll realize that doesn't bode well for your plans. As for me, being Hannah's mother, neither scenario appeals to me in the least, but I would certainly choose having Hannah with you over Agremon any day of the week. He's a loose cannon and wants to murder my child."

She leaned back in her seat and folded her hands on her lap, feeling more confident with each breath she took. "I know you need my daughter. I know you need her power, and it comes from her blood. But one doesn't have to murder to achieve that. I will only allow you to have as much as is absolutely necessary of her blood if you get her away from Agremon, tonight, within the hour. And you get the added benefit of dealing with Agremon's betrayal. I want from you the promise of getting my daughter back alive and safe from this point on."

"You know who I am? And you still dare to strike a bargain?" he scoffed with raw arrogance. "Your love for your daughter is touching, to say the least, Ms. Livingston. But I don't think you realize the magnitude of what you're offering and its consequences. You think you've got it all wrapped up neat and tidy, but I assure you, there is so much more to this than your daughter's life. She, my dear, is the catalyst for a major shift in world domination."

"She'll be nothing to you if you don't get her away from Agremon. I think I've offered you a very good deal. I just want my daughter back."

"And where are your Brethren friends?"

Emma flinched. *Damn it! Poker is so not my game.*

"Oh yes, I know they're here. Very well-shielded, I do give them points for that, but remember who you're dealing with here. Where do they fit into your simple plan?" Namirha stood and began circling her, making her feel as if she were his prey. Her confidence was being tested, but her heart remained steady, her breath calm. She refused to yield.

"They know nothing of this. I chose to come on my own as an act of good faith to you. Whatever it is you have against The Brethren, or they against you, I want no part of it. I simply want my daughter. Time is wasting, Namirha, what do you say? Do we have a deal?" Emma stood her ground against his ever predatory strides.

"You've devised a foolproof bargain, my dear; one that assures your daughter's safety when our deal is done. The only thing you didn't bargain for was yours as well. So, rest assured, your daughter will be safe, but you will have given your life in her stead. Now do we still have a deal, Ms. Livingston?"

Chapter Twenty-Four

"Of course, we have a deal," Emma responded without a moment's hesitation. There was never any doubt she'd put Hannah's life before hers. She hoped Michael would be able to forgive her at some point during his immortal life. She knew better than to expect it while she was alive. "So, now what? Do you know where Agremon could have taken her?" She wasn't about to give up the fact that she'd already known their last position or had powers of her own. It could very well be the only thing to come in handy when the two evils faced off.

"If he's got her, then he's taken her to the mountaintop altar. I had it erected as soon as I found this area. We'll go there now." Emma started to walk out of the tent. "Uh no, Ms. Livingston. We'll go my way. It's quicker." He grabbed her by the arms. "Hang on tight. It'll only take a moment."

Emma thought her body had been completely torn apart, disintegrated and reintegrated within a span of five seconds. Within those five seconds, however, she felt absolutely nothing, no pain, no fear, no joy, no existence. When she realized they had actually traveled to the top of one of the peaks in the mountain range, she came undone. She screamed and her hands did a quick check to make sure all body parts were where they were supposed to be. "Heaven, help me!" she blurted out with relief.

"It's a little too late for that, Ms. Livingston. But let me assure you, you are quite all right. All of your body parts are where they should be. In fact, they are put together quite nicely."

"Ugh!" Emma groaned, disgusted. It was bad enough that his crusty hands had held her through the flashing. "Don't even start, Namirha, I didn't bargain for that! Let's just find my daughter, shall we?"

"Pity, we could actually make a grand family, the three of us," he mused aloud. "I could rule the world, and the two of you could sit around and watch me."

Ignoring him at this point, Emma walked away towards what looked like a clearing. She recognized that they were on flattened ground, but all around her were edges that dropped off to oblivion. Great! No easy way up or down.

She hadn't needed to worry about getting there, but leaving there was another matter entirely. She was counting on Namirha to castrate Agremon and get her and Hannah out of there. If he couldn't, they were stuck without an exit plan. Who goes into something like this without an exit plan?

The further she walked into the clearing, the more she noticed the elaborate setup Namirha had constructed for the blood ritual. There was a circular formation of stone statues stretching at least twenty feet into the air. It was one thing to be in the midst of ancient stone statues as in Rome or Greece, or even Easter Island, and something completely different when she saw what stood before her.

Grotesque, monstrous, misshapen figures of all manner of beasts glared down upon her. She coughed and wheezed and fell to her knees, not able to get enough air into her lungs. Namirha shuffled over to her nonchalantly and waved his hand over her back. She immediately felt better and stood up. She knew better than to thank him. That would be admitting that she now owed him something, and since she'd already bargained away her life, she figured that was plenty already.

"You and Agremon! You both have a keen sense of the macabre, don't you," Emma balked. Namirha smirked.

"It's not all horror. Take a look in the center of the ring. See the beauty that was carved into a plain slab of stone?" A striking likeness of Hannah's face was carved into each side. "Only the best for our little one, who will lie upon it and give her powerful energy to me. Then I will be able to take my rightful place as ruler of this world for eternity!"

"Easy there, bucko, you don't get to do shit until you get her back. So where is she?" Emma demanded.

"We'll have to wait for Agremon to appear, naturally. He will, too. There's no doubt about that. He knows this is the only place she can be sacrificed, ritually, of course." Emma raised her brow dubiously, but accepted his response. "Let's move off to the side so when he does appear he doesn't go flashing off immediately should he see us."

God, but she hated waiting, and she hated Namirha with every fiber of her being. She prayed silently that Agremon would indeed bring Hannah here.

"Can't you keep him here when he does appear? I mean what's the point of being here if you can't trap him and finish him off?" Emma was getting more and more unsettled with this lamebrain scheme of hers.

"Don't worry so, Ms. Livingston. Yes, I can trap him here. And I can do worse, and shall. A bargain is a bargain. I keep my bargains. Now hush and let me concentrate on detecting his threaded signature."

Emma obeyed, as she secretly tried to relocate Hannah's thread herself. She had lost it when they flashed to the ritual site. She detected something faint. It could be her. It was easier to grab the thread when Michael was with her. There was something to be said for the Trinity. As she focused harder on the wisp of a thread, she could tell they weren't in the abandoned mine anymore.

The thread's energy signature was increasing, and suddenly, she felt Hannah as close as a breath away. Emma gasped and brought her hands up to her mouth to silence herself as well as to keep from reaching out to her daughter. Hannah and Agremon were here! It was then that she recognized another fatal flaw to her idiotic plan. The Brethren wouldn't be far behind.

"Don't you think Emma should have been back by now?" Raphael was a little miffed. "I mean, what could possibly be taking her this long?"

"I don't know and I don't like it. Not one bit. I'd better go see what she—"

"Hey, the knife's gone!" Nathanael swept into the tent like a tornado. "Agremon must have gotten there before the prayer service began."

"Damn it all!" Kemuel's frustration finally bubbled over and he slammed his water bottle to the ground. "He evades us at every turn. He plays us like we're fools. And we are fools unless we can gain some solid footing here. Damn it all."

"Well, there's only one thing left to do," Gabriel said, closing his laptop. "Let's go get Hannah. We know where she is, and we don't have much time."

"I'll go see what's keeping Emma," Michael said. "Be right back." He hadn't been able to sense Emma's thread for a while now. It was possible to shield one's threaded signature if you wanted privacy. He hadn't thought much of it at first. And he had to admit, it could get pretty disconcerting to have someone's thoughts as well as your own active in one's mind. But now, he had an uneasy notion walking towards their tent. He entered only to find it empty. "Emma?" he called out anyway. "Emma! Damn it!"

He ran back to the warrior's tent. "She's gone!"

"What the hell do you mean she's gone?" Raphael asked. He stood up and confronted Michael. "Gone where?"

"I don't know, Raph, she's just gone." Michael's arms fell to his sides. Confusion struck him. Where could she be? "We've got to find her, now."

Cassiel tossed a few almonds in his mouth and stood up as

well. "Can't you feel her thread? I thought you were connected and all with that Trinity thing, you have going on. What gives?"

"Yeah, well she shut me out. That's what gives," Michael snapped. "Her powers are growing."

"Oh, that's not good, brother. Agremon's gone, Hannah's gone, and now Emma's gone. You don't think, I mean, could she be that stupid? Do you think she went after them?"

"She's not stupid, Cass! She's a mother who's desperate to save her child. Wouldn't you try something, anything to get her back?" Michael's appeal fell like a lead ball. "All right, so she's stupid and desperate. God willing, she isn't fool enough to get herself killed."

Kemuel stepped up to Michael, putting a hand on his shoulder. "All right, everyone, we're moving out. We know at least where Hannah is, up on that mesa north of the big peak. Who knows, Emma could be with her. Warriors, call up the troops. Have them ready for combat. Let's go!"

Chapter Twenty-Five

*F*rom what Emma could see from her vantage point, Agremon had tied Hannah's hands behind her back. When she shifted a bit to get a better look, she found that Agremon had also attached a collar around her neck and a leash attached to that. He was pulling her like a dog towards the stone slab altar. She couldn't stop her impulses to run to her daughter, but Namirha's strong hold settled her back in her spot, silently conveying he had it all under control.

"Well, well, well, what have we here? You're starting the party without me?" Namirha quickly waved his hand to secure Agremon to the very spot where he stood. For all his efforts, Agremon could not pick up his feet, and his arms were sealed to his sides. "Don't you know how rude that is? In fact this party's not supposed to happen until Thursday, isn't that right, Hannah? Your birthday is on Thursday. You must have gotten your dates wrong, Agremon. Tell me you got the dates wrong, and I shall not punish you too severely."

Agremon roared and shook with rage. "Father, I'm so glad you're here!" Hannah cried out. "I knew you wouldn't let him hurt me, I just knew you wouldn't!" She ran to Namirha, leash dragging on the ground but stopped short.

Emma watched as she turned her way, and for a brief

moment, they locked eyes. Namirha saw the brief exchange between mother and daughter and quickly grabbed hold of Hannah. "Remember our deal, Emma," he intimated, and thrust Hannah into her arms.

"I remember, Namirha," she replied bravely, hugging her daughter for the first time in what felt like a lifetime.

"What is he talking about, Mama?" Hannah asked.

"It's nothing to worry yourself about right now, my angel. Just be happy that you're out of Agremon's clutches," she hedged dismissively.

She quickly untied Hannah's hands and removed the collar from around her neck, checking all the while for any injuries. Hannah's neck was red from chafing, as were her wrists. Emma unobtrusively waved her hands over the reddened areas and sent her healing warmth. Since they were minor, it took a fraction of a moment to return her abraded skin to normal.

"I shall not be denied, Namirha!" Agremon snarled. "I shall succeed where you have failed! I shall destroy all and reign over the universe and you will bow down to me!" He struggled against his invisible bindings and tore his arms away from his body, then used both hands to tear his legs from their moorings. Namirha raised an eyebrow at Agremon's prowess. He'd managed to get one leg free when Namirha spoke.

"My, but you've become a bucking bronco, Agremon. You know what they do to broncos, don't you? They break their spirit! They squeeze the life out of them! Just like what I am going to do to you." Namirha reached a hand out towards Agremon, and as he did so, it formed into a boa constrictor that slowly made its way up and around the leg still attached to the ground, then circled around Agremon's waist. "And when I'm finished, you'll know who is Master and Ruler of the universe. Me!"

Before Namirha could finish what he'd begun, the ground beneath them suddenly shook and pulsed like a heartbeat, or a drum. Everyone froze. Namirha's arm, distracted by the sound, recoiled back to its normal state.

Looking victorious, Agremon crowed, "Ah! Namirha, do you

recognize that sound? It's the sound of the last few seconds of your life. Your death toll. My minions have arrived!" He pulled his other leg free and loped to the mesa's edge. "My insurance that Hannah's blood will be spilled this evening for my own glory has arrived," Agremon howled.

"Your minions? You must be delirious. I am their ruler and I hold dominion. I called to them, and they came for me not for you, you sorry excuse for a demon."

"We shall see who they call master in a few short moments," Agremon taunted.

Namirha and Agremon circled around each other like lions ready to pounce. Emma walked up to the edge with Hannah in tow, only to find a darkness encroaching on the mesa from as far as the eye could see, a darkness teaming with all forms of undead and immortal demon-kind. She shivered and held Hannah close. So it was really happening. The war between Good and Evil was about to begin. Emma wasn't religious by nature, more spiritual than anything else. But today, that didn't seem to matter. *God help us all*, she prayed.

With Hannah temporarily forgotten by both Namirha and Agremon, Emma and she could inch themselves further away from the two. They daren't speak aloud, only with their minds.

Agremon has the knife sheathed and strapped to his back, Mama. The scary things down below were called by Agremon, not Namirha. So Namirha is bluffing.

Namirha is going to keep Agremon from slaughtering you, and he isn't going to murder you either.

The Brethren are coming.

"Crap!" Emma swore aloud. Back inside her mind, she told Hannah of her plans for Namirha and Agremon to annihilate each other before any Brethren showed up. It looked like it was actually working, too, although, the minions below them had Emma's stomach trembling like a nest of angry bees.

"Hannah, darling, why don't you come by your father and lay on, I mean sit at the table of honor."

"I don't think so, Daddy darling."

"Oh you do hurt me so, Hannah. After all I've done for you since we've met," Namirha scolded icily, "I would have expected a little more obedience."

"You were expecting this to make me your dog, hmm?" the Ancient Warrior retorted while stripping his amulet from her neck. "Not a chance."

"Namirha, aren't you forgetting something? You can't do the ritual without the knife. Gee, I wonder who has the knife," Agremon goaded. "Oh yes, I forgot, I do! She's mine, Namirha, I worked too hard to get her, and no one can stop me from taking what's mine. Come here, girl. I'm not going to hurt you. I'm just going to..."

"Slice and dice me for your dinner? You really need to take up vegetarianism. It's much healthier and would improve your disposition."

Agremon growled and made a grab for Hannah. She countered with her fingernails and dug deep trenches in his arms. He hissed as he took a step back.

"Enough of this!" Emma snapped, stepping forward. She whipped her head around to Namirha. "We have a deal, Namirha. I suggest you tend to it." Through their threaded connection, she told Hannah to do whatever Namirha told her to do. Hannah's face flushed a brilliant red.

"What have you done, Mother? What have you done?" she shouted angrily.

"The only thing I could, angel. I saved your life." Emma reached to caress Hannah's cheek. She kneeled down and kissed her and whispered, "I love you." She waited, praying that she would hear those blessed words one last time.

"I love you more," Hannah choked out.

"I love you most," Emma said, letting out the breath she'd been holding.

"You win, Mama," Hannah cried out as she hugged her. Emma agonized. *Lord, she knows something is up. I can feel it. God forgive me.*

"Yes, angel, I win." Emma tenderly and with resolve set

Hannah away from her, turned to Namirha, and ordered harshly, "Get her out of here, now."

With no more than a nod, Namirha grabbed Hannah and flashed her to his mountain dwelling

"No!" Agremon roared, running about frantically, and then he settled his gaze on Emma. "You! You planned this. I'll kill you with my bare hands and take pleasure in tearing you apart limb from limb!"

He charged towards her, and before she could even think what to do next or flat out run, the Brethren arrived. And how they arrived astonished her. As if flying down from Heaven itself, she saw nine glowing men, with outstretched wings and swords raised in their mighty hands, descend upon the mesa. She thought they were truly magnificent to behold, this army of angels.

Emma dropped to the ground like a lead balloon, right on her behind, and stared in awe at the men. How different they all looked in their leather pants, muscles glistening from sweat, and their wings unfurled. Indestructible and unyielding, an impenetrable wall of immortal flesh now stood solidly before her. Agremon slowed to a stop. Emma gathered her wits, got up, and began searching for Michael. It didn't take long, and his murderous expression gave her pause. He moved to her and stood protectively by her side.

"We know Namirha has Hannah. You will tell me about that later," Michael demanded pointedly.

Emma nodded silently.

"Michael! Brethren!" Agremon shouted. "Long time no see. Come for a rumble, have you?"

"Come to serve justice swiftly and permanently, Agremon!" Kemuel answered, walking towards him.

"Ha! I look forward to you trying!" Agremon quickly flashed himself off the mesa to join his minions below. "Agremon has back up," Emma shared. "Did you see the masses down there?"

"The Brethren have backup, too. Gabriel!" Michael shouted. Gabriel blew his horn, and suddenly, the sky was ablaze. She covered her ears and looked up. The sound of beating wings was deafening.

What she saw defied explanation. Legions of angels swarmed in the air, and descended on Agremon's minions who were already decimating the towns surrounding the mountain. All the Brethren, save Michael, quickly took flight and joined in the descent. Just like Hannah's pictures, Emma marveled.

Well, if those pictures were accurate, I wonder what others will be, too.

Michael shook her out of her wonderment. She seemed a little dazed when he yelled, "The war's begun, Emma! You're going to be needed down there soon to heal the angels and mortals. That's your job now. I'll be with you to protect you. That's my job. You see, we both have jobs that complement each other. We go hand in hand, not alone, Emma, never alone."

She caught his message and turned away, ashamed. He trailed his hands from her shoulders down to her hands and held them. "So tell me what you've done, Emma. Whatever you've done alone, we'll face it and get through it together. Why did you shield yourself from me? Why did you leave the encampment alone? What were you doing here before us? And why did you let Namirha take Hannah?"

She gazed into his eyes, those dazzling orbs that could see straight into her soul and set her heart on fire. She would miss them. And when she could look no longer, she turned away and found she couldn't utter one word for fear of losing all the courage she'd built up 'til now. So she let down her shields and all of her thoughts and images went cascading down the thread she shared with him. She leaned her head against his chest, not wanting to see the inevitable shock and disappointment on his face.

"Oh, my God, Emma. Oh, my God," he whispered as he stepped back from her. His wings trembled. "I refuse to believe this. This—this is completely unacceptable. You weren't in your right mind when you struck that deal. You were distraught. Your daughter was going to be brutally murdered. E.L. can work with this. I know he can. I can protect you to the best of my ability, but E.L. has ways. He's dealt with Namirha personally before. He can fix this. He owes me this much!" His voice took on a grizzly and desperate tone. "I love you, Emma. I refuse to accept this!"

"Michael, listen to me. Listen to me," she repeated as she stepped back into his arms and caressed his cheek. "This isn't what's important right now. What's important is winning this war and keeping Hannah safe. Namirha saved her just now. He promised he wouldn't kill her and I have to have faith that he will do as he said. I have to, Michael. And you're right; I have a job to do.

"I have three days until I need to think about me. That's three days I know Hannah will be safe, and three days knowing you love me. When it's all done, and we've won, promise me one thing. Promise me that you'll watch over Hannah. See that she does well in school and has a happy life. I pray you'll do this for me. Do this so I can go, knowing I did what was right for my daughter."

He held her tightly in his arms, cradling her head to his chest. "But this isn't right! She needs you, Emma! I need you!" She heard his heartbeat quicken, and sensed love and fury literally wrap a tight coil around his heart. Her own heart ached and was rent in two. "I must answer your prayer, and as I have done once before, I will do it again."

Begrudgingly, he agreed to the last wishes of the woman he loved. By law, he was bound to them, for a prayer made in desperation wrapped in love for another had to be answered. But inside, shielded from her, he vowed not to be alone at the end of this war. He'd already lost his first family at the hands of Evil; he wouldn't lose this one, as well. He'd find a way to break her deal with Namirha and make damn sure both Hannah and Emma were still alive and well when this war was over.

There were no other options.

Chapter Twenty-Six

"I'm sorry but I must leave you alone here." Namirha released Hannah's arms. "It seems the party back at the mesa just became adult-only. By the way, you should know your mother was a very brave woman. You should also know she traded her life for yours. I plan to be as honorable as can be, given who I am, and hold up my end of the bargain. What a grand birthday you shall have, my dear! We'll toast your mother and her valiant effort to save you."

She raised her fists in defiance and shook them fiercely at Namirha. "You're lying! I don't believe you! No!" The ground rumbled beneath her. The walls of the mine shook with such force that it began a rippling effect. Moans and groans, as though the mine were crying out with pain, tore through the cavernous room, and then there were snapping sounds, like tree limbs flexed to their limits and beyond. Rocks tumbled one upon another, effectively entombing her in Namirha's lair. He sneered and disappeared.

Namirha appeared back at the stone altar and found himself alone. Damn it, he needed that knife! As he looked out over the mesa's edge, he saw the fighting going on in earnest. He had to find Agremon as quickly as possible. He knew those minions were fighting for Agremon, not him. His powers had waned so that he prioritized when and how he used them. Controlling minions wasn't a priority until after he'd gone through the blood ritual with Hannah.

Right now, his energies were better spent on the impenetrable shield around her, as well as transporting himself wherever he needed to be. That left precious little for anything else, save a few tricks at best. But even those tricks had lost their effectiveness. He needed Hannah's energy!

He couldn't sense Agremon's signature anywhere, and then out of the corner of his eye, Namirha caught sight of him down in the midst of the mêlée. So, he was shielding himself, was he? That took considerable energy. How strong had Agremon really become?

The thought of Agremon being more powerful was unsettling and completely unacceptable. It fueled his anger, and he quickly flashed himself into the fray, far enough from Agremon so as not to be noticed, yet near enough to do what he had to do.

He could tell Agremon was enjoying every minute of the battle, as he watched him rip through mortals and angels alike with his bare hands and needlelike teeth, then laugh maniacally as he tossed the bodies aside.

⌭

So, Namirha had taken Hannah back to his dwelling. Agremon could feel the powerful shield he had erected to keep him away from her. But he had the knife. Each had a piece of the prize, which without the other rendered them both useless. Agremon snarled as he ripped into another hapless human.

But wait, he thought, he was in the perfect position to bargain. Each had what the other one wanted. Namirha would never give up Hannah, and he would never give up the knife. Perhaps they could, dare he think it, share, and both gain Hannah's powers? Preposterous! But, he could let Namirha at least think so. He was willing to wager that Namirha was struggling at this point and would yield. And then, when the time came, Agremon would strike and absorb all of Hannah's powers.

He grabbed another human and sent him to an untimely death. He could sense Namirha's arrival behind him. He felt a tugging on the sheathed knife, but he had shielded it so it wouldn't budge. Agremon swiftly turned around and saw Namirha standing there puzzled.

"What, did you think I would leave the knife unshielded? Even your mind is showing signs of deterioration, Namirha," Agremon jeered. "These foolish angels have already tried to take it from me and found it impossible. I think it's time we made a deal. I have a proposition for you that will benefit us both in the end. Come, let's leave the angels and demons to their war, while you and I work out how to reap the mutual benefits."

"You intrigue me as much as you disappoint me, Agremon. While I admire your audacity to think you can best me, I find your betrayal repugnant. But, I see we are indeed at an impasse, with you holding the knife and I holding the girl. So I will agree to hear your proposition, but understand this. I'd sooner have neither of us win than see you rule. Keep that in mind while you make your proposal."

"Very well, Namirha. I suggest we go to neutral territory for this discussion." Agremon grabbed hold of Namirha and flashed them both to, of all places, Hannah's home.

Darkness had long since fallen over the battlefield that had once been the scene of quiet serenity. Emma looked all about her and saw the sturdy cacti dotting the area now neighbored with human remains from the carnage. Pools of coppery-smelling blood, that brought bile to the back of her throat, was quickly absorbed into the parched earth, and Emma had only a moment to wonder if the cacti would eventually turn red. Helpful was it that the usual moonlight and star-filled sky were replaced with the glow of angels. The howling that pierced through Emma's skull like an arrow was not that of the coyote, but of the demons, as angels sent them back to Hell with swift thrusts of their swords.

The Warriors' battalions of angels were challenged at every turn—fighting for their own immortal lives while warring against those who attacked the humans. The minions were cutting down hundreds of people as they screamed and ran for their lives. Emma could hear their prayers for someone to come and save them. But she knew no one outside the area had any clue of the devastation being wrought; and she knew, as well, that no one would come, for the Brethren had secured the area with a shield to prohibit the influx of any more innocent people. Protectors flew around the battlefield casting shields around as many groups of innocents as possible. Buildings lay in demolished charred heaps, having previously stood strong against many a sandstorm and monsoon.

Emma, along with the other Saviors, was up to her eyeballs with healing the fallen. As soon as one was healed, two more would fall in their place. The Saviors were tireless immortals, who kept up their lightening pace of healing anyone who had even the slightest thread of life to cling to.

It was grueling work, especially so for Emma, who felt every bit of her mortality coursing through her weary muscles and bones. But she carried on, mustering every ounce of energy she could, hoping, though, there would be a break in the action. She honestly didn't know how much longer she could keep up the pace. She would look at Michael from time to time, who'd been by her side steadfast and true, sharing his energy with her as she needed. She would pause at those moments, and thoughts would enter her mind. It was Michael, trying to give her hope. She'd pushed every one of those thoughts away and gotten back to work more feverishly than before, giving her no time to think about anything. Thinking was the last thing she wanted to do.

Plumes of dust settled over broken bits of furniture while

small rocks continued to topple precariously around Hannah. She had assumed that when the cave-in began that she was not long for this world. But as she stood there in her stupor, gazing at the destruction she had unwittingly wrought, she realized that nothing had touched nor harmed her in the least. There wasn't a trace of dust or debris to be found anywhere on her body. Namirha's protections must have created an impenetrable zone around her.

She had thought herself sealed in forever, but when the air had cleared of the dust and debris well enough, a shaft of light shined down in front of her feet. She followed its path with her eyes and found herself looking at a hole in the roof about the size of her bed pillow. Her freedom was close at hand!

Namirha had put her in the so-called living room area of the dwelling. Moving cautiously about and looking through the rubble, she saw that most everything was broken. But if chosen well, she could still make a workable staircase from the wreckage. Being only a small child, the opening appeared miles high even though it wasn't too far from the floor.

She chose a large trunk, that hadn't suffered too badly, to begin her staircase, and placed a side table on top. Then she put a couple of chairs on top of that. With those pieces stacked, she figured she could climb through the hole and hoist herself up and out. She took a deep breath, said a little prayer, and started her ascent. When she reached to put her hands through the hole, she was met with the unexpected: an invisible wall. She patted her palms against this wall to find that it completely covered the opening.

She let out a frustrated yell, but quickly stifled it for fear of another cave-in. Namirha must have shielded the entire room so Agremon couldn't get in. But now, she couldn't get out!

"Crap, crap, crap!" Hannah muttered. Then she did something completely bizarre considering her tenuous situation, she giggled. If her mother knew she'd said that word, she'd wash her mouth out with soap. And then her giggle became a chuckle, which turned into a belly laugh. Her laughter became almost maniacal. And then her laughter turned to sobbing. Her mother. She'd give anything to hear her mother scold her right now.

Hannah fell to the floor in a tiny heap. She needed her mother desperately. She was only a six-year-old girl, not even. She didn't know what she was supposed to do now. "I want my Mama!" she wailed. And then, as she listened to her own crying, she realized hers was the only voice in her head. Hers was the only heart beating. Where was the Ancient Warrior soul? She thought it silly, but she lifted her head to look around and, of course, saw no one.

As she rested her head on her arms again, someone rested theirs on her shoulder. A tender gesture meant to give encouragement. She peered up to find a smiling angel dressed in a golden suit of armor sitting beside her. The angel was no bigger than she, its wings spanning wider than its height. She reached out to touch this angel, and her hand passed right through its body. She knew then she was looking at the Ancient Warrior itself.

"I am not Mother, nor Father, but I can be both for you, now. I am here for you, child, as you have been most gracious in welcoming me. Come and rest in my arms, little Hannah. There is so much yet for us to do. Until we are free to do so, I will surround you with my presence and give you the peaceful rest you so richly deserve."

The Ancient Warrior beckoned her to its lap. Hannah crawled over and quickly nestled in its arms. She looked up at the Ancient Warrior's face and said simply, "Thank you." Its wings enveloped her. Safe and comforted, she drifted off to sleep.

Agremon knew Namirha would be pissed when they flashed into Hannah's home. He'd dared to touch Namirha and handled him with little finesse when doing so. But Agremon was in charge here, and it felt good.

Namirha turned around, surveying the lay of the land. They

were in a cozy room with a fireplace and a mantle filled with pictures. He recognized the child in the photo as Hannah. "So this is where you took us—Hannah's home. How apropos for our discussion. Don't waste my time Agremon," Namirha spat out with disdain. He absently picked up a picture frame and then tossed it to the floor. "Tell me what you want."

"I'll get straight to it, then." Agremon sat down on the oversized chair, leaned back and folded his arms, exude overwhelming confidence. "You need the knife, I need the girl. I say we pool our resources and both go after the prize."

Namirha rested a hand on the mantle and turned, his face holding no expression. "You're offering a deal to share the girl's powers between us?"

"Yes, I am willing to share. As you can see, I've proven to be a worthy adversary or should you choose, a wise partner. It's up to you. I do have the means to retrieve the girl and go it alone. I thought I'd offer you a partnership given how long we've known each other. A professional courtesy, if you will. So that is my offer. Take it or leave it. One way or the other, I will have the girl's powers."

Agremon couldn't wait to see Namirha's reaction to his win/win proposal. Now who's the Master? he thought smugly.

Namirha was silent for a few moments. He walked to the window, turned, and paced back toward the fireplace. He pointed a decrepit finger at Agremon. "If you want a share of the girl's powers, then you'll have to do it my way. We wait for her birthday as originally planned." Namirha fidgeted with his hands and rubbed them as though putting on lotion. "Since we'll be sharing them, it is vital that we wait for her powers to be at full strength. You bring the knife and I'll bring the girl to the stone altar on Thursday by six o'clock. We'll sacrifice her together at precisely six minutes after six. When her blood mixes with ours, we shall be more powerful than any immortal creature."

"Agreed." Agremon stood, easily towering over the withering Master of Evil. He intentionally stood close enough to look down upon him. "Nice doing business with you, Namirha. I knew you'd see things my way." He eased off a bit, leaning against the mantle and knocking off the remaining pictures in the process. "Now, about these Brethren. You know they're going to try everything in the book to keep this sacrifice from happening. I say we increase our minions to keep them good and busy for the next few days."

"I agree. Keep them occupied round the clock. Even their powers can fade over time without some kind of regeneration."

"Then they'll be vulnerable and I can rid us of them once and for all."

"Oh, Agremon, you know better than that," Namirha reminded him glibly. "You can hurt them and drain their powers temporarily, but you can't kill them."

"Yes, of course you're right, Namirha. I guess I got carried away with the thought of ultimate power at my fingertips." *Stupid ass, Agremon scolded himself. You almost gave yourself away! Just shut up and don't fuck it up!* "Thursday, then. Don't try anything screwy, Namirha. I'll be watching you."

"As I you, Agremon." He quickly flashed out of Hannah's house.

Chapter Twenty-Seven

*N*amirha decided it was best not to return to his lair. He was confident his shields held Hannah within while keeping others out. Besides, knowing that she was there was too enticing. He didn't care about the deal he'd made with Emma. He'd gotten Hannah away from Agremon to benefit himself. He did care, however, that he should get all of Hannah's powers, and that wouldn't be possible for three days. Three impossible days. So he decided to head to The Source's vacant headquarters and wait it out, while keeping a close eye on Agremon's movements. He would surely pay for his betrayal. Namirha relished the many possibilities he could unleash for the rest of Agremon's eternity. Those very evil possibilities improved his disposition exponentially.

Just as it looked to Kemuel as though the angels had gotten the upper hand, another wave of demons appeared to start the onslaught anew. Thousands of angels reasserted their lethal dominance, led stalwartly by Nathanael, Seraphiel, and him. But Kemuel knew the Brethren were tiring and would need a break soon.

Nathanael, Seraphiel! Kemuel called out through his mind. *We should rotate command so we can renew our powers. We can't keep this up indefinitely, and I've a feeling when these hordes are dispatched, there will be more right behind them.*

You got it! Nathanael called back. *You go first, Kemuel, we'll keep things running like a well-oiled machine.*

Fifteen minutes. That's all I need, brother. And with that, Kemuel flew off. As he did, he cursed their manifested constraints of human form.

Night turned into day which blended into night and day once again, with no sign of the war letting up. As weary as Emma had thought she was, and worried she wouldn't be able to continue past the first few hours of healing, miraculously, she indeed trudged on. Something had grown within her, a never-ending source of power and determination that kept her diligently saving those who could be saved.

She made her way across the battlefield and was horrified by the scenes around her. The brutal carnage that Saviors were too late to stop, the regret that hung in the air as angelic souls made their way home for the last time, was nearly too much for her to comprehend. That this wasn't some sort of nightmare, that it was a reality she wished no one would ever have to endure ever again sliced through her heart like a thousand daggers. She could hear Raphael's voice in her head at one point. "We can never save them all, Emma. It is the way of things."

"Well, in my opinion, that is absolutely unacceptable. These people are innocents! How dare they be used as fodder in a war between immortals!" Emma spit back.

"It is the way of things," Raphael spoke plainly, and he returned to his healing.

"Well it's not my way, Raphael. I will find a way to save them all, mark my words!" But she got no reply.

cᴥ

Hannah remained secure in the arms of the Ancient Warrior. She slept for hour upon hour, day upon day, dreaming the most vivid of dreams. In her dream, she stood before a council of seven ancient souls, sitting on a golden dais, in a chamber whose very walls glowed with energy and radiated off soothing warmth. There was no ceiling above them, just a cloudy mist. Beneath her lay a smooth marble tile that cooled her feet. She was not afraid of these council members, but had the utmost of respect for them. They were talking in whispers to each other and then turned to her.

One spoke, "We are the Council of Ancient Souls. You are here because it has been ordained that you, Hannah, daughter of Emma, granddaughter of Mica, great granddaughter of Sima, shall be one part of the Trinity to usher in a new era of peace. In order to do so, we are giving you gifts that will lead us to victory over the darkness that threatens to expand its hold over our world."

Another spoke, "Your first gift you have already received. The Ancient Warrior soul resides within you and shall remain with you until Evil has been vanquished. You have been afraid of letting the Ancient Warrior have all the control. Trust it, our child, and let this soul guide your hand and mind in battle.

"The second gift is the gift of immortality. You are but a child now, and you shall continue to grow and age as any mortal child. Yet when you reach your thirty-sixth birthday, you shall assume your immortal state and become one of the Brethren, as the leader of the Warriors.

"The third and final gift is that you alone will then possess the power to create or annihilate. Although your intuition will never steer you wrong, use this power with extreme discretion."

"So is this why Namirha and Agremon want me? They want these powers?" Hannah asked.

"Indeed. As you can see, given the nature of these powers, they cannot gain possession of them or our reign over the universe will cease and Evil will rule," one council member confirmed. "And now, Hannah, you must wake up and rejoin your Ancient Warrior soul. Namirha comes for you. You must be ready for the battle that is awaiting you at the stone altar. Good luck, our child. The prayers of millions are waiting to be answered and prophecy must be fulfilled."

Hannah awoke alone, with a renewed sense of hope and purpose. She would let Namirha take her to the stone altar and wage the final assault with the Brethren at her side. She breathed deeply and tried to reconnect with her warriors, but it was no use. Namirha's shield was blocking her efforts. She would have to wait until she reached the mesa before alerting them.

Light was blazing through the hole in the ceiling. She knew it was afternoon, but what she didn't know was of what day. The council member had said Namirha was coming for her. Did that mean she had slept for nearly four days straight? Was Namirha going to show up any minute? Was today her birthday? Had it been a normal birthday, she would have called herself a big girl now. But she didn't feel like a big girl. She still wanted her dolls, her stuffed toys, and her Mama.

She thought of her mother, and then thought better of it. Certainly, no good would come of that. Whatever her mother had done had been for Hannah's protection. She had a dreadful feeling that she'd done something that could never be taken back, and Hannah would be living with that decision for the rest of her life. Not just any life, she thought absently, an eternity! She would be immortal! It was unfathomable to the child.

Suddenly, Hannah felt a little sizzle of energy nearby, and just that fast, the Ancient Warrior's soul took over, having tucked little Hannah safely back into her corner. This time, there was no fear, no resistance. Namirha flashed before her and she took a defiant stance. Namirha's eyes flashed with anger, and then let out a haughty laugh.

"Oh, Hannah, my daughter, you are as enchanting as you are petulant. Now, put your violent nature aside. By the looks of things around here, you can't quite control the damage it can wield."

"It will be a cold day in You-Know-Where when I ever think of myself as being your daughter, Namirha," Hannah lashed out with an acid tongue.

"Well, bundle up, darling, because You-Know-Where's about to freeze over," Namirha snickered. "You see, your mother and I had a deal."

"You said that before, and I'm not interested in your lies, Namirha. You're trying to scare me, is all."

"Oh, but it is no lie. Your mother bargained for your safety, you see. I am to keep you away from Agremon and tonight, I am allowed to partake of some of your blood, your power-rich blood. I'm not to sacrifice you, though, such is the pity. And since your mother has agreed to do that duty, well, you're going to need a father to watch over you while you grow into a young lady and adult. I happen to fit the bill. That was our deal, Hannah; her life for yours. Are you getting chilly yet, 'cause it's getting mighty cold in Hell already. Come to Papa!" Namirha held out his arms as though waiting for her to embrace him.

Hannah was stunned and the Ancient Warrior soul was having difficulty navigating her back to her corner. She raised her fists, wishing she had her sword to run him through over and over again until he was good and dead. Her arms stayed steady as her legs took stilted steps toward him. Namirha moved a wary step back.

Easy little one, the Ancient Warrior soul soothed, *we mustn't let him get to your heart. We have a job to do. We must get to the battlefield and end this war. Go back to your corner, little one. I will handle it from here. Trust me.* Hannah slowly lowered her balled hands and stood firm once again.

"You came to get me, didn't you? Are we going back to the stone altar? Is it my birthday?" Hannah asked.

"Well, we've finally gotten around to the reason for my visit. And the answer is yes. I'm sure all of your guests are eagerly awaiting your appearance."

"Do you have the ritual knife?"

"Don't you worry your pretty little head over the details. I'll have it when I need it, rest assured."

So he doesn't have the knife yet. That wasn't the best news.

Agremon was definitely stronger than Namirha right now, and definitely the most lethal. She would have to be very cautious when trying to retrieve the ritual knife from its sheath. Agremon had a shield on it. She would have Michael render it null and void first.

"Time to go, my dear, and uh, no more questions. I don't fancy you'll like any answers I'll have for you."

"Just so you know, if I had my sword, I'd slice your hands off your arms so fast you wouldn't even realize they were gone until you reached to pick your nose."

"What a vivid image you've produced in my head, child. You really do have potential for evil. Such a pity you were born on the wrong side of the tracks. Yes, such the pity." Namirha grabbed her arms and flashed them to the mesa, where the stone altar stood ready.

While trying to contain her impotent fury at having lost her sword, Hannah could hear screams and howls from below and knew the war waged on. She hoped that her mother and the Brethren were still alive. She instantly opened herself to feel for any threaded signature of her mother and what amounted to her extended family. Yes! They were all alive!

She called to them. *I'm here at the stone altar. Come quickly! Namirha is waiting for Agremon to show with the ritual knife. I shall take it from him after Michael tears his shields to shreds. Warriors can then turn ugly on them both. Timing is everything right now. Come!*

Chapter Twenty-Eight

*E*mma felt her daughter's thread come crashing through her latest attempt at saving one of the angels. *Thank the heavens she's alive,* she thought. But not out of danger. She looked over her shoulder to her rock and protector, who had been unwavering in his support during the past three days.

"It's her birthday, Michael," she lamented. "She's six years old today. My baby's six years old." She shut her eyes for a moment and gathered herself together. So far, Namirha had kept to their deal. Hannah was alive and at the altar. She had to go to her, to see her one last time.

"I know. We have to go. She's waiting for us," Michael urged softly. He grabbed her and then flew them to the top of the mesa. Her stomach fluttered as her feet left the ground, and she closed her eyes tightly, holding onto him with a death grip. But her trust was strong, and her need to see her daughter, stronger. She fully expected to arrive at the altar in perfect health. And then she could say goodbye. Rather than go into this final showdown blind, she bravely opened her eyes as they approached the top of the mesa.

Agremon was nowhere to be seen, but Namirha was there dressed in a red robe, Hannah beside him. The other Brethren were close behind, leaving their battalions to handle whatever else came their way. What happened now, at the altar, took top priority for the elite group.

Emma barely had her feet on the ground when she took off running toward Hannah. "Not so fast!" Namirha shouted, and with a wave of his hand he forced Emma to stop in her tracks. "Although a reunion would be quite touching, it is not prudent. You'll keep your distance, Mother dear, or I shall indeed sacrifice her."

"Hannah, are you okay?" Emma minded Namirha's threat.

"Firmly rooted in place, Mother, but I'm fine, and you?"

"Looks like I'm firmly rooted, as well. Don't worry about me, angel. I'm fine," she answered, brightening her voice to compensate for the emotional pain flowing through every fiber of her being.

The Brethren surrounded Namirha, swords in hands, and ready to battle. "I would think better of your position right now, gentlemen. Take one step closer to me and the girl dies." He had brandished a dagger while grabbing Hannah close and held it up to her neck.

"No!" Emma screamed, and ran in front of the warriors to push them back. It was like trying to move the Great Wall of China.

"Now, what good would that do you, killing the girl? You've waited a long time for her. I don't think you'd damage your chances of ruling the world, Namirha," Michael said, calling his bluff.

Agremon flashed in right next to Namirha. "I have to agree, although agreeing with Mr. Protector here, is causing me a bit of chafing. Namirha, put the dagger away. You're going to get someone hurt, most likely Hannah or me."

As soon as Agremon had appeared, Michael muttered under his breath the sacred words that would shred the threads of protection over the ritual knife. "I'm not taking this dagger away from her throat."

"Then let's get on with the real business we're here for. Bring the girl over to the altar." He turned to the Brethren standing with swords ready, yet not moving. "Anyone follows, and you're dead."

All bluster, Agremon was. Until Seraphiel saw an opening to retrieve the knife. As Namirha, Hannah, and Agremon turned to walk toward the altar, Seraphiel leapt to Agremon's back and unsheathed the knife. But he was slow on the retreat and found himself hoisted up and over Agremon's head like a pillow to stand before him.

"You are one stupid, stupid angel, aren't you?" Agremon remarked with a maniacal smile, showing all of his needlelike teeth in their glory. "Say goodnight to all your friends."

Before Seraphiel had a chance to throw the knife to any of the Brethren, Agremon grabbed it with his free hand. He then flung Seraphiel around so that his back was facing him. Opening his mouth, Agremon thrust his head forward and bit deeply into Seraphiel's left wing and actually tore it off, spitting it out to the side like a discarded piece of gristle. Seraphiel let out a wail that rivaled the banshees of Ireland. Agremon dropped him unceremoniously to the ground and turned to face the Brethren, each in utter shock.

"Oh, my God! Seraphiel!" Emma screamed, breaking the stunned silence.

"Who's next to die?" Agremon shouted exuberantly, spraying blood as he spoke. "Come on! I dare you!"

Seraphiel lay on the ground unmoving. Raphael was closest and hurried to his aid. Nothing he tried was working. He looked over at Cassiel, and waved him over. Cassiel rushed over to lend his powers, and they started up their efforts again in earnest.

Emma was about to go over, as well, but saw Namirha had taken Hannah to the stone altar. Emma watched him like a hawk as he laid her down, dagger still a threat to her neck.

"Agremon, stop playing around!" Namirha shouted impatiently. "Get over here with that knife."

"Not on your life, Namirha. I've waited too long for this moment to have you rush me through it. Brethren are going to die tonight!" Agremon growled.

Knowing he was outnumbered by the remaining Brethren, rather than fight them all at once, with a wave of his hand, Agremon sent all but Michael back down to the battlefield, and threw up a shield to keep them at bay if they tried to come back.

"How do you know?" Michael whispered fiercely. "Only E.L. and I were to know. How do you know how we can die?"

"So you've finally caught on, eh Michael? Yes, your big secret's blown. I've known for a long time. I know how to kill the Brethren! I know much about E.L. and his secrets, having been a favorite and then spurned so long ago. Remind me to share with you sometime. Oh wait, you're going to be dead soon, too. Well, you'll just have to die knowing I screwed you, again. You know, I've been biding my time, waiting for the right moment. And now seems the perfect time to stick it to you yet again." Agremon was swinging the ritual knife around, nonchalantly teasing Namirha and Michael.

"You think to taunt me with your words and your knowledge, but you don't fool me Agremon. You have no power over me. You're still an outcast and always will be. You think you've been waiting a long time for this? Well, I've been waiting longer. I will see you die this night, Agremon, at my hands alone. I will take great pleasure sending you to the deepest, darkest region of Hell to wallow forever in your failures." Michael wielded his sword and lunged forward to launch his offensive.

Emma screamed, "No, Michael!"

As he came down through the air, he roared, "This is for Beth and our unborn child." He sliced through Agremon's chest and retreated a few steps. It happened so fast that Agremon stood shocked for the briefest of moments. He bellowed and charged at the Protector. Michael flew up and over Agremon, grabbing the ritual knife along the way down.

He called out, "Emma! Catch this, and for God's sake, hold onto it!" He gently tossed the knife to Emma, who caught it by its handle, and returned his attention to Agremon. The demon had turned and was charging at him once again. Michael readied his sword to slash when Agremon disappeared right in front of him.

Michael tensed and swung about looking everywhere for Agremon to pop up. "Where are you, you cowardly bastard?"

Agremon goaded, "I'm right behind you, you useless sack of shit."

Michael piveted with his blade ready to do some heavy damage, but only managed to nick Agremon's cheek. Then he lunged, aiming for Agremon's heart, but Agremon leaned away and instead got nailed in his left shoulder. Agremon swatted the next blow away with his forearm. Back and forth they went meeting each other blow for blow.

Torn, Emma kept one eye on Namirha and her daughter, and the other on the two fighting. Agremon and Michael were tangled together, grappling on the ground and in the air. She noted how Michael kept his back from the demon at all times, keeping his wings protected and out of Agremon's reach. Emma was so concerned for Michael's safety she'd turned her full attention on them.

Namirha made a grab for the knife. "Give it to me!"

"No! I won't let you have it!" She tightened her grip, her own strength surpassing Namirha's in his already weakened state. She found herself dragged to the altar, unwilling to relinquish her hold. Hannah yelled for Michael. Emma jerked her head in her Protector's direction. As if in slow motion, she saw a dagger fly towards him. Her heart dropped to the pit of her stomach. Michael caught it by its handle and plunged it deep into Agremon's heart. Relieved, she turned her attention back to Namirha and the ritual knife.

"Now Hannah is all mine." Namirha tugged at the ritual knife, drawing Emma back to her current predicament. "As you shall be, too, my dear."

Chapter Twenty-Nine

*N*amirha immediately took hold of Emma's hands around the knife and made ready to plunge it into Hannah's little body. She looked on in horror as Namirha seemed poised for a complete sacrifice. With her hands still on the sword, she would effectively be killing her own daughter. Adrenaline surged. Her maternal instincts to protect her child kicked into high gear.

"No! It's not time yet! Don't do this! It won't work!" Emma struggled to keep the knife away from her daughter. "We had a deal, damn it!"

In her head, Hannah spoke. *Let go of the handle and grab the blade with your hand. I will, too. Trust me!* Emma did as she was told. She grabbed the blade with her hand as Hannah did. Its well-honed edge cut deeply into her palm. Hannah yelled, "Duck!"

As Emma ducked her head, Hannah kicked Namirha in the face. He let go of the knife and staggered backward. Hannah yanked on her mother, and still holding the blade, they rolled to the ground, out of Namirha's reach. As he howled his outrage, another sound echoed and died away. Agremon, with a final burst of immortal life, reached up and gripped Michael's left wing. He tore it away from the angel's body. Both collapsed lifeless on the ground.

Emma and Hannah froze. Time, itself, seemed to stand still. "Michael!" Hannah screeched. And Emma burst into action. She scrambled over to him, Hannah right behind, noticing Agremon's lifeless body. But she saw, too, Michael's left wing lying beside him, bloodied like his shoulder blade.

"Oh, my God! Michael! No!" Trying to save him would be futile. That's what she was told. How could this be possible? This couldn't really be the end for him, for them, for the Trinity. Inconceivable!

Hannah rested a hand on her head. "I know how to fix this, Mama. We need to put our hands together, your special powers and mine, combine them with the knife, and touch Michael's shoulder. It will heal him and save him from certain death."

"It's not going to help. You saw Seraphiel," Emma sobbed.

"Mama, we can't let Michael die. We are the Trinity. We're special. It can't be this easy to get rid of us. It has to work. The Ancient Warrior says so. Do it!"

Hannah forced their bloodied hands with the knife onto Michael's left shoulder, where the wing should have been. Instantly, Emma and Hannah felt a jolt of energy.

"Mama, my hand is getting really warm. How about yours?"

"Uh huh, mine is, too. And now I'm feeling a strong throbbing, too."

A brilliant light shot up from Michael's shoulder blade and knocked their hands away. The ritual knife burst into a million tiny fragments that floated up into the air. Out from his shoulder blade sprouted a new wing. Michael was still unconscious, but Emma could see he was breathing.

"Michael, can you hear me? Michael, it's Emma. Come back to me, my angel. Come back to us." Emma held Hannah strong in her arms while stroking Michael's newly sprouted wing with a hand that had miraculously healed from its deep cut, leaving behind a faint scar as a reminder.

"You've both been very naughty girls. Father's none too pleased," Namirha snarled as he stalked over to the Trinity. Emma turned and gasped, squeezing Hannah even tighter. She'd forgotten about him in the frenzy to save Michael. "And now you both shall pay for your misdeeds. Say goodbye to your mother, Hannah. A deal is a deal. And this deal I'm not about to break!"

Before Hannah or Emma could say anything, Namirha grabbed Emma by the throat, tearing her out of her daughter's arms and disappeared. Michael awakened to see Namirha flash away with his love.

"Mama!"

"Emma!"

Michael and Hannah turned to each other, astonished, looked at where Emma had sat, and faced each other again. Hannah crawled into his lap and they clung to each other. "I'll get her back, Hannah. I promise you, I will move Heaven and Earth to get her back."

"You're going to have to move Hell, too, Michael."

Chapter Thirty

*E*mma was still reaching out towards Hannah when she found her surroundings disappear and change from the stone altar to a hole dug into the earth. She turned feverishly around and around to get her bearings. The hole she was in had to have been no bigger than five feet in diameter and twice as deep.

"Namirha! Namirha!" she cried out. All she saw was his demonic face peering over the edge. "Namirha! Where am I?"

"I'd say you were in a holding tank, of sorts, in my dungeon under my home. Thanks to your lack of honor and your insufferable daughter, I have not the energy necessary to make the trip back to Hell just yet. So you'll have to stay here until I'm strong enough to bring us both there."

"Am I—am I—" She couldn't even say the word aloud.

"Dead? Is that what you were wondering? Are you dead? Not yet, but you'll wish you were. Oh no, since our deal took a turn for the worse, I've got something different in mind for you. Death would be too easy, and not at all what you deserve for ripping ultimate domination out of my very hands! Emma, my darling betrayer, your fate is much worse than death. And it begins now!" Namirha moved out of Emma's line of sight.

Emma didn't know what to expect but feared the worst. She still had all of her protections on her and hoped that they would help, but she wasn't counting on it.

"Meet your neighbor, Emma. I found him on the floor by the manacles and chains I have hanging on the walls up here. Oh, but you'll know what I'm talking about soon enough." Namirha grunted as he threw something into the hole. Emma screamed and moved aside as quickly as she could to avoid getting pummeled.

When she looked at what had been tossed in as if it were trash, she shrieked at the top of her lungs and scuttled as far from it as she could, which wasn't saying much. Namirha had tossed in a man's dead body with no regard. She recognized it as the body Agremon had possessed days ago. This poor soul had already begun to decompose, with maggots having a feast on his eyes, mouth, nose, and open wounds. The horrific sight and the putrid smell emanating from him made Emma wretch immediately. Having not eaten for days, there wasn't much to bring up, so dry heaves quickly took over.

"Getting to know your friend there, Emma? From the sound of it, you're the only one holding up the conversation," Namirha mocked from somewhere above her. "Just as well, he seemed dead on his feet. Give him a little time, though. He may prove to be an interesting companion."

"Damn you!" was all she could muster.

"That would be rather redundant, now wouldn't it?" There was silence. Nothing and no one around that was alive it seemed, but her.

Oh, dear Lord! What had she done? Emma thought to herself. She'd saved her daughter, and Michael was alive. She'd seen that and their shock, before being whisked away. "But our bargain was my life for hers, my death not hers. I didn't bargain for eternal torture!" she yelled out loud. She had to get out of there, somehow. She checked the wall surrounding her only to find it smooth, with nary a foothold or handhold to be found.

With the dead body taking up most of the usable space, Emma stood in place, closed her eyes and quieted herself. If she meditated she'd come up with some kind of plan. Before she could take her second deep breath, however, she found herself flashed out of the hole. Not quite sure what to make of this, she quickly looked around. But as she turned, something restricted her movement. Her ankles had been shackled to the floor. She looked at her wrists and they, too, were shackled, but loosely. Namirha's voice suddenly filled the cavernous room in the earth, but he couldn't be seen. "Treat number two is on its way."

She found her wrists involuntarily raised above her head until she felt stretched to her limit and on her tiptoes. She was completely at a loss, and unable to do anything to free herself.

"My hounds want to play, Emma. It's funny, but whatever I give them to play with, they destroy so quickly. Maybe you could be their everlasting chew toy, hmm? See, if you get too chewed up, I could always return you to your normal state. You'd be good as new and ready to be played with all over again."

Emma could hear snarling coming from all around her but saw nothing. She prayed her protections would hold against whatever physical pain these hounds would surely try to inflict. The snarling got louder and closer and still she saw neither a whisker nor a tail. So it was to be blind terror, then.

Suddenly, Emma heard a scrabbling on the ground, as if an animal had begun racing towards her. She turned her head away from the sound, unable to move an inch of her body, and held her breath. She immediately heard something slam into a wall and a subsequent yelp. She had felt a vibration around her and could only assume the wall in question was her protective shield, the yelp, a hurt invisible hound of Hell. As soon as that hound backed off, another took over, and another, each taking a pounding from the impenetrable force. The problem was, it was taking the same pounding, and she wondered how long it would be before it would start wearing thin.

Gabriel and Urie had finally broken through the roadblocks of energy Agremon had installed to keep them away from the business on top of the mesa. With the last of Agremon's minions sent back to Hell, the Warrior's battalions ascended to their home, save one, while the Brethren quickly flew back to the stone altar, swords ready to do battle. The first thing they saw was their brother, Seraphiel, lying lifeless on the ground, his left wing in tatters next to him. Raphael quickly assigned the angel that had followed them the task of bringing Seraphiel's body and wing back home. Scanning to the right of him lay Agremon on his back with a dagger stuck in his chest to the hilt. And finally, at his feet, in a crumpled, heaving mass were Michael and Hannah.

"Where's Namirha? Where's Emma?" Raphael asked no one in particular, turning this way and that.

Urie had walked over to Michael and Hannah. He knelt down and put a gentle yet strong hand on Michael's shoulder.

"Michael?" Urie asked gently. "Michael, where's Emma?"

Michael looked up without seeing, barely registering the existence of anyone other than Hannah. "He took her," he answered as a single tear escaped and made the solitary journey down his cheek. And as it dropped to the ground, it sizzled and scarred the earth. "And I'm going to get her back." The haze of grief slowly clearing got him standing on his feet again, Hannah still in his arms. "I don't care about any deal that was made between them. He made the wrong move first. By my accounts, the deal is null and void." He gently placed Hannah on her feet again. She hugged his leg.

"I can't feel her, Michael. Can you?" She peered up at him anxiously.

"No, Hannah, I can't. But that doesn't mean that she's dead. Namirha could have shields around her so we can't sense each other." The wheels churned mightily in Michael's head. "If that's the case, he hasn't killed her, and that means that she's still here. If she's still here, we can find her. There are a limited amount of places Namirha can go with the little powers he has left. In fact, I don't think he can even make it back to Hell given all the energy he's expended. What do you think, Gabriel?"

"I think you're on to something," Gabriel replied. "If we can assume Namirha is too weak to leap to Hell with Emma, then he's stuck here until he builds up his strength again. I hate to say it, but it's not a guarantee that he hasn't killed her already. Now, you know me. I'm not a pessimist, but we have to look at this realistically."

"I know, I know. Any demons left down below?"

"All gone, angel battalions, too," Kemuel reported. "Thanks to Emma and the Saviors, the immortal losses are quite minimal. Mortal losses, well that's another story. We have a massive cleanup to tend to later thanks to our dearly departed Agremon."

"Son of a bitch," he muttered. "Well, if everyone's gone, that makes our job of finding Emma easier. No barriers, no road blocks, just a failing Namirha to contend with."

"So where do you want to start?" Kemuel asked.

Hannah walked over to the Brethren as they spoke, and stood at Michael's side. "There are only two places Namirha could have taken my mother—the compound or his dwelling."

"His dwelling? Where's that?" Michael asked.

"I don't know, but Nathanael does. I was always flashed to and from there, but I can describe what I saw while I was in there. Maybe that will help."

"Yes, please, anything you know will help. In the meantime, let's split into two groups. Kemuel will lead one party going through the compound," Michael ordered. "Nathanael, you'll stay here and lead the party going to Namirha's dwelling."

"Will do, Michael. Cassiel, Urie, you're with me," Kemuel called out as he took to the air.

"Hannah, can you tell us what you know?" Michael asked. "Hannah," he repeated, pulling her from watching the Brethren fly off.

"Sorry. Well, first of all I was underground. The walls were made of stone, but not the kind you build with. It was like being in a stone cave. The ground was dirt. I remember walking down a long hallway that could have been like a tunnel, because it felt closed-in to me, so if I reached my hands out and jumped, I would touch the ceiling.

"When I was flashed there by Namirha, I was so angry I screamed. My scream actually caused rocks and stuff to cave-in. An opening appeared in the ceiling of the room I was stashed in. If it weren't for the shields, I could have climbed out myself."

"You caused a cave-in? Impressive." Gabriel smiled. "Michael, it sounds like she was in an abandoned mine. Let's go back to my tent. I can get the exact location from some maps I downloaded and saved."

"Let's hope the tent is still standing!" Michael huffed. Without another word, the remaining team took flight and headed back to the encampment. "Hannah, are you ready to fly, darlin'?"

"As ready as I'm ever gonna be," she answered excitedly.

"All right, now don't worry. I'll have you, but it's easier if you hang on, too."

Hannah clung to him like a koala bear and off they went. It was exhilarating to feel the wind on her face and neck as it drove the sweat and heat away. She actually felt joyful for a brief moment. Before she knew it, they were at Gabriel's tent.

"Well, what did you think of your first flight?" Michael asked as he gently touched down.

"It beats the heck out of flashing in and out of places. You get to see all the in-between places!"

Invigoration quickly died along with her delight when she saw the devastation around her. A battle in which she was supposed to lead the Warriors to victory had been fought without her, and she felt guilt and frustration for having been used as a pawn instead. A few tents remained standing; luckily, Gabriel's was counted amongst them.

"Oh Michael," Hannah murmured, "it must have been terrible."

"Yes, well, it's over now. We won, the evil guy lost, and all will be right with the world when we get your mother back," Michael replied tersely. "So, what do you have for us, Gabriel? How do we get to that abandoned mine?"

"Well, if you look at this map, it looks like there's an

abandoned mine at the base of this mountain here," he explained, pointing to an area he had enlarged. "It's part of the Goldfield Mountains, right next to the Superstitions. From the looks of it, I figure that's exactly where the entrance is. But Hannah, you mentioned something about a cave-in?"

"Yes, but I don't know how far-reaching it is. It definitely blocked my way out of the chamber I was in, though. And I heard rumbling for quite a few seconds after it began. This could be a problem, couldn't it? I mean, you don't flash around like Namirha does."

"Yes, it could turn out to be a very big problem, depending on how extensive the cave-in is, and where your mother is being held," Gabriel conceded. "But we won't know until we're there, will we?"

"All right then, let's head out. Gabriel, we follow you, brother," Michael decided, and then whispered, "Lead us to her, Gabriel. I mustn't fail her again."

"With all that is in my power, brother, I shall," he vowed solemnly.

Emma didn't know how long it had been since the hounds of Hell started charging and snapping at her, but it was long enough that her shields were starting to tear and the damned dogs knew it. They were a perfect blend of patience and impatience, tenacity and eagerness. The fact that she hadn't been able to see them at all before was a good thing. As they tore away at her shields, she was beginning to get glimpses of what they really were, and abject terror was quickly setting in.

Through those tears she could see about a dozen pairs of red glowing eyes and frothing mouths that could barely contain the protruding rows of jagged teeth. She shuddered every time one of the hounds would come slamming into her shields, now knowing what awaited her when her shields finally failed.

One hound was finally able to get his muzzle through a tear

and bit her thigh as though it were the tastiest chop from the butcher. It held on and shook his head like her leg was, indeed, a chew toy. She howled in agony, helpless to shake the demon dog off. It let go after a time and backed up. Her head slumped to her shoulders with the reprieve.

But before she could catch her breath, another set upon her, opening the shield's breach even wider. This time the jaw clamped down on her hip while claws were able to reach through and tear ribbons of flesh from her belly and back. The pain was excruciating and Emma fell into a pain-filled stupor knowing she was near death.

On and on the demon dogs came at her, with a ferocity that could only be produced from a creation of Hell.

Emma regained semi-consciousness some time later and sensed she was no longer vertical or chained. She lay on the ground, and when she tried to move her legs, besides the pain stopping any further movement, so did a wall. She figured she was back in the hole as she lost consciousness again.

The mine's entrance was in ruins. All of the Protectors worked feverishly with their unsealing incantations to blast a new opening, but the cave-in was irreparable.

"Damn it!" shouted Michael in utter frustration. "I'm calling E.L. right now!" He took out his cell phone and started punching numbers.

"Whoa! Wait a minute," Nathanael yelled, grabbing at Michael's arm. "I'm sure if we fly around, we can find another opening."

"No! I've had enough. If we waste any more time Emma could be dead. He owes me, Nathanael! He fucking owes me!" Michael tore away from Nathanael. "E.L.? Michael."

A deep timber reverberated in his ear. "Hello, Michael. Nice job on saving the world this week. The company is quite pleased with the results and I'll be sending out a formal response to everyone shortly."

"Yeah, well we're not quite done yet, and I require your unique services. Given the fact that you destroyed my life and family, I figured you owe me. Big time."

"I see. Well we may have a difference of opinion on some events that occurred in the past, but I'm willing to overlook the discrepancy. What unique services are you in need of, Michael?"

"I believe Emma's being held against her will, by Namirha, in an abandoned mine. We can't get in and she's in grave danger. You can get her out. With a blink of an eye, you know you can get her out."

"Now Michael, you know better than to ask that of me."

"I'm not asking you. I'm telling you. You're going to get her out and we'll call ourselves even."

"I can't do it, Michael. It would disrupt the order of things. But, I can help you get to her if you're sure she's there. Yes, I could do that," E.L. acquiesced decisively.

"E.L. we're not sure of anything. We have a strong suspicion that she's here. That's the best you're going to get."

"Well, that's not quite true. You have our Warrior Child with you?"

"Yes, why?"

"She has a scar on her right palm. So does her mother. And you have a scar where you lost your wing. You are all bound to each other in a way that no power can destroy. Focus both of your energies on your scars. You will be able to tell where her mother is. If she is indeed in that abandoned mine, I will clear your way, but that is all I can do."

"Stay on the line. Hannah, you have a scar on your right palm?" She nodded and showed him. "I need you to focus your energies on it. Somehow it will let you know if your mother is here."

Hannah closed her eyes and Michael could see her brow wrinkle in concentration. It only took moments. "Michael, it's tingling. And it's getting warm. What does that mean?" she asked excitedly. He focused on his scar as well. It was behaving in the same way.

"E.L., we've both got tingling and warmth. What does that mean?" Michael asked urgently.

"She's there. I've cleared a path from the entrance through the tunnels. You'll know you're getting close to her when the tingling gets stronger. You're on your own from here. We're even." Dead air came across the other end.

"Hannah, she's here. Hey, everyone, she's here! If she's here, Namirha's here, too. Nathanael, call Kemuel and get the other team here on the double."

"On it. You don't go anywhere 'til they're here. Got it?" Nathanael ordered. "We don't need you going in there hell-bent without backup."

"He has backup," Hannah spoke up. "Me."

Michael looked at Hannah and knew she wouldn't wait any longer either. "You're a fine warrior, Hannah. I'd be honored to have you as backup. Let's go!"

Emma was coming to again. Each time she surfaced her body and soul were weaker than before. She feared that the next time she went under she might not make it back. It was then that she felt a mild tingling in her right palm along the scar line left by the ritual knife. She rubbed at it absently with her thumb. But the tingling persisted. As she rubbed it again she noticed that besides the tingling, her palm was also very warm. "Hannah—Michael," she whispered. A single tear made its way down her ravaged cheek, and she fell into the deep darkness once again.

Chapter Thirty-One

$\mathcal{M}$ichael suggested Hannah take over the lead through the mine since her palm was behaving like a compass. Providing the necessary light with his aura to guide them through the dark passages, they continued their tedious hike bringing them deeper and deeper into the earth. He had hoped he could fly them through the tunnels, but they were far too narrow to navigate safely, and would have slowed them down tremendously.

As they made their way deeper into the mine, he noticed that the juncture where his wing joined his shoulder was tingling so strongly it was on the verge of pain.

"Michael, the tingling is getting stronger." A bend in the tunnel revealed a stone stairway leading downward. Hannah turned back to him as if to question the next move.

"We go down, of course," he responded. "Let me go first, though, I don't want you falling and hurting yourself. I'm not the healer around here, you know."

The stairway was simple and old, and the treads had been so worn, that by the time they reached the midpoint, Michael picked her up and floated the rest of the way down. They immediately found themselves in a chamber, the size of a huge master bedroom, with no exit. It had to have been some kind of storage room in the past, but from the looks of it now, he knew it had been used as of late for something much more dark and malevolent.

Hanging from the ceiling, rather than a chandelier, were manacles. Bolted to the floor beneath them were shackles as well. Michael immediately raised his wings to shield the young girl from seeing the rest of the horror. The walls were splattered with blood and on the ground was a bloody trail that led to the far left corner and disappeared into blackness. What that blackness was, he couldn't tell yet. As for the blood, he prayed that it wasn't Emma's but knew better in his heart.

"Hannah, you shouldn't be seeing this. I want you to go up a few steps and sit there while I check things out."

"I'll do no such thing! My hand is about ready to burn off. She's here, Michael. Right here! Don't get all Principal D'Angelo on me. Whatever is to be seen, I'll handle it. I'm an Ancient Warrior, you recall. Little Hannah can be a tough cookie, and I'm here to protect her when she's not." She gently moved his wing aside and entered the chamber. Michael's light illuminated more and more of their surroundings.

They followed the bloody trail to the corner and his light revealed a hole, a pit, perfect for throwing refuse in, big enough to hold a person. He scrambled to its edge to have a look.

Half of him wanted to find Emma. The other half prayed he wouldn't.

The second team finally caught up with them as he was approaching the pit. They took up positions on either side of Hannah. Michael gave no sign that he had even heard them enter the chamber, so fixed was his gaze on the pit.

"Have you found her?" Kemuel asked.

"I think so," Hannah whispered.

Michael leaned over the side of the pit, and what he saw defied words. He was initially puzzled seeing two bodies lying on the floor of the pit, even more so at the state of decomposition of one of them. Recognizing that the body was that of a male calmed him slightly. But then his eyes floated to the next body, and his heart stopped. Under the shreds of clothing and dried blood covering most of her body lay Emma, as still as the dead.

"It's her," he croaked hoarsely, and immediately flew into the pit to retrieve her.

He knelt beside her, sick with anguish and rage. He looked for a place he could check for a pulse, but with the many punctures and rips shredding her skin, it was near impossible. He decided simply to put his ear to her chest and listened. Although faint and far too slow for a human, she still had a heartbeat. "She's alive, but barely!" he shouted up to the group above. Her breathing was ragged and shallow as if a lung perhaps had been punctured. Wasting no more time, he gingerly lifted her from the ground into his arms and flew up and out of the pit.

"Raphael, Cassiel, come quick!" he ordered as he rested Emma on the floor of the chamber. Her body had been so mutilated that she resembled a ragdoll put through a shredder. Kemuel immediately took Hannah into his arms and turned her away from the gruesome sight. She did not resist.

"Dear God in heaven!" Raphael gasped. "Cassiel, quickly, we must heal the inside first, then we'll move to the outer parts." Cassiel moved quickly into position as they both began the tedious work of bringing a life back from the brink of death. And not just any life, but their Great Savior Mother.

Hours, it seemed, went by in utter silence as they wielded their energies to knit together internal organs, reattach torn muscles, and repair broken bones. Once those life-saving tasks were accomplished, the feverish speed with which they worked slowed considerably to a more comfortable pace. Suturing her surface wounds, even by their alternative methods, was a delicate process considering the depths of some of the scratches and punctures. They wanted to make sure no scar would mar her skin. They wanted no reminders of the cruelty she must have endured to haunt her.

Through it all, Michael held her hand, the right one with the scarred palm. It was the only place, oddly enough, that had no signs of damage. Through it all, as well, Emma hadn't stirred, and that concerned Michael greatly.

᪆

As the healing continued, Raphael left Cassiel to finish the surface wounds, and he switched positions to sit by Emma's head. He breathed deeply, placing one hand on her heart and one hand on her head, and began the healing again.

An immediate change came over him. His hands shook, his body convulsed and he let out a howl so raw, the others covered their ears from the piercing pain of it. Raphael's hands leapt off of Emma's body as though they had touched fire, and his body was thrown clear across the chamber. Nathanael was closest to him and rushed to his aid.

"I'm all right, I'm all right," he assured everyone, a bit breathless as he slowly got to his feet again. "Thanks."

"What the hell happened?" Nathanael asked.

"Everything was fine until I went to heal her heart and mind. Nathanael, I can't begin to describe what I saw and felt. What she went through—I can't fix it, brother. I can't fix it," he faltered, shaking his head and looking completely defeated.

"What's going on?" Michael called out. "Come on back here and finish her healing."

"I-I can't, Michael. I could fix everything else, but I can't fix this. It's horrible in there, man. And Cassiel certainly can't. Together, all the Saviors are still no match to heal her heart and mind. It's far too powerful and dark. I-I'm sorry, brother. I'm so sorry." He turned away to sit down, and put his head in his hands.

"So that's it? Her body is fine but her heart and mind are lost to us forever?" Michael began stroking her hair compulsively. "Why, that's absurd. It won't do, you hear? I won't let it be over. There has to be something else you can do. There has to be!" He stood with fists raised in defiance. "I didn't come this far only to be denied my future. My future lies with Emma and Hannah. Don't you understand? We're the Trinity. We're supposed to be together. How can we be together if you can't fix her?" He walked, blinded by grief, to the stairway and pounded his fists against it. His body slumped against the wall in abject misery.

Hannah quietly walked over to her mother and lay beside her. She snuggled up against her as if she were going to sleep. And she whispered, "Mama, what should we do? You always know. You're the one who always saves me. Tell me what to do." She grabbed her mother's scarred hand in her own and held it close, stroking her own cheek with it for comfort. She felt a glimmer of an idea begin to surface. Her mother must be communicating with her somehow! She listened with her heart, and made a plan with her mind.

Hannah kissed her mother's cheek, walked over to Michael, and placed a gentle hand on his left wing. Feeling her child's hand, he turned to her and fell on his knees. This time there was no stopping the barrage of tears that fell. "I failed her, Hannah. I failed you. Just damn me to Hell. I'm halfway there already."

She wiped away his tears and it was little Hannah who spoke. "Don't cry, Michael. Mama's going to be okay. Come with me, come." She pulled him over to where Emma lay unmoving. "We can fix her heart and mind, Michael. Mama told me how. Remember when we saved you?" He nodded silently. "Mama and I had cut our hands on the ritual knife and were bleeding. We put our hands on your shoulder where you were bleeding. We fixed you. You have your wing back and you're not dead."

"But we don't have the ritual knife anymore, honey. How do you think we can fix your Mama?"

"Watch and follow me. Mama told me what to do. We've got nothing left to lose and everything to win."

"You are one courageous, little girl. You know that?"

Hannah smiled at Michael and sat by Emma's right arm. Michael sat by her left. "Let's hold hands and place them over Mama's heart and forehead."

Michael obeyed.

"I know you're not a Savior, Michael. I'm not either, but Mama is, and I know she will find her way back to us if we do exactly what she told me to do. I just know it."

"I'm ready, are you?" he asked.

"Ready," she answered, finally seeing a spark of hope light up his eyes.

They linked hands as Hannah had described, took two deep breaths and closed their eyes. Hannah's scar began to throb and glow just like Emma's. Michael's wing glowed as well, and fluttered erratically. They were instantly aware of Emma's desperation to return to her family and forget the horrors of her torture.

At first, there was only a glimmer of light emanating from them. That glimmer grew stronger and brighter until it became the brilliant aura that had encompassed the three in Emma's backyard. And then, Michael heard something that was music to his ears.

"Hannah." Emma spoke in little more than a whisper.

"Mama!" Hannah cried out. "You came back! I knew you would come back!" But Emma didn't respond. Hannah nudged her. "Mama? Michael, she's not saying anything."

"Let's try it again. I don't think she's really back yet. Maybe we need to do this holding hands thing a little longer this time."

"Come on, then!" She grabbed Michael's hands quickly and they poked and prodded Emma's heart and mind back to them for good this time.

Emma opened her eyes a crack, and Hannah smiled.

"Hannah, my angel," Emma cooed weakly. "You heard me. I thought I was dreaming; that it was too good to be true. But you really heard me."

"We're magic, Mama. Remember?"

"Yes, sweetheart. We're magic." Hannah felt the comforting squeeze of her mother's hand. "Michael, where's Michael?"

"I'm right here, honey. Welcome back. We've missed you something fierce." Michael took up her hand and layered kisses firmly on her palm.

"I've missed you, too." A watershed of tears flowed down her temples. "You two were the only things keeping me going. Thank God you're both okay."

Emma pulled Michael and Hannah to her and embraced them both. She kissed Hannah atop her head, and then kissed Michael gently but soundly on his lips, right in front of her. And Hannah didn't mind it at all.

"All right! Break it up! Break it up! Let us have a chance to welcome Emma back to the land of the living!" Cassiel snorted, shoving his way through the crowd. "Can you turn off the lightshow, though? I'm bound to be the first blind angel in history."

Michael laughed, shaking his head, and as they released each other from their grasp, the brilliant aura faded. "You're a real pain in the ass, Cassiel," he admonished, giving him a shove. "But you're young still, so I'll forgive you. For now."

Michael watched as one by one the other Brethren kneeled down, kissed Emma's cheek, and gave her their biggest, brightest smiles along with well wishes. She smiled back.

He hoisted Emma in his arms, making ready to leave.

"Raphael, there's another body in the pit. It's in bad shape. We should give him a proper burial." Raphael immediately flew down first to see if there was any identification on him. That way they could notify his next of kin.

"I know who that is," Emma remarked. "It's the body of the man Agremon possessed when he came to me and took Hannah."

Raphael came back up with a wallet in his hands. "Says here his name is Jared Sikes. Lived in Sedona. There's a picture, too. Looks like it's of him and a girlfriend or sister, maybe. I'll take it with me and see what we can do about finding family." Raphael stuck it in his back pocket. The Brethren made quick work of filling the pit, saying a few prayers, and marking the improvised grave.

Nathanael led them out of the chamber and back through the twisting tunnels of the mine. "Is Namirha gone, Michael? Is it over?" Emma whispered in his ear.

"No, we haven't seen him or sensed him in a while. He's bound to make an appearance, I'm sure. But don't worry; we won't let him get to you or Hannah. We're ready for him."

She relaxed in his arms and watched as the Brethren ahead of her exited the mine. The three of them were just reaching the opening when Namirha suddenly appeared, providing an effective roadblock between them and the rest of the Brethren. Emma noticed the others hadn't turned around. *Why aren't they turning around?* Michael slowly lowered her to her feet, so that the three of them stood side by side.

"Emma, great to see you looking so well," Namirha sneered. "Michael, you, too. Hannah, my prodigal daughter. Are you ready to return to my loving arms?"

He looks different from when I saw him last, Emma noted. His face had grown gaunt and ashen. And even though he wore a robe, she could tell the rest of his body was skin and bones. His failure to retrieve Hannah's powers had left him depleted, with no chance to bounce back.

"Get out of our way, Namirha," Michael commanded. "You waged your war and failed. And if I were a betting man, I'd say you just used up the last of any power you may have had shielding your presence from us. So go back to Hell and have your hounds lick your wounds. It's over."

"My influence is rooted deeply all over this world. Evil is everywhere. I may have lost this war, but I'll be back. It's not over. It's never over."

Before Namirha could say or do anything, Michael calmly directed, "Hands, now." Emma grabbed his and Hannah's in hers and their aura immediately erupted. With Namirha temporarily blinded, Emma pulled the two behind her, and moved them past Namirha and out of the mine. Then, they all raised their hands and pushed their energy towards Namirha until their arms were completely outstretched. The Trinity's enormous surge of energy slammed Namirha against an inner cave wall, his entire body becoming entombed like a fossil. The blast was so strong that it caused another cave-in, sealing the entrance to the mine with tons of rock and debris.

"You're right, now it's over." Michael dusted off his leather pants as best he could and shook his wings to free the little granules that had fallen in between the feathers.

Emma heard a stifled giggle escape from Hannah. "What's so funny?"

"You!" Hannah giggled, pointing to Michael. "You look like a goose doing that!" She laughed even louder.

"A goose!" Michael balked, looking shocked. "I look like a goose to you? Geez, I'm an angel, I just saved our lives, and all you can say is I look like a goose. I don't even rate looking like a swan? Come here, you! I'm gonna have to teach you a lesson on the difference between a goose and an angel!"

Emma watched, amused as Michael swept Hannah off her feet and squeezed her. She squealed with delight. "You see, a goose couldn't do this with you, now could it?" Michael tossed Hannah high into the air, and as she fell back to earth, he soared up to catch her. "How about that?" He then planted her gently back on her own two feet firmly on the ground.

"Wow," was all she could muster.

"Brothers!" Michael called out to the Brethren who had finally turned around to see what was holding up the Trinity. "Namirha has been defeated."

The Brethren cheered as they unsheathed their swords, raised them in the air, and touched the points. The inscriptions on the blades glowed and hummed for a moment, and then returned to their regular state. With the swords safely sheathed once more, it was time to return home.

"Can you take Hannah back to her house, Cassiel?"

"No problem. Hey, I'm starving! Anyone else? I wonder if the pizza place is still standing." Cassiel blathered on while flying away with her.

"So," Michael said, turning to face Emma.

"So."

"So, I guess you'll be needing a lift home?"

"Looks that way. It seems like my friends have run off with my daughter, and abandoned me. But are you going my way?"

"Whatever way you're going is my way, forever and always."

"Yeah, about that," she began as he picked her up in his arms. "You see, um, well, I don't know if you noticed while you and Hannah were healing me, but um, oh, how do I put this?" Emma was stumbling over her words again.

"You"—he kissed her cheek—"and Hannah"—he kissed her other cheek—"have become immortal." He kissed the tip of her nose.

"Yes!" Emma chirped. "I can feel it in the both of us. But I'm not sure how it happened, although I do have my suspicions regarding that ritual knife."

"We'll figure it out, as soon as I get you home and make love to you for a couple of weeks or months or years, straight."

As they flew home, Emma knew her shivers had nothing to do with the cool night air and everything to do with the glorious anticipation of Michael's decree.

Chapter Thirty-Two

"*Happy birthday to you! Happy birthday to you! Happy birthday, dear Hannah! Happy birthday to you!*" The cheerful song was thunderous in the house as the Brethren bellowed it out, and Emma loved it. Although it was sung over a pizza rather than a cake, she could see Hannah didn't care. It was still her birthday for another six minutes.

"Make a wish, honey," Emma coaxed, rumpling Hannah's hair.

Hannah closed her eyes and opened them. She announced stubbornly, "You know, I think I deserve more than one wish after all that's happened, so I'm going to make wishes and I want you all to hear them."

"Well, okay then, Miss Warrior, let's hear them."

"First, I wish that I could have a swimming pool in the backyard. Second, I wish that Seraphiel could come back to us. Third, I wish that everything in those towns would be back to the way it was. That's what I want. Oh, and that Mama and Michael get married!" She blew out her seven candles, one for each year, and one for good luck. "There! Now, can I have a piece of pizza, please?"

"Absolutely, Birthday Girl." Emma chuckled and began serving up the pieces to everyone. "Seems we have some negotiating to do with some of those wishes, little one." When slices of pizza were duly passed around, and the Brethren were deeply involved in their meals, she took Michael aside.

"Michael, is there anything to be done about Seraphiel? Can he be brought back to us?"

"I'm not sure. Agremon knew the only way to kill one of us, and it's forever as far as I know."

"And what about all the mortals that died and the towns that lay in ruins? Can they be saved?"

"You know, you saw what we were able to do to Namirha when the three of us worked together. It's worth a shot to see what else we can do," Michael ventured. "Maybe we can turn things to rights. I mean, you're a Savior, I'm a Protector, and Hannah's a Warrior. We are The Trinity, are we not?"

"Why yes we are. Let's finish our birthday pizza then, and after, we can see about fixing things."

"That sound like a great idea," Michael agreed.

They walked back to join the others who were eagerly dipping into the newly opened boxes of assorted pizzas. It truly was a time to feast, Emma thought, whether it was to be fit for a king or a six-year-old. As their hunger was finally appeased, they began to focus conversation on what was to happen next.

"We're going to try and put those towns back together," Michael said, "and return the mortals back to the land of the living." Hannah jumped and skipped around the family room, barely able to contain her joy.

"Well, I don't know about anybody else," Cassiel declared, "but I've got a caseload waiting for me back at the office. E.L.'s probably going to call a meeting to debrief us on the war, and that could take another week all by itself. If I don't get to work, I'll be drowning in even more paperwork."

After a round of handshakes, hugs, and kisses goodbye, one by one the Brethren left. Knowing that they'd see them soon enough didn't make their leaving any easier for Emma. Where once they were only two, they now had a family of ten, and it felt wonderful. She watched and waved from the threshold until all the Brethren were gone.

"Emma, before Raphael left, he told me what we need to do if we're to be successful with our plan. We have to increase our powers more than what simple meditation can do for us. Let's go to Hannah's room."

"Okay, but why? We can meditate just as easily in the family room, and more comfortably, I might add."

"Remember what Raphael said about this house, this land being on one of those magnetic lines of a vortex?" She nodded. "Well, the line runs right under Hannah's bedroom."

"Oh my. Well that explains a lot, doesn't it?"

Michael had them sit in a circle on the floor and hold hands. As they closed their eyes, the Trinity's aura began to glow brilliantly for a few moments and then dimmed. Hannah's and Emma's scars tingled like a low electric volt was passing through their palms. Michael experienced the same feeling in his left shoulder blade. As the discomfort grew stronger, their strength and energy increased tenfold. Simultaneously, their eyes opened and radiated a brilliant white light for a matter of seconds before returning to their normal state.

"Whoa," Hannah muttered.

"Whoa is right," Emma agreed.

"I think we're ready. Let's get to work, shall we?" Michael offered a hand up to Emma. His wings unfurled and as they made their way outside, he grabbed both Hannah and Emma.

"Hold on, everyone! Here we go!" He lifted off the ground and came back down sharply. He received cross glares from both Emma and Hannah. He tried again, and came back to earth.

"Only fooling!" He laughed, and took flight with the ease of a swallow.

When they reached the top of the mesa and settled back to the ground, they stood at the edge to witness the devastation the war had wrought, and a silent reverence fell upon them. Only an atomic bomb could have done more damage. It occurred to Michael that Hannah's pictures of the devastation rang eerily true.

"Are we ready?" Michael asked quietly.

"Yes," Emma and Hannah answered together with eagerness.

"Then, let's hold hands, and focus our combined energy on bringing life back to the dead and restoring the towns to their original glory."

The Trinity's aura burst through their fingertips and eyes, and fanned out towards the battlefield below. Michael felt as though they were the sun, sending rays of light and hope over the land. He had them stand this way until their aura faded completely, knowing that all that could be done was done. Gazing out, he blinked a few times to make sure what he saw was true.

Lampposts that had been uprooted and twisted like shoelaces were now casting a warm glow over the towns' streets. Buildings that had been demolished were back to their normal state. Roads that had been pocked with craters from fireballs spewed by some demon of darkness were smoothly paved. Cars and trucks that had become charred skeletons sat pristine in their parking spaces. But the people, where were the people?

"Michael, where are the people?" Emma asked in a hushed whisper.

"I don't know," he replied, puzzled.

"I do." They both stared at Hannah. Michael was surprised to see a smile on her face.

"Where are they, angel?" Emma asked softly as she touched her cheek.

"They're home, sleeping. It's the middle of the night! What would people think if they found themselves walking around the streets in the middle of the night?" Hannah reasoned. She raised her fists in triumph. "We did it! We really did it!"

"We sure did, Hannah. We sure did!" Michael picked her up and swung her around. "Hey, what's the matter, honey? Just a second ago you were cheering. Now you look all sad."

"It's time to say goodbye."

"Goodbye? Goodbye to whom?"

"Goodbye to the Ancient Warrior soul. It's time for it to go."

"I thought you'd be happy to be little Hannah all the time

again, sweetie."

"Oh, I will be. It's just that, well, it's been with me for a while now and I kinda got used to having it around."

"Well, maybe you'll come across it again when you're older," Michael suggested. "You never know."

"Can you guys leave me alone for a couple of minutes while I say goodbye?" she asked.

Michael and Emma looked at each other and with silent agreement, Emma replied, "Sure, we'll be over by the altar. Let us know when you're ready to leave."

Hannah sat on the ground and closed her eyes. Immediately she felt the hands of the Ancient Warrior soul on her shoulders. She opened her eyes and turned to find the angel, luminous as ever.

"I must go," it proclaimed. "My duty here is done."

"I know. I'm going to miss you."

"Oh, I was a nuisance most of the time."

"No you weren't! You protected me, fought for me, and gave me courage when I didn't have any!" She paused and reached out to the Ancient Warrior as she smiled. "There are big things ahead for me, you know. Will I ever see you again? Will you be there for the big things?" Hannah asked hopefully.

"Yes, my warrior, I will be there for the big things. I shall always look out for you. But I shall be there to watch from the sidelines as you come into your own." With a breath of a kiss on each cheek and a wave, the Ancient Warrior soul faded from sight.

Hannah stood, feeling empty yet at peace. "Mama!" she hollered.

Emma ran over to her. "What is it, honey?" she asked nervously.

"I'm back, Mama, for good!" And she jumped into her mother's arms, giving her the biggest squeeze.

"I'm so glad, my baby, so glad!" Emma choked through the tears and sobs. "Let's go home then. It's been a very long and busy day for you, and way past your bedtime."

"Aw, Mama! But I'm not tired! Really!" Hannah argued jokingly.

"I've got two seats available for transport over to the Livingston residence," Michael announced. "Do I have any takers?"

"Me!" Emma cried out.

"Me, too!" Hannah added, raising her hand.

"Well then, climb aboard!" Michael opened his arms and they both ran to him. "Angel Airways, ready for takeoff!"

Hannah looked out at all the in-between places as they flew home. Emma had eyes only for Michael.

⌘

With Hannah finally tucked into bed, lights off, Emma and Michael found themselves alone. With a quick glance and a nervous smile at Michael, Emma walked back into the kitchen, and began cleaning away all the pizza boxes and cans of soda left on the table. Shame, guilt, and doubt had wormed their way back into her mind since returning from the mesa. She'd behaved like an ass. She'd been so afraid to trust, yet wound up being the untrustworthy one in all of this. She wouldn't be surprised if he had second thoughts and called it quits right here and now. But she'd be damned if she let him see her cry over it. She'd wait for him to leave.

Michael had followed her in, and as she reached for yet another empty box, he took her trembling hand. She froze and closed her eyes. *I can do this. I can keep it together.* She willed herself not to breakdown.

"Emma, cleanup can wait," he reproved. "Come here, love." He coaxed her into his arms. "Let me hold you. You've been through quite an ordeal that, quite frankly, could break even the strongest of us immortals." He held her good and strong. "It destroyed me, you know, seeing you in that pit, thinking I'd lost you forever." She felt his lips press against the top of her head.

His touch was so good and right and perfect. *And I'm totally undeserving of his words and attention.* "None of it would have happened if I'd just followed the plan," she rebuked. "But I wavered and let everybody down. I don't know. Something came over me, frustration mixed with a compulsion, to go it alone. I thought I could pit one evil against the other and they'd cancel each other out. It almost worked, too. But at the end of the day, no matter how I look at it, it's still my fault, Michael, and mine alone. My impetuousness is the reason I suffered and nearly died, and put you and Hannah through hell, literally, to save me. I'll bear that black mark for the rest of, well, eternity it seems." Angry, remorseful tears trailed silently down her cheek.

"We all have crosses of some kind to bear, love," he admitted, stroking her hair gently and kissing her temple. "It's what keeps us grounded. You did what you thought was right at the time for the sake of your daughter. No one is holding that against you. No one."

He didn't say we're finished, did he? I didn't hear him say we're through. "You're not mad? You're not leaving, then?"

"Oh, I'm fuming that you put yourself in the hands of the Devil himself. But I understand. I would have done the same thing, truth be told." He held her away from him. "And no, I have no plans on leaving you, ever." She looked up into his eyes—eyes that forgave and told her she had nothing to fear ever again. "Do you remember it at all, Emma, the torture you had to endure?"

"I remember the hounds. I remember their eyes, their teeth, and their viciousness. But I don't remember the pain or the fear they inflicted," she affirmed. "That's what you and Hannah released from me. I will always remember the hounds, and their capabilities, but I will never feel the paralyzing fear ever again. It may serve me well in years to come, I should think."

"I know I promised you I'd make love to you for weeks upon weeks, but with Hannah around, reality has set in rather sharply. Would you settle for hour upon hour?"

"From now until forever is all I'm settling for, with some breaks in between for eating and working and taking care of Hannah, oh and—" Emma's next words were smothered by what she thought was the most flaming kiss ever recorded in the history books.

"I can live with that," Michael interrupted, lifting her off the ground as he plundered her mouth yet again with his.

Emma basked in the glory of Michael's attentions. Forgiven, accepted, and loved were more than she could have hoped for. Having her body worshipped by an angel sent her over the edge into pure bliss. Before they even reached the bed, Michael had peeled away her clothes as well as his. He unleashed wings that shimmered enticingly in the natural glow of the moonlight streaming through the window. Emma reveled in the splendor of their bodies touching, gliding, and moving in rhythmic harmony. His hands roamed all over her body, touching those places that had set her on fire before, and then found new ones to ignite. Emma's hands, in turn, kneaded the muscles that had pulled her from the brink of death, stroked the wings that flew her to freedom, and journeyed across the expansive landscape of Michael's body. He had teased her with his tongue, and she now teased him with her lips.

"Michael," Emma whispered, frantic with a desire that would not be extinguished. "I need you inside me, now!"

"God, yes! Right—now—"

She gasped as he sought and found the shelter of her waiting love.

They came together in a fevered pitch of lust and love and unrestrained emotion. After, totally spent by their ardent lovemaking, Emma clung to Michael in her drowsy state as though afraid he would disappear.

"God, I want you all over again, my immortal lady. In truth, I don't think I'll ever be able to harness the passion and ecstasy you bring about in me. So be it." He caressed her cheek with his thumb.

"Say you'll marry me, Emma," Michael whispered into her hair.

Emma's grip unintentionally tightened. She leaned up onto his chest. "You know, forever is a long time when you're talking about marriage. Are you sure you can endure forever with me, Michael?"

He laid his hands gently upon her face and professed, "I'm sure I can't endure it without you." He kissed her so sweet and tender, it brought tears to her eyes.

"I'll marry you, Michael, now, forever, and always."

Epilogue

"Okay now, push! Push! Real hard, Emma! That's a girl!" Michael was yelling, sweat pouring down his face. Emma was huffing and puffing and pushing like crazy, her face turning beet red.

"Blow it out your ears, Michael! You want it so badly, you push! Ahhh!" Emma cried out. "In fact, why don't you take over for me right now? Ohhh! If I'd known you could do this to me, you jerk, why I'd, oohh! Look at you, standing there, feeling no pain, you bastard! Ahhh!"

"One more time, honey, push real hard! Push for your scheming, low-down, son of a bitch husband! Push!" Michael yelled, taking no offense at the thrashing he was getting from the woman giving birth to his first child.

"That's it, Emma, Michael. You have a beautiful baby girl!" The doctor proclaimed. A wail beyond all wails erupted from her tiny mouth.

"And she's got a great set of lungs on her, too!" Michael boasted. With trembling hands, he cut the cord.

The doctor brought the baby to Emma after cleaning her up and checking her vitals, and placed her in her arms. Emma looked at Michael and then upon her baby, and brought her to feed upon her breast. She counted out loud ten fingers and ten toes. She closed her eyes for a moment and then they suddenly opened wide like saucers.

"Oh! Ready for number two, everyone, 'cause I am!" Emma cried out. "Ohhh! Oh, dear God help me!"

The doctor rushed over and moved the nurse aside to take a look. "Here we go, baby number two."

"Push, Emma! I promise this one will be quick!"

"Ohhh!" Emma bore down and as she took a deep cleansing breath, she heard the wail, as strong as the first, come from her daughter's twin. Again, Michael cut the cord, the baby was cleansed, and vitals checked.

"A boy!" Michael announced, and brought him over for her to hold and check over. "Ten fingers, ten toes, just like your sister. Perfect!" she gushed, kissing his cheek and putting him to her breast.

Michael bent over Emma to plant a kiss on her forehead, but she looked up and he connected with her full on the mouth. He wasn't one to shy away from her lips, so he lingered, drowning in the succulence that was his wife and now mother to his children.

"You know," she said nuzzling his chin, "I didn't really mean any of those nasty things I said, really."

"I know you didn't. Remember, I'm to forgive you for your scathing tongue," he cajoled. "If there ever was a time that called for it, I'd say this was it."

"Would you get our daughter, please, and then get our newly crowned big sister in here? I'm dying to have our family all around me."

"Sure thing, love." Michael brought their baby daughter to rest in her other arm, and then went to the hall to get Hannah.

The hallway was filled with anxious faces and frayed nerves. Ending the suspense, he announced, "It's a girl! And a boy!"

Whoops and hollers filled the air. Michael was swarmed with hearty pats on the back and handshakes from the Brethren. All the while, he looked around for Hannah. She was a bit of a thing and was easily lost amongst them.

"Hannah? Where are you?" he called out.

"Over here, Daddy!" she yelled from on top of a chair a few doors down. God, how he loved that she'd started calling him that!

"Would you mind passing my daughter over to me, please? She has a sister and brother to meet!" he shouted to the crowd.

Hannah was passed through a sea of Brethren arms until she eventually came to rest in his. "Come on, big sister. Time to meet your new baby sister and brother."

As the tumult and fussing finally died down, and all of the doctors and nurses left for a while, Emma and Michael were alone with their children. With the babies in Emma's arms, Hannah next to her on the bed, and him standing by his wife's side, he felt complete.

"Let's welcome our babies, Blessing and Asher, to our family," he suggested.

In an embrace that spoke volumes, they welcomed the babies. The Trinity's aura began to glow and grow, encompassing not only the Trinity, but now the babies as well.

"I can't wait to show you what wonders await you, my children," Michael murmured.

"Welcome to our family, little ones," Hannah cooed.

Emma softly whispered, "Welcome to Eternity, my angels."

Michael returned Blessing and Asher to their bassinets, and then escorted Hannah out of the room to Kemuel's waiting arms. He would be taking her back home and playing nanny for a while. Back inside Emma's room, Michael walked over to the babies who were nestled snuggly in their bassinets sleeping like the little angels they were. In fact, Michael could already see their individual auras glowing.

He then tiptoed towards Emma's bed and stopped. Emma's eyes were closed and her skin was still dewy and blushed from her exertions. It was then he decided he'd never seen her look more beautiful, and was overcome by the devastating love he felt for her.

Emma stirred and caught him staring. She covered her face with her hands. "Ugh! Don't look at me that way, I'm a mess! I'm all sweaty and gross, you silly man!"

He closed the distance between them in two strides, gently removed her hands and settled his own around her face. "You're the most beautiful woman I have ever laid eyes upon, and you're glowing. Like our babies. They are truly a blessing," he stammered, choked with emotion.

"As are you, my angel." Emma turned her face to kiss both palms. "You answered my prayer and forever changed my life, our lives. Any regrets?"

"Only that eternity won't be enough time to show how much I love you."

"Well, that settles it then," Emma proclaimed with a playful glimmer in her eye. "We'll just have to make eternity last forever."

~ABOUT THE AUTHOR~

It was the mystique of Arizona's history and landscape that called to Deena and catapulted her career as an author. When she's not writing novels and poetry in the wee, small hours of the morning or in the deep, dark of night, Deena teaches language arts to middle school students. She currently lives in Gilbert with her husband and two children, but New Jersey will always tug at the heartstrings.

Deena loves talking to her fans. You can reach her at deenaremiel@yahoo.com. For updated information on the Brethren, visit Deena at her website, *www.deenaremiel.com*

Book Two of the Brethren Series

Decadent Publishing
www.decadentpublishing.com